"Continuing the narrative of comic evangelist Leo Bebb begun with *Lion Country,* Frederick Buechner's novel *Open Heart* is a memorable, comedy-leavened interpretation of human relationships written with innate common sense." —*ALA Booklist*

"That strong and refreshing comic sense so abundantly revealed in Buechner's novels is once more on display in this slyly composed new book. . . . Mr. Buechner has many gifts. He is resourceful, ingenious, a stylist, and uncommonly effective with his ribald wit." —*Virginia Quarterly*

"Buechner is a master at putting together a religious novel without sentimentality or dogma. *Open Heart* is an extraordinary book." —**Joan Joffe Hall,** *The Houston Post*

"*Open Heart* should establish Frederick Buechner as one of the leading fiction writers of the decade. He has composed a very well-written, striking, humorous story. It is a pleasure to read and difficult to put down." —**Peter Rowley,** *Chicago Sun-Times*

"*Open Heart* has many pleasant treats for the reader." —**Augusta Gottlieb,** *St. Louis Post-Dispatch*

"Fun to read." —**Joel Kramer,** *Newsday*

"Good to read, vastly entertaining, never for a second dull. . . . Mr. Buechner is a warm, and I suspect a wise, novelist." —**Guy Davenport,** *National Review*

"Deliciously comic. . . . Buechner has made farce and faith compatible. . . . As crisp and witty as DeVries. . . . *Open Heart* can be read for sheer fun, but if you want to get serious about it, there's a lot to ponder." —**Ervin J. Gaines,** *Minneapolis Tribune*

"An entirely satisfying entertainment." —*The Kirkus Reviews*

"Frederick Buechner has somehow performed the magic of creating a story that is even more pleasant to remember than to read. If you do the latter, Buechner will enable you to do the former." —**Robert Baker,** *The Christian Century*

OPEN HEART

Books by Frederick Buechner

Novels

GODRIC 1980

THE BOOK OF BEBB 1979

TREASURE HUNT 1977

LOVE FEAST 1974

OPEN HEART 1972

LION COUNTRY 1971

THE ENTRANCE TO PORLOCK 1970

THE FINAL BEAST 1965

THE RETURN OF ANSEL GIBBS 1958

THE SEASONS' DIFFERENCE 1952

A LONG DAY'S DYING 1950

Non-Fiction

A ROOM CALLED REMEMBER 1984

NOW AND THEN 1983

THE SACRED JOURNEY 1982

PECULIAR TREASURES: A BIBLICAL WHO'S WHO 1979

TELLING THE TRUTH: THE GOSPEL AS TRAGEDY, COMEDY AND FAIRY TALE 1977

THE FACES OF JESUS 1974

WISHFUL THINKING: A THEOLOGICAL ABC 1973

THE ALPHABET OF GRACE 1970

THE HUNGERING DARK 1969

THE MAGNIFICENT DEFEAT 1966

Frederick Buechner

Open Heart

A Novel

Part 2 of The Book of Bebb

Harper & Row, Publishers, San Francisco
Cambridge, Hagerstown, New York, Philadelphia
London, Mexico City, São Paulo, Singapore, Sydney

This book was originally published in hardcover by Atheneum Publishers and in a collected work entitled *The Book of Bebb*. Reprinted by arrangement of Atheneum Publishers.

 For information address Harper & Row, Publishers, Inc., 10 East 53rd Street, New York, NY 10022. Published simultaneously in Canada by Fitzhenry & Whiteside, Limited, Toronto.

First Harper & Row paperback edition published in 1984.

Library of Congress Cataloging in Publication Data

Buechner, Frederick, DATE
Open heart.

(The Book of Bebb ; pt. 2)
I. Title. II. Series: Buechner, Frederick, DATE.
Book of Bebb ; pt. 2.
[PS3552.U3506 1984] 813′.54 84-47715
ISBN 0-06-061166-9 (pbk.)

---

84 85 86 87 88 10 9 8 7 6 5 4 3 2 1

For Jamie and Jackie

OPEN HEART

One

"GET UP, Herman Redpath," my father-in-law Leo Bebb said. His fat face was slippery with sweat and his eyes tight shut as though he'd gotten soap in them. The box had not been lowered into the ground yet but still hung cradled in canvas straps. Inside the box, Herman Redpath was laid out in his brown silk shirt and chocolate-brown suit with a Navajo blanket tucked around him at the waist. Possibly there were damp spots on the blanket. My father-in-law crowded him with his prayer as though if he didn't, the old man might dawdle there indefinitely.

"It's time to move out," Leo Bebb said. "So get going, Herman Redpath. Go forth now from strength unto strength. Rise up now from glory unto glory." Bebb made it sound uphill all the way. If I had been Herman Redpath, I would have pretended not to hear. It was a muggy spring day with thunder in the air.

Herman Redpath, that comic-strip Indian and Cherokee Croesus. I was informed later that he did hear. He set forth across impossible prairies. He clambered up mountains that only seemed to be mountains. He padded down canyons that he must have known weren't really canyons. He came at last to a place that was not a place, and he was challenged there by a stranger who was not a stranger. So I was told anyway, although on authority that I must admit was not unimpeachable. Who knows? Maybe it was so. Maybe a lot more began for Herman Redpath with his death than ended for him. And for the rest of us too.

Certainly for me his passing opened more doors than it closed. And even for Bebb it did although no one would have guessed it at the time since Bebb worked for the old man after all, was his beadsman, his medicine man, his charm against the evil eye. When the old man went, Bebb's job went with him. But if a chapter was ending for Leo Bebb as he stood there in his maroon Holy Love robe nagging at Herman Redpath, at the same time, in ways we were unaware of, a brand new chapter was just getting started. And for Sharon too, my young wife, who should have been there with her father and me but wasn't—because of the baby, she said in a wild flight of fancy. It was Chris, our eighteen-year-old nephew, who worried about the baby.

Bebb wired me as soon as he saw that Herman Redpath was dying, and I caught a plane out of Kennedy that got me there while he was still alive, after a manner of speaking. In the Red Path Ranch there were many mansions—stucco, mostly, with patios and tiled roofs—and the one in which Herman Redpath drew his last breath was built like an L lying on its back with its foot sticking up in the air. This foot was the living room which was two stories high to accommodate the pipes of the organ that Herman Redpath had had installed there. He did not play the organ himself and neither did any of his Indians as far as I know, but every once in a while somebody would turn up who did. Sometimes of an evening he would get Bebb to bluff his way through a hymn or two. With some slow, fuzzy chords in the background, Bebb used his scratchy tenor to carry most of what there was in the way of a tune. *When the Roll Is Called Up Yonder*, Bebb would sing, or *The Old Rugged Cross*, or *Rock of Ages*, and Herman Redpath would sit listening in the dead center of the settee with his hand on Mrs. Trionka's enormous thigh. He died without much in the way of organ accompaniment, but it was in this large, high-ceilinged room that he did it.

I arrived there about the same time he did. A tall brave in a gag T-shirt with *Alcatraz 12230015* stenciled on it came in carrying him in his arms and propped him up like the Infant Jesus of Prague in an overstuffed armchair. He had had them dress him in the same chocolate-brown clothes they later buried him in, and he wore a string tie with a Mexican silver medallion which moved when he swallowed, the Adam's apple bobbling and the silver glittering each time he tried to choke down what little spit he must have had left by then. His skin was stretched so tight he could hardly close his lips over his teeth, and long after the brave who carried him in had left, he kept his gaze directed up to the empty place where the brave's face had been. Someone set a bench in front of him to prop his bare feet against so that he wouldn't slip down. His feet were too swollen to get his shoes on.

The place was crowded with Indians, and when Bebb brought me up to pay my respects, I wasn't sure that Herman Redpath knew that I wasn't just another of them. I said, "I'm the one that married Bebb's daughter. You remember me. Antonio Parr."

He didn't look as if he even remembered what it meant to remember. I said, "Armadillo. We met in Armadillo, Florida, five years ago. We were both there to see Bebb."

I said, "I'm teaching school in Connecticut these days," as if the poor old Cherokee gave a damn. Eyebrows raised, eyes goggling, dry teeth parted, he looked as though I'd made some unprecedented disclosure: that for years before she died I'd been half in love with my twin sister, Miriam; that even in the sack there lay some queer sadness between my young wife and me.

I said, "Sharon. You remember Sharon Bebb. I'm the one that married her." It was to be my last stab at self-identification, the single most substantial piece of evidence I could think to offer either him or myself that I truly existed, and this time it seemed to work.

He raised one hand a little off the arm of his chair and said something. What I thought he said was something like "sweet little *butt* on her," a reference I had heard him make in happier days to that aspect of Sharon's charm that he found especially congenial. But Bebb said he was either clearing his throat or possibly asking somebody to undo some *button* somewhere. In either case, he didn't seem inclined to pursue the conversation with me any further.

Bebb said, "Herman Redpath, they're all here, and now Antonio is here too. But if you added up the total number, you'd come out one short. The reason is there's one other one that's here too only there's not anybody can see him because he's invisible. But he faileth not. He's on deck with the rest of us."

Herman Redpath had not tried to close his mouth since whatever it was he may have tried to say to me. His tongue looked humped and dry like a parrot's. His next words, however, came through with surprising clarity. "Harry Hocktaw," he said. It was only the last name I wasn't sure of—Hoptoad, Hotstraw—but Bebb recognized it immediately.

"Harry," Bebb said, looking back over his shoulder. "Harry Hocktaw," he said. He snapped his fingers like a maître d'hôtel.

Harry Hocktaw turned out to be one of the Indians I remembered from earlier visits. He looked less Indian to me than he did Eskimo. He reminded me of Jack Oakie. He was wearing a Hawaiian shirt and squatting not far from Herman Redpath's chair with his back to a circle of children who had some comic books spread out among them on the floor. When Bebb snapped his fingers, Harry Hocktaw started to get up, but Herman Redpath stopped him by suddenly raising one arm. "Harry Hocktaw," he said in the same parrot accent. Harry Hocktaw sank back to his heels and waited.

Herman Redpath curled the fingers of his raised hand carefully down into a fist as though he was picking something dangerous out of the air and then drew the thumb in tight over the knuckles like a latch. For a few moments he held the fist motionless. Then he gave it a few small, rapid shakes. Then he stopped. Harry Hocktaw was watching, and so were Bebb and

I. A lot of the Indians were watching too but trying to look as if they weren't. Then Herman Redpath shook his fist again. He shook it more fiercely than the first time but delicately too. He was looking straight at Harry Hocktaw now instead of at the empty place in the air, and this time Harry Hocktaw caught the old man's meaning. Like the squirt of a water pistol, he caught it full in the face, and a tabby smile swelled his cheeks. His eyes came alive with a look of hilarious recognition, and he reached into the pocket of his green and yellow pineapple shirt and pulled out a rattle. It was one of those rattles you find in Latin American dance bands made out of a dried gourd filled with seeds. I knew there was a special name for it, but I couldn't remember what the name was, and off and on the whole afternoon of Herman Redpath's dying I kept trying to remember it. In any case, Harry Hocktaw held his rattle up and gave it a few rapid shakes just the way Herman Redpath had shaken his fist. You could tell from the way the old man let his hand fall back to the arm of his chair that this was what he had wanted right along.

The sound the gourd made was less of a rattle the way Harry Hocktaw shook it than a kind of hiss. Sometimes he made it sound like footsteps on a gravel drive, sometimes like the dithering of crickets before rain, sometimes like dice in a cup. After he'd shaken it, he would stop for a while before shaking it some more. Sometimes he stopped so long between shakes that you'd think he'd stopped for good, but then he would shake it again, his arm crooked out in front of him and all the movement limited to his hairless, brown wrist. I assumed at first that there was no pattern to his rattling, but as the afternoon wore on, I began to wonder. It was like the stars at night. Either there is no pattern at all or a pattern so vast and simple nobody can figure it out.

I also couldn't figure out the purpose of the rattle. Was it a sound to scare death off with—Herman Redpath sitting there barefoot in the big chair while death waited under the comic book or in the organ pipes for a silence just the right size and shape to slip in through? Or was it to give death a beat to enter by—a noise to bump and grind to as it postured its way in through the Indians? Maybe the rattle was death itself. Maybe Harry Hocktaw had smuggled death in with him in the pocket of his Hawaiian shirt and had kept it hidden there till Herman Redpath gave him the signal. Crowded between the great, round cheeks, Harry Hocktaw's nose and upper lip looked stitched together like a cat's with several stray black whiskers at the seam. The bare feet of Herman Redpath angled out from the heels like halves of a broken ivory fan.

The big room was full of Indians who were there to be with him when he died presumably, but none of them seemed to be paying him any particular attention. The three flat-faced Trionka sisters were watching a quiz show on TV, and their huge mother sat dozing over a copy of *Life* spread out on her knees. There was a poker game going on between four Indians, one of them the man in the Alcatraz T-shirt and another wearing a cap made of a handkerchief knotted at the corners. An old woman in a peekaboo blouse was sitting at the organ. She was mending something flesh-colored, using the keyboard to hold her sewing equipment, and every so often in reaching for something she would strike a note by accident, usually one of the higher, shriller ones, which made a more inscrutable music still out of the inscrutable rhythms of Harry Hocktaw. One small boy, naked except for an orange life jacket, came up behind Herman Redpath, who had his mouth wide open now as if he was trying to sing something, and started to urinate on the back of the chair before a woman in a bathing suit snatched him away. There were children of all ages milling in and out, brown-faced, dark-eyed children, and many of them, I knew Herman Redpath would have said, had been begotten by him on one kinswoman or another.

Children maybe and grandchildren certainly, great-grandchildren, they were all there that afternoon with the nephews and nieces, the wives and cousins and hangers-on, none of them paying much attention to the small chocolate figure melting slowly away in the armchair although from time to time one of them would come up and stand near him for a moment or two. Once I saw a woman with a braid down her back offer him her naked breast the way a nurse might or a mother whereupon with one hand the old man covered his mouth and with the other seemed to be trying to push her away. I suppose he thought they were just trying to force down his throat some final bitterness. And then suddenly the hiss of the snake again, the clatter of dice in a cup, and *marimba, cucaracha, hacienda . . .* ? For the life of me I couldn't remember the name for a dried gourd filled with seeds.

A middle-aged Indian in jeans that smelled of

horse came up to me where I was standing not far from the trio of Trionka sisters. His upper front teeth all had their own little frames of gold, like cufflinks, He said, "Your wife. How she doing these days?"

I said she was doing well. Home taking care of the baby.

He said, "How many babies you got now anyway?"

"Just the one baby," I said. To take some of the curse off, I said it was a boy.

"Just one baby?" he said. He pushed a finger into his cheek. "Who's going to believe that, a big boy like you?"

I said, "What's with that thing Harry Hocktaw keeps rattling?"

He said, "Hocktaw? I don't hear him rattling nothing."

"He's got it in his hand," I said. "In a second he'll hold it up and start rattling it again."

"I don't see Hocktaw's got anything in his hand," the Indian said. Almost as soon as he said it, Harry started it again, a barely punctuated trembling of sound this time, not unlike the sizzle of rain on a sidewalk. I kept my eyes on the Indian's face the whole time it lasted. When it was over, he smiled at me handsomely.

Through his golden teeth he clucked out the syllables rapidly, "Chicka-chicka, chicka-chicka, chicka-chicka." He said, "The cicadas they sing sometime. Could be that's what you think was Hocktaw. Just one baby." He sucked in his breath through puckered lips, a backward whistle. "Better get going, boy." He went over and sank down in front of the quiz show at the feet of one of the Trionkas.

I had the feeling death himself was there in that room like a celebrity. All of them except me had spotted him, and out of the corners of their eyes they were watching every move he made. Like a movie star he was there in some transparent disguise which they were all tactfully pretending not to see through. The poker players, the old woman at the organ, fat Mrs. Trionka dozing over *Life*—it was their air of utter unconcern that was the dead giveaway. You couldn't look that unconcerned without working at it. Harry Hocktaw shaking his rattle at odd moments as though nothing could matter less than whether he shook it or not. My friend saying it was cicadas. Everybody in that room except me knew that one of those Indians wasn't an Indian.

I found a telephone and called Sharon. Herman Redpath was melting fast. One arm had already started to run down the side of his chair, and some parts of his face were starting to go. One of those Indians was death warmed up, and I was homesick for life. I called Sharon up because for better or for worse she was the alivest thing I knew.

"That sonofabitch Tony," she said, referring to the younger of my two nephews, Miriam's boys, who lived with us. "When he got home from practice this afternoon, he put the African violets in his jockstrap and hung it on the hall light so when Anita came in with my guitar, it practically totaled her. You should have heard him knocking himself out over it in the can upstairs. He gives me a pain in the butt."

"Butt reminds me," I said. "Herman Redpath asked after you first thing."

"Old Herman," she said. "Has he made it to the happy hunting ground yet?"

I said, "Not yet, but he's struck his wigwam. One of the papooses tried to take a leak on him."

"I bet he got a bang out of that," Sharon said.

"What are you up to?" I asked her.

"Not much," she said. "I think there's going to be a thunderstorm. Chris has got the baby's bottle heating, and two-ton Tony's out lifting weights to keep from doing his homework. I was just about to wash my hair. I left the water running."

She was upstairs then. I could see her sitting on our bed long-legged, barefoot, with one foot up on the bed beside her so she could pick at a toenail. She was looking down at her foot so all you could see of her profile was a patch of forehead and the bridge of her nose.

I said, "I'm sorry about yesterday. We can't let a swami come between us."

"He's not a swami," she said. "He just teaches yoga. He comes from Beloit, Michigan."

"Wisconsin," I said.

"Have it your way," Sharon said.

I said, "How's the baby?"

"Chris thinks he's going to start walking soon," she said. "I wish to God he'd start getting some hair first. Tell Bip he looks more like him every day, I'm afraid. What's Bip think he's going to do anyway? After Herman croaks."

"I haven't asked him," I said.

She said, "Tell him for me he better start taking it to the Lord in prayer."

"Listen," I said. "Everybody's hanging around to

see old Herman off, and there's this Eskimo with a rattle and a lot of kids and old squaws all playing it real cool except I've got an idea the whole bunch of them is doing something basic and subtle to help something happen or not happen and I'm the only one who isn't in on it. I've got a strong hunch every Indian in there knows something I ought to know too only I don't. When they think nobody's watching, they've all got their eyes on something I can't see. Maybe it's just as well."

"Have you checked your zipper lately?" Sharon said.

"How old are you anyway?" I asked her.

"Going on twenty-seven," Sharon said.

"Well don't go on," I said. "Just stay where you are, kid, and don't go on."

"Lucille's been dosing you with Tropicanas," she said.

"No such luck," I said. "I haven't laid eyes on Lucille yet."

She said, "It must be Herman then. Is it pretty bad for him?"

I said, "It's not bad at all. That's what's bad about it. A child could do it without half trying. You go back and wash your hair now and leave a lamp in the window. Tell Tony he's sixteen now. It's time to stop acting like a sixteen year old."

Sharon said, "You should have seen Anita's face when she figured out what the damned thing was. I think it's the closest to the real McCoy she's ever been." She said, "Tell Herman hello for me. Tell him something for me anyway. Tell him happy hunting. Say happy hunting to old Herman Redpath for me, will you, Antonio?" And when she hung up, I could see her sitting there barefoot a few moments more before getting up and moving across that messy room to the bathroom. I could see the way her hair divided over her ears and the lazy, loose-limbed way she had of walking, and I decided that if it was true that it was only "Button" that Herman Redpath had said when I mentioned her to him, he had already slipped farther than I thought.

I might still have made it back to him in time if at that point I had not heard the sudden scraping back of a chair and the sound of breaking glass. The phone I had been using was in the kitchen, and the noise came from a dining alcove around the corner. There was a bay window filled with potted plants that were glowing gold and green in the afternoon sun. There was a table and some chairs, and in one of them, sitting up straight as a stick with her eyebrows arched into a question above her black glasses sat Lucille Bebb, my mother-in-law. She said, "Find me a Handiwipe, will you? I was going to come tell Sharon hey, and then I spilled my Tropicana all over Herman Redpath's linoleum."

I said, "You wouldn't happen to have another one on hand, would you?"

"Are you kidding?" she said. "These days Bebb makes Tropicanas for me one at a time."

The sun through the leaves gave a soft, greenish light as if we were meeting at the bottom of the sea. I sponged up what I could of the Tropicana and broken glass and sat down across from her at the table. She was even skinnier than when I'd seen her last, and instead of limiting herself to her usual cropped utterances thrown out take-it-or-leave-it, she seemed almost talkative.

She said, "I heard what you were saying to Sharon, and there's one thing I can tell you. You hit the nail on the head about those Indians. They know plenty, and they're not talking. They're born knowing plenty that folks with white skin don't know and won't ever know. Except Bebb. I think Bebb knows just about everything Indians know and then some. I'll tell you something else. When it comes to Indians, I'm fed. I haven't anything to say against Herman Redpath, especially now. He has always behaved like a gentleman in front of me. So I've got nothing but good to say about Herman Redpath, and I would never have wished on him what's happening to him in there right this minute. But as long as it's got to happen and there's not a thing in this world anybody can do about it, I don't mind saying it suits me just fine because I know as soon as it's happened we'll be getting the hell out. I'm up to here with Indians. They've got a rancid odor to them, and like you say, they know too much. Sharon says the way they look at you sometimes, it's like they knew the last time you had the period."

It may have been the longest speech I ever heard her make. She must have cut her finger trying to pick up the broken glass because she was holding a wad of Kleenex pressed against it, and I thought to myself she didn't look as if she had any extra blood to throw around.

"What else do those Indians know that we don't?" I asked her.

She said, "You tell me." She was back to her usual conversational style. "Ask Bebb," she said.

I said, "You think he knows?"

"Look," she said. "I don't think. I live with the man. He's from outer space." A huge elephant's ear turned into green fire behind her.

I said, "Maybe you're from outer space yourself. It takes one to know one."

"Listen," Lucille said, straightening her black glasses. "I could tell you plenty."

If you get to gazing out the window for a certain length of time with other things on your mind, you can look at something for quite a while before you actually see it, and in the same way, I suppose, you can listen to something quite a while before you actually hear it. Off and on the whole time I'd been out there in the kitchen with my mother-in-law, the sound of Harry Hocktaw's rattle must have been perfectly audible—there was only a hall between us and both doors were open—but it was not until this point that I became conscious of it again. It had speeded up considerably—*chicka-chicka chicka-chicka chicka-chicka chicka-chicka*—with hardly so much as a breath in between chickas, and it was also louder. If, before, it had been someone walking on gravel, now it was someone running, or something running—something heavy-footed and in a terrible hurry. That was not all. There was a hollow tock-tock of wood against wood such as you might hear in a kabuki theater, about four of these, very sharp and forceful with shuddering pauses of silent air in between them. Then, so help me, there was a desperate, flapping sound like a flushed partridge. The tocking had plainly come from the big room, but the wings could have been anywhere—wings in the big room, wings in the hallway, wings even in the kitchen with Lucille and me and the plants.

Some windowshade fluttering in a freak gust of wind? Some echo of Mrs. Trionka waving her copy of *Life* around her head in a sudden assault of grief? Or could it really have been, as I'm sure at the time I wanted it to be, the soul of Herman Redpath mounting up like an eagle, that chocolate-clad Cherokee flip-flapping his way through the house to be gathered to his fathers at last? I see him swooping out of the window all hung with sharks' teeth and wampum with his hands together like a diver's to cleave the humid Texas dusk. There was an electric fan in the bathroom, and Lucille told me later that what I heard was the sound an electric fan makes if it gets blowing toward a shower curtain.

The third noise was the last. As children my sister Miriam and I were taken to see an early movie version of Rider Haggard's *She*, I think it was, and there was a scene in Aisha's underground jungle palace where Aisha herself came rising up out of a flaming crater, and all around it writhing savage women in grass skirts and Theda Bara headdresses joined together in a foreboding, choral wail. This was the sound I heard again in the kitchen with Lucille except that it flickered off and on a few times like a phonograph when you pick up the needle. A foreboding, choral wail. Then we heard footsteps running down the hall, and in a moment Bebb stuck his head in.

His plump, white face was closed tight, his mouth

sprung shut, but his eyes were round and quick as a bird's.

He said, "Antonio, tell it not in Gath, publish it not in Askelon lest the daughters of the uncircumcised triumph. Herman Redpath now rests in the bosom of Abraham."

"Believe me," Lucille said, wiping some Tropicana off the table with her bloody Kleenex, "I could tell you plenty."

Two

LEO BEBB sits halfway down the porch steps watching the sun set over the Red Path Ranch. Between his socks and his trouser cuffs, his hairless calves are the color of skimmed milk. The color of the sky is orange with a few long, flat clouds. There is no sound. He says, "Antonio, it is easier for a camel to go through the eye of a needle than for a rich man to enter the Kingdom of Heaven. That miserable Brownie, he claims the true translation is that it's as easy as a needle going through the eye of a camel." In his lapel he wears a little gold cross made up of LOVE going across and HOLY going down. Identical crosses are available at the gift shop attached to the church that Herman Redpath built for him. Also available are postcards including one of Bebb in his maroon robe with his right hand raised in benediction and another one of Herman Redpath in a feathered headdress and business suit presenting a pipe of peace to Lyndon B. Johnson.

Leo Bebb is washing his hands in a men's room in a Houston gas station. His nostrils are swelled out and his lips pressed together. He is humming a tune. Looking at himself in the mirror, he turns his head a little to the right and then a little to the left. He pulls his handkerchief up by the points just enough for the monogram B to show. He starts to leave but then comes back and swings open the door of the cubicle where the toilet is. On the inside of the door there is a heart with an arrow through it drawn with a ball-point pen.

The sun is setting, and in the two-story room the old woman in the peekaboo blouse is taking her turn keeping the flies off Herman Redpath. Outside, on the porch steps, the only thing that is moving is the trick eyelid of Leo Bebb.

Leo Bebb stands at the bedroom door and knocks. In his right hand he is carrying Lucille's Tropicana with half as much gin as usual and twice as much orange juice.

Bebb hates to fly, but he flies anyway. When he is flying, if you took away the plane, the crew and all the other passengers, what you would have left in the sky would be just Bebb. He is sitting there above the clouds with his knees pressed together and his eyes shut. His chicken sandwich is untouched. Depths have never bothered him, but he is scared stiff of heights.

"Dear Bip," I wrote him once from the top of a Green Line bus between London and Hampton Court. "Did you really raise Brownie from the dead in Knoxville, Tennessee? What was it, if anything, that really *happened* that day with the children in Miami Beach? Have you ever forgiven Lucille about the baby? I don't care so much how you answer. Just answer." Bebb was sitting in the front seat of the bus peering down at the traffic so he could get the feel of driving on the left, he said, in case Gertrude Conover should ask him someday to take the wheel of her rented Daimler. I never gave him the letter.

The sun had almost set when Mrs. Trionka came out of the house and joined Bebb and me on the porch steps. She was wearing a white terrycloth bathrobe and had rollers in her hair. She was carrying a glass of rootbeer with a scoop of vanilla ice cream in it. It was her favorite warm-weather drink, she said. She called it a brown cow. She was a brown cow herself, but in the gathering twilight her robe made her look more like Pope John XXIII.

She said, "Things aren't going to be the same around here without Herman." The brown cow had left her with a white mustache.

Bebb said, "In a way that is true, but in another way it is not true. When the right time comes—later," he said, interrupting himself, "later on I'm going to explain what that means."

Mrs. Trionka said, "Watching the sun go down always makes a person think. It makes a person wonder what's it all about anyway."

Bebb said, "Antonio, you've had a college education, and you're a deep thinker. In there they've got Herman Redpath laid out in his brown suit, a fine Christian gentleman snatched away when there was still plenty of mileage left in him. Out here the Almighty is washing the underside of those clouds with gold same as if today was no different from yesterday or tomorrow. You tell Mrs. Trionka and I what it's all about."

He wasn't trying to put me on. I don't think he believed I could tell him but thought it might be worth a try. The horizon was the color of smoked salmon as he turned away from it to see what I was going to say. I was sitting behind him on the top step. Mrs. Trionka was standing by the door of the house with her white robe almost touching the ground at her heels but hiked up to her shins in front.

Without being sure why, I found myself answering this metaphysical question by giving him and Mrs. Trionka a detailed description of something I had been making in a shed off the garage. Before marrying Sharon, I had tried making things out of odd pieces of scrap iron dipped in Rustoleum black. Since then I had turned to making things out of wood.

The thing I described to them was a six foot high triangle of raw pine planking. From the apex hung down thin tongues of wood of different lengths, some spear-shaped at the end, some spatulate, some notched or rounded. The three vertical planks that side by side made each leg of the triangle had spaces between them, and fastened into those spaces were wooden balls and cubes and discs that could be turned on their axes. The planks of one leg were not always pierced to match the planks of the opposite leg—a square hole on one side might face a circular hole on the other, a star a diamond, an *X* an *O*—but wherever there was a triangle cut out of one leg, there was an identical triangle cut out in a comparable position across from it. I have no idea why. Between the two legs and somewhat nearer the top than the bottom there was a bridge made of three strips of wood each a few inches above, and thus a few inches shorter than, the other. These strips had been slotted so that the tongues from the top could pass through without touching the slots. The base of the triangle was an open wooden grille at the center of which I thought someday I might put a smaller triangle which would duplicate the large triangle and inside that maybe a smaller triangle still. The whole construction was suspended by a chain from the roof of the shed and hung about eighteen inches off the floor. The shed was not air-tight, and sometimes when I was out there after dark with the light on, the thing swayed a little from its chain and made complicated shadows on the floor and walls.

To Bebb and Mrs. Trionka I said, "It's made of wood, and it's got a woody smell. It holds together. The air moves around inside it. But if you asked me what it was all about, I couldn't tell you. I don't know what it's all about. So when it comes to what Herman Redpath is all about and the sun setting, I can't tell you that either. That's your department," I added to my father-in-law.

Bebb said, "It's good for a man to have work for his hands, Antonio." He sat there on the steps gazing west.

Mrs. Trionka said, "When it comes time for us to go, we all of us got to go, and it don't make a bit of difference if we know what it's all about or not." She sloshed her glass back and forth a few times and then tipped her head back like a sword-swallower to drain it. The scoop of ice cream must have rolled down against her lips. I could hear the sounds she made dealing with it inside the glass.

It wasn't until she had left that Bebb spoke again. By this time it was nearly dark. At Holy Love they had switched on the recorded chimes, and *Abide with Me* went trembling out over the fading grassland. Bebb said, "I didn't want to talk about it in front of Beatrice Trionka, but I'll tell you one thing about what it's all about, and that is that it's hard, Antonio. It's all of it hard. Right down to the end. Even the things are supposed to be easy, they're hard too. You take what Herman Redpath's up against now. 'In the twinkling of an eye we shall all be changed,' Scripture says. *In the twinkling of an eye*, Antonio, like it was the easiest thing in the world. It is not easy. Out there somewhere now Herman Redpath and his Maker are sweating like horses. You ever seen anything getting born looked easy, Antonio, let alone anything getting born again?"

From behind, Bebb had no neck to speak of, just a coil of fat above his collar. He looked diminished against the huge sky.

I said, "At least it's nice you believe there's something left of Herman Redpath to sweat with."

"Listen," Bebb said. "That's not even a half of what I believe."

"What else do you believe?" I said.

"Antonio," Bebb said. "I believe everything."

It was a remark of such classic grandeur that for a few moments I sat there in the twilight silent before the sheer magnitude of it.

"You make it sound almost easy," I said finally.

'Don't kid yourself," Bebb said, turning slowly to where he could look at me. "It's hard as hell."

The building where Bebb and Lucille lived was near Herman Redpath's and much like it except that the living-room ceiling was of normal height. I stayed with them the two days I was down there, and the second night—Herman Redpath had died the day before, and the funeral was to take place the day after—I had a hard time getting to sleep. I was almost there—drifting toward it like leaves, like smoke—when, at the very threshold, I tripped over something. I could feel the bed springs bounce under me as I came down on them, and the next moment I was more awake than awake, which is to say afflicted with that awesome clairvoyance of insomnia where even through closed eyelids you can't help seeing, and past, present, and future are all there to see at once.

I thought about home. I thought about my unfinished masterpiece hanging forgotten in the shed month after month while daylight came and went and the seasons changed and weather happened. I pictured it turning pink at daybreak or with snow falling past the window. I pictured a spider using it for something, or a mouse. I thought of the soft and steady downward pull of its suspended weight, the cumbersome woodenness of it with dusty shafts of sunlight sometimes lighting up random surfaces and quirks of it. I thought about the imponderable innocence and gravity of inanimate things, and how even with nobody to watch it, it must sometimes move on its chain.

And I thought about Sharon, of course. The swami from Beloit gave his yoga lessons in the Masonic hall over the bank, and she would drive home from them in her Volkswagen wearing her black leotards with maybe a raincoat thrown over them. Almost as soon as she stepped into the house she would start practicing. She would lie there with her hair spread out on the living-room rug or sitting in the lotus posture with her hands palms up in her lap.

Earlier on the same day that I flew down to Herman Redpath's death-bed, I had come home for lunch to find there was no lunch ready. Chris and the baby were upstairs and Sharon was on her back with her legs so far over her head that her toes were touching the floor behind it. Then Chris came down and said in his muted way that the diaper had slipped out of his hand while he was flushing it out in the toilet and now the toilet was plugged and overflowing onto the bathroom floor. There in the warm Texas night with the sound of either Bebb or Lucille snoring down at the other end of the hall, I relived the low comedy of what had followed—my elephantine sarcasms, the banging doors, the bitter silence as I made my own sandwich in the kitchen. Through closed eyelids I saw Sharon the way she had stood there in her black tights. She told me I was a shit and for God's sake not to hurry home.

No man is ever quite sane in the night, Mark Twain said, and in the dark I reached out for her as if she was actually there only to feel hurt and betrayed all over again when I found my fingers coming down on emptiness. I threw the top sheet off and lay on my stomach with the knuckles of one hand touching the bare floor.

It wasn't the yoga lessons that I held against her. It was the speed reading too. She would sit on the lawn with the sun on her bare back as she drew her fingers in sinuous zigzags down the pages, flipping them over one after the other at a rate sufficient to get her through most of the Sunday *Times* in an hour. Yoga to control her mind and Evelyn Wood to pack it full at increasing speeds—it was like going to the Tour d'Argent with your belt tightened, I told her. Her answer was, "Everybody in this whole damned house can *do* something except me."

It was the closest she ever came to an explanation, and it never seemed to me to explain much. Tony was a raging jock who probably couldn't have gotten through the Sunday *Times* in a month. At eighteen Chris had read all of Virginia Woolf and a good deal of Henry James, got an occasional poem in the senior literary sheet, and was Cinna the poet in the winter production of *Julius Caesar*; but he was bookish as distinct from bright, I'm afraid, got mediocre grades in History and English and flunked math two marking periods in a row. As for me, I taught sixteen year olds *Cry the Beloved Country* and how to identify iambic pentameter and what was wrong with "like a cigarette should." I coached track. I had my six foot mobile casting complicated shadows in a shed off the garage. That was all we could *do*, the rest of us, but maybe it was enough to have precipitated Sharon's remark. I don't know. But whatever the motive, she studied the guitar too, took it up, in fact, before she'd even heard of Evelyn Wood or the swami.

She bought a secondhand Goya when she was seven months pregnant and found a woman named Anita with a grey crew-cut and a face like an unshelled walnut to teach her to play it. She bought a shoulder strap and for weeks carried it all over the house with her playing "I've got a little gal in Kingston town" until I feared for the sanity of our unborn child. Under Anita's supervision, however, her repertoire grew considerably, and it became the only one of her extracurricular interests that I did not begrudge her. Leonard Cohen's *Suzanne* was one of her best. "Jesus was a sailor when he walked upon the water" she would sing with her head to one side so that her hair touched her bare forearm.

And I thought of our unborn child who in spite of everything managed to be born. When they told Sharon it was a boy, she said, "That house of ours is so full of balls it's turning into a goddamn bowling alley." It was the first time I ever saw her cry. Just her eyes cried—none of the rest of her face seemed to have anything to do with it. Under the fluorescent hospital lights the tears turned her cheeks silver. I don't know why she cried. I'm sure it had nothing to do with the baby's being a boy. Maybe it was just that for the first time she felt the walls closing in around her and hadn't yet found Evelyn Wood and the swami to come to her rescue. If that was what she found them for. Anyway, we called the baby William because she thought just plain Bill would be a good antidote for Sharon on one side and Antonio on the other. Right from the beginning he was a good baby. He slept nights. He took his bottle without a fuss. He didn't seem to mind that his mother turned most of the care of him over to a soft-spoken, introspective eighteen year old who had played Cinna the poet in *Julius Caesar.*

My son lies on his stomach in his play-pen. It is a warm spring day, and he has nothing on but his diapers and a pair of rubber pants. He has rings of fat around his arms and legs and looks like the Michelin tire man. Near him on the grass is my nephew Chris. Narrow chested and white, he looks out of place in a bathing suit. He is reading *The Prophet* and every once in a while, without having to look up, he moves the wooden beads of the play-pen abacus with his bare foot to keep the baby entertained.

That is the scene I finally went to sleep on. There was no luxurious moment of knowing that at last sleep was on its way, of feeling it lap around the edges of me like a warm tide. It fell sudden and heavy like a headsman's ax. When I woke up, my father-in-law was standing by my bed in a saucer-shape of sunlight softly tapping me on the shoulder with a copy of the last will and testament of Herman Redpath.

Three

THERE WERE times when I wondered whether Bebb ever went to bed. He was always fully dressed when I went to bed myself, and he was always fully dressed when I got up the next morning. If he slept in between times, I never saw any evidence of it. I can't imagine him asleep. I can't picture him abandoning that overcrowded face even temporarily, can't imagine those busybody eyes turned inward on the puzzle of some dream. The most I can picture is Bebb tucked in like a tin soldier. He's got on his Palm Beach suit, and his arms are stiff at his sides. He is staring up into the dark.

He said, "Antonio, wake up and take a look at a wealthy man. This is the third day for Herman Redpath, and with Herman Redpath I will arise from the dead and shine too. How beautiful upon the mountain, Antonio, are the feet of him that bringeth good tidings. You can read it for yourself when you've had your coffee. One hundred thousand dollars is what it says. One hundred thousand dollars to my loyal friend and pastor Leo Bebb."

I had never seen him more excited. I was still half

asleep, and the whole room seemed to be turning to gold, the shallow pool of sunshine where he was standing, sun on the wall, sun drenching the curtains, sun on my pillow and in my eyes.

He said, "Think what a man could do with a sum like that, Antonio."

"I do hereby devise and bequeath," I read out loud with my hair in my eyes. "To my loyal friend and pastor."

Bebb said, "There is absolutely nothing in the—hardly anything in this world a man could not do with wealth like that."

He stood there by my bedside dressed for Herman Redpath's funeral in his gents'-furnishings suit with his shoulders too square and his ribbed silk tie and his pointed black shoes, and "Expensive clothes," I said, "and expensive women and an air-conditioned Cadillac automobile and color TV in every room. For openers."

Bebb was not listening. He was dreaming. He was glittering in the morning sunshine, his face powdery pale. He said, "Yes, that is so, Antonio. All the kingdoms of the earth spread out at my feet like a wall-to-wall rug. My father was a house painter. He took a bad fall when I was small and spent most of the rest of his life in bed. His fingernails were always dirty. I never did see how a man could get his fingernails dirty just laying around in bed all the time, but he did. Someday I will tell you more about him. My mother was a hard-working woman, a good woman, but she didn't have a particle of charity, Antonio, and without charity her goodness didn't profit anybody anything, herself included. Makes you wonder what a pair like that would have done with a hundred thousand dollars in cash money. They wouldn't have even believed it, most likely."

I had never thought of his having had a mother and father. I said, "Tell me more, Bip."

The one lazy eyelid flickered down for a moment, and I was afraid I had put him on his guard. He said, "Antonio, I will tell you this much for now. I was born and raised outside of Spartanburg, South Carolina, and that is where I got acquainted with sin and death for the first time, and many other things besides. The first time I got acquainted with death was in the railway depot. I don't suppose I was more than six. There was a big, long box sitting out on a hand car waiting to be loaded on to the Atlanta train, and I asked my mother what was inside it. Well, she didn't want to say, naturally, what was in it, but I wormed it out of her. She said it was a dead man was in it being shipped to the crematory with his name written out on the shipping labels just like there was horse feed in there or dry goods. The peculiar thing, Antonio, is I knew it wasn't a dead man. I knew it was a dead woman. It was an old woman, and I could see her in there plain as if I had x-ray eyes. Now you explain that any way you want. She had got on a pair of pink bloomers and a summer dress, and they'd put sticking plaster over her mouth, don't ask me why. It was the first meeting between me and death, Antonio. I have never forgotten it."

He was sitting on the edge of my bed with his hands on his knees looking down at the sun on the floor. I had a momentary impulse to run my finger down his stubby profile the way you might with a statue or a child. Instead, I said, "How about the first meeting between you and sin, Bip?"

Bebb said, "Around Spartanburg it's a lot of good peach country. You wouldn't think so maybe to look at all the red clay, but it is. One summer they commenced dumping peaches to keep the price up. There was piles of peaches heaped up all along the sides of the roads and in the orchards. Antonio, there was peaches every place you looked nearly—big, pinky-yellow, juicy peaches enough to make your mouth water—and there they were, going brown and rotten in the sun. It made you sick the same way as sin makes you sick." His jaw snapped shut as though on a spring.

Bebb said, "Sin is waste, Antonio. Sin is life wasted. Now you take this," he added. Reaching forward he took the last will and testament of Herman Redpath out of my hand. He said, "Everything is accounted for here, and that means nothing is wasted. Everybody has come in for his share, Antonio. I'm fixing to explain it all out later at the funeral." Someone was knocking at my bedroom door, but Bebb took no notice of it. "Jesus has come in for his share too," he said. "A trust has been created to take care of the operating expenses of Gospel Faith College, and there won't have to be any 'Closing Out' sign hung up on the door of Holy Love either. I wanted you to be among the first to know, Antonio. Nobody has been left out in the cold, not even Jesus."

I said, "Maybe that's Jesus now. The knocking."

It was Brownie. He had been off on some errand for Bebb when I had arrived the day before, and I got out of bed now to greet him. He said, "I'm sorry for the sad occasion that's brought us together, dear," and when he smiled, I decided that the way to do Brownie's smile properly would be first to form the expression of a man who has just been kicked in the crotch and then to say "cheese."

Brownie turned to Bebb and said, "I was just over to the church checking on the flowers, and I thought I ought to let you know that I noticed a certain person hanging around outside again. Mrs. Bebb said she found him in the gift shop when she got over and he bought five postcards of you. She said afterwards when she come to look at the money he'd given her, she found this."

Bebb took the object that Brownie handed him and examined it carefully. It had apparently come from one of those machines they used to have in the waiting rooms of big railway stations where you put a quarter in a slot and, by turning a wheel with the alphabet on it, could stamp out your name on a perforated aluminum disc about the size of a fifty cent piece. The one that Brownie handed Bebb had no name on it, however, but just the word SWEETHEART. On the upper rim were printed the words GOOD LUCK.

"Good luck, Sweetheart," Brownie said.

Bebb put the piece in his pocket and said, "Brownie, did he say anything to you when you saw him?"

"He was standing out there in the wet grass like he was reading the bulletin board," Brownie said, "I told him the church was going to be closed to the public today because we were conducting a private funeral."

Bebb said, "What did he say when you told him

that?" They were standing together in the morning sunlight. Bebb had the knob of his chin thrust forward a little, the flesh beneath it slightly in motion.

Brownie said, "He didn't say a word. He just gave me a real friendly smile and started walking away. The bottoms of his trousers were all wet from the grass. That man must weigh a good two hundred and seventy-five stripped."

Bebb said, "You strip him, Brownie." He stood there at the window looking out with his thumbs linked behind him. Without turning around, he said, "Antonio, some of those big government agencies won't stop at anything. The Federal Trade Commission, the U.S. Post Office Department, the Better Business Bureau, you name it. I've had my set-to's with all of them on account of Gospel Faith, and one time or another they've all sent plainclothesmen down here to snoop around. He's one of them probably."

"Why don't you ask him?" I said.

Brownie said, "Dear, that is just the trouble. Up till today he never came close enough to talk to. Before, you might catch sight of him looking out at you through the dime-store window or hanging around by the swimming pool the day Herman Redpath had open house for Rotary, but he never came near enough so as you could get a chance to have a conversation with him."

I said, "Maybe he's bashful."

Brownie said, "Maybe he is, dear." Like Bebb, he had on a dark suit for Herman Redpath's service.

Bebb said, "Good luck, Sweetheart. You don't

generally wish a man good luck unless you think he's going to need it."

"What's he look like?" I asked.

Bebb said, "He looks flat. He looks like he was cut out with a cookie-cutter."

"Flat," Brownie said, "but wide. Very wide, dear."

When Bebb picked Herman Redpath's will off the bed to put it back in his pocket, the reflection of it flickered in the window like a white bird. He said, "If you stick around for a while you may get a look at him yourself, Antonio."

I did stick around, of course—for the funeral that morning and for the burial afterwards—and before I caught the plane back north, I did get a look at him as Bebb had predicted, but not before getting a look at a variety of other things first. There were times during the funeral when I couldn't believe what I was looking at and these are the times I remember best.

There were no special pews reserved for the family because one way or another they were all family. I took a place near Mrs. Trionka toward the back because it gave me a good view of the whole church, and when I was settled down I said a kind of prayer for Herman Redpath. I tried to picture him and his maker sweating it out together the way Bebb had described it and wished them both a happy issue out of their labors. When that was finished, I passed the time until the service was to begin by seeing how many of the Indians I could identify. The Trionka sisters were easy, the three of them drifted together like snow in their flowing white dresses, several rows in front of their mother and me, and I had no trouble with Harry Hocktaw or the small boy who had urinated on Herman Redpath's chair. I recognized the woman who had offered Herman Redpath her breast and the old woman who for the first time in my experience was wearing not a peekaboo blouse but something high-collared and Victorian that buttoned up the back. I looked a long time for Lucille before I discovered her sitting by herself in the choir loft with her dark glasses in place. There were also a few children whose faces I remembered from one visit or another, and of course there was Herman Redpath himself. The coffin was open, and by raising myself slightly in my pew I could just see his nose jutting up out of the white satin like the fin of a shark.

It wasn't until everybody stood up for the opening hymn that I discovered that several members of the congregation were as far as I could see naked. There were just a few of them scattered here and there among the fully clothed ones, and apart from their nakedness they didn't seem to have anything else in common, some male and some female, some old and some young. They did not turn out to have any special role to play in the service either but just stood up and sat down with the rest of us. I convinced myself at one point that they were possibly a little taller and handsomer than the others and wondered if they could have been special favorites of Herman Redpath's who were using this device to say so. Or was it conceivably their way of dramatizing that they had been dealt with inadequately in the will and thus sadly reduced? Or could it just be an overreaction to the Texas heat that day? I don't know. When I asked

Bebb later, he said he didn't know either. In any case, nobody seemed to pay them any particular attention, and I am surprised how quickly I reached the point myself where a bare brown shoulder or buttock or breast seemed no more out of place than a straw hat or a hymn book.

After the funeral was over, Bebb was able to explain to me at least something about the eccentric behavior of John Turtle, but at the time I was unprepared for it. Bebb said, "Seems like every one of your big family groups has got what they call a Joking Cousin, and for Herman Redpath's family group it's John Turtle. A Joking Cousin's main job is to make jokes, but he doesn't make your run-of-the-mill jokes, and he doesn't make them at run-of-the-mill times either. Say there's a marriage being arranged and the heads of both families are there all dressed up to make terms. Or say a man's dying or just died and the women have come over to pay their last respects. Maybe a girl gets herself in trouble, and there's a pow-wow what to do about finding her a husband. They're the times when the Joking Cousin does his stuff. Seems as if the Joking Cousin is the Indians themselves mocking and blaspheming their own holiest times so as nobody else will. Seems to me like an Indian thinks if he mocks the holiest times he's got, maybe then the evil spirits will be fooled into letting the holy times alone. Maybe even God will let them alone then, Antonio."

I don't know about Bebb's explanation. I know only that at the funeral of Herman Redpath at Holy Love, John Turtle played the part of the Joking Cousin. John Turtle turned out to be the one who had teeth like cufflinks and had told me he couldn't hear or see Harry Hocktaw's rattle.

"I am the resurrection and the life," Bebb said from the pulpit pale as death, and John Turtle stood behind him holding two fingers up over Bebb's head like rabbit ears. When Bebb was winding up his eulogy of Herman Redpath by giving out the details of the will—explaining how even from the grave Herman Redpath would continue to finance the ranch indefinitely and everyone was going to have his share including Jesus—John Turtle picked his nose on the chancel steps. At several points in the service, he even tried to get Bebb to enter into dialogue with him.

"The Lord is my shepherd, I shall not want," Bebb read from the lectern, his face glistening with perspiration, and "I know what *you* want right enough," John Turtle said from the foot of the casket.

Bebb said, "He maketh me to lie down in green pastures, He leadeth me beside the still waters," and John Turtle said, "I know a girl what lives on a hill. If she won't do it, her sister will." You have to hand it to Bebb. He never batted an eye.

"Chicka-chicka boom, chicka-boom, chicka-boom," went the Joking Cousin not unlike the sound of Harry Hocktaw's rattle all through the Lord's Prayer. And during one of the hymns he ate a slice of watermelon. When he finished it, he made the motions of turning a crank in his neck and made his head tilt slowly backward like an anti-aircraft gun. When he reached maximum elevation, he turned another crank to make his head swivel around to face the congregation. With his lips puckered out to a point and his cheeks puffed he waited until the Amen came and then pulled one ear to fire. Watermelon seeds flew out toward the front pews like shrapnel.

Unlike the small boy in the orange life preserver, nobody came up to snatch the Joking Cousin away when just after the benediction he walked over and either took or pretended to take a leak into Herman Redpath's open coffin.

Oddly enough, the most vivid memory I have of Herman Redpath's obsequies involves none of these extraordinary events but one which was comparatively speaking rather ordinary. The whole congregation was standing up for a hymn, and when it was over, Bebb patted the air with one hand to indicate that everybody was to sit down and said in his pulpit voice, "Brothers and sisters, let us bow our heads in prayer." As far as I could tell, everybody obeyed and sat down and bowed their heads. I bowed my head too but not so far as to keep me from seeing what was going on.

At first I thought that for once there was nothing going on. Bebb was praying his prayer, getting more and more vehement with God about something. Even John Turtle was for the moment quiet. The Indians had arranged themselves in varying attitudes of worship and inattention—some with their faces in their hands or their foreheads resting on the pew in front of them, some half-sitting and half-kneeling, several with their heads down almost in their laps as if they were trying to keep themselves from being sick. A few pews in front of me I noticed that the shoulders of one of the Trionka girls were heaving and wondered if it was from grief or some dark spasm of mirth. A naked boy was leaning forward with his head cradled in his arms on the pew in front of him, and under one arm I could see the hair dark and luxuriant as fur. It wasn't for some moments that I glanced in the other direction and discovered that one member of the congregation had remained on his feet. He was standing there with his hands in his pockets, and as soon as I saw him, I knew that he was the stranger Bebb and Brownie had been discussing that morning.

From shoulder to shoulder, hip to hip, he was a very wide man, and anybody meeting him head-on would have thought he was enormous. Seeing him from the side, however, I appreciated the accuracy of Bebb's remark about the cookie-cutter. From back to front he was not enormous, and the only place where his thickness came near to matching his width was below the waist. It was not a paunch because it was too low for that and too spread out laterally. It was as if he was wearing some kind of inner tube or bolster which had slipped down over his loins, a massive eave of flesh swelling out over his crotch. His face was sallow and wrinkled, but when for no apparent reason he smiled at one point, his teeth showed strong and white and young. It was the smile of a pretty girl.

There he stood in the midst of Holy Love, cumbersome, relaxed, while all around him everybody else including myself were sitting or kneeling with our heads bowed. What made the moment so peculiarly vivid, I suppose, was the sense I had that he was the one we were bowing to. Bebb went on praying with his eyes screwed tight shut, and when the stranger smiled that oddly gay and youthful smile, it seemed a kind of graceful acknowledgement that even the prayer was addressed to him.

After the service was over, I hoped that I could get close enough to hear what his voice sounded like, perhaps even to speak to him, but I lost him in the crowd while I was waiting to shake hands with Bebb on the way out and caught only one more glimpse of him later. He was way off beyond the parking lot by then, drifting along through the high grass like an oddly shaped swarm of bees.

Later that afternoon when we had come back from the cemetery, Bebb and Lucille drove me to the airport to catch my plane home. Brownie came along for the ride, and when it turned out that the plane was going to be more than an hour late, Lucille insisted we all go into the lounge for some refreshment. Through the picture window you could see planes landing and taking off into the hot, pearly sky. Bebb and Brownie both had iced tea, and I joined Lucille in an airport lounge version of a Tropicana.

After a while Lucille said, "Golden, Brownie. When he bought those postcards, I asked him what his name was, and he said his name was Golden." It was a statement, but she left it hanging like a question. Bebb seemed remote and preoccupied, watching a big airliner go taxiing down the runway. Lucille and Brownie sat looking at each other in silence, Lucille behind her black glasses and Brownie behind his horn rims. "That's one for the books," Lucille said.

Brownie smiled dimly. He said, "I've heard stranger names than that in my time. I knew a boy once named ToeWater. Fred ToeWater."

There was another long, interrogatory silence

during which Lucille lifted her glass to her lips and stared at Brownie over the rim of it, her eyebrows raised. She said finally, "Golden's a Jewish name."

Brownie said, "Some of my very dear friends are Jewish."

Lucille said, "If that man's Jewish, I'm a nigger."

Bebb turned slightly more toward the window like a man stirring in his sleep. Over the loudspeaker a voice read a long list of flight numbers. Brownie placed his hands palms down on the table in front of him. He wore three rings which looked like fraternity rings and a gold spring-band watch around one hairy wrist. Without looking up from his hands, he said, "What are you getting at, dear?"

Lucille dropped her lower jaw slightly. She said, "You tell me."

Brownie shrugged his shoulders and laid one hand on top of the other.

Lucille said, "He's no more Jewish than Bebb is, but when I asked him what his name was, he said it was Golden. That's Jewish."

"Are you inferring that Golden is an alias, dear?" Brownie said.

Lucille said, "The only thing I'm inferring is suppose he hadn't said his name was Golden. Suppose he said it was Silver."

Bebb's face looked vigorous and fresh as he interrupted them. He said, "Brownie, how'd you like to start being number one man at Holy Love?"

It had been a long, hot day. I was starting to feel a little drowsy from the Tropicana, and didn't listen as carefully as I might have otherwise to the conversation that followed. When I got home late that evening, Sharon was irritated by my incomplete and garbled account of it. She said, "My God, all our lives are at stake and you weren't even listening. What kind of peckerhead are you anyway?" And of course she was right. One way or another our lives were at stake.

All the time Bebb had been praying in his maroon robe with the sweat running down, all the time John Turtle had been trying to distract the evil spirits or God or whoever it was, all the time we had stood there under the low clouds waiting until Herman Redpath's urine-stained coffin was finally lowered into the Texas soil, Bebb had apparently been making plans. There in the airport against a backdrop of silver wings and pewter clouds he had revealed them rapidly, one after another, like a magician pulling silk scarves out of somebody's ear.

What I remembered best was how he talked about the money Herman Redpath had left him. "One hundred thousand in cash, Antonio, with no strings attached," and he made it dance there, stringless, on the Formica before us. The money was power, it was promise, it was all the benevolence of Herman Redpath rolled into one. The money was freedom and adventure and fun, and as he stacked his words higher and higher, I wondered if he was thinking of his bed-ridden father again with the dirty fingernails in Spartanburg, South Carolina, and the piles of golden peaches abandoned along the roads to keep the price up. "The sky is the limit," he said—the sky behind his bald head looking electric and dangerous—and he stuck his finger into his tea and stirred the ice around until it rattled.

Herman Redpath had endowed both Holy Love and Gospel Faith in perpetuity, *saecula saeculorum*, so he, Bebb, was no longer needed there, he said. He had planted the seed and watered it with the sweat of his brow and tended the young shoots, and now he would leave it to Brownie to supervise the harvesting. Even Brownie should be able to handle things from here on out, Bebb said, and Brownie sat there in his short sleeves listening to him.

Bebb said, "Antonio, I have heard the voice of the Lord saying, 'Whom shall I send?' and I have said, 'Here am I. Leo Bebb. Send me.' I have labored in these Texas vineyards long enough. I may not be the man I once was, but I am not an old man yet either. There are souls to be saved same as there always was and always will be, and one hundred thousand dollars will take me a long piece down the road toward saving them. Indians aren't the only lost sheep of the House of Israel."

Lucille said, "I've got your Indians up to here," and drew one horizontal hand across her face at nose level, knocking her glasses crooked along the way. "That Turtle wasn't just pretending to piss on Herman Redpath. I was sitting upstairs by myself, and I could look right down and see it soaking into the Navajo blanket. Show me an Indian," she said, "and I'll show you a slob. I'm getting out of here if I have to push a peanut with my nose clear to Savannah."

Bebb talked about the North, I remember, with such poetry and zeal that it took me a while before I was sure what he was talking about. "The pilgrim's pride," he said. "The place they landed at in their old-time hats with buckles on their shoes and kneeled right down on that rock-bound coast with the waves pounding in their ears to return thanks to the Almighty. I am proud to be a Southerner born and bred, Antonio, but North is where the history was made and where the history is still being made to this very day. North is where the money is. North is where the power is. And the great whore is in the North too, Antonio, holding a golden cup in her hand full of the abominations and filthiness of her fornications. We have not been called to sit on our tails by the swimming pool forever and break bread with multi-millionaires of Indian descent. We are called to the North where the fighting is thickest. That's where we must work and fight while we can, for the night is coming. At any moment the end may come, Antonio. Like a thief in the night."

It was on this part of my report that Sharon questioned me most closely later. Did Bip mean that he was coming north to *us?* Could he possibly mean that he and Lucille were going to live in our house? Did he plan to create a new Holy Love right there with Tony going around hanging up African violets in his jock strap and me having a hemorrhage every time my lunch wasn't ready on the dot? Did he say *when* he was coming—like next year or next month or next week?

I failed miserably to give her the information she wanted. It was the rhetoric I remembered, not the facts. I wasn't even sure whether Bebb himself had given facts. I was sure that there was no need to start emptying bureau drawers that night, I told her, but that was all I was sure of.

The boys had both gone to bed before I got home,

and the baby was asleep. The house was stuffy and still smelled of hamburger and onions so we were sitting outside under the spring stars. Even outside it was very warm, but, unlike Houston, there was at least a little movement in the air. When I finished my lame recital, Sharon did something she had learned in yoga maybe. I was lying face down in the damp grass, and she got up and stood on my back in her bare feet. She stood on the small of my back. She stood with one foot on my neck and the other between my shoulder blades. I could feel the cool soles of her feet through my shirt, and sometimes when she changed position the weight of her pressed the breath right out of me, but I could also feel it ironing out all the soreness and snarls left by my hours of sleeplessness the night before and by the long flight north and by my memories of how Herman Redpath's nose had looked jutting up out of the white satin.

Being stepped on almost put me to sleep before she was through, but she didn't let it. I was lying on my stomach, and she slipped one bare foot underneath me and did something unexpected and just painful enough down there to remind me that where her foot had touched was also part of who I was and that the three whole days and nights I had been away, that part too had been living, however obscure and neglected, a life of its own which she restored now, that accomplished young acrobat, that speedy reader, that guitarist, on whose charms Herman Redpath may or may not have expended the last words I ever heard him speak.

Four

I SUPPOSE it is from my days as a schoolteacher and from my own school days that I have inherited the feeling that the year really starts in the fall. Fall is the time when the long dream of summer comes to an end and you settle down to the true business of your life. Spring, on the other hand, is the time of ending, and it is the season when I feel most vulnerable and anxious and haunted. Something more than just school is coming to a close, and all the poignant and beautiful things that are happening in nature only serve to heighten by contrast all the dim and disturbing things that are happening in me.

For the first few days after I got back from Texas, much of this vague, floating malaise tended to attach itself to my uncertainty about what Bebb's next move was going to be and Sharon's growing horror that he and Lucille were probably about to arrive on our doorstep as permanent guests. She didn't want to call or write to find out his plans for fear of pushing him into something he might not yet quite have decided on so she just moved around from lesson to lesson in a somber, inflammable state waiting for our doom to be announced. The boys stayed out of her way as much as they could, Chris drifting around the second floor like a ghost and even Tony making a visible effort to use up less oxygen than usual. As for me, I found sanctuary in the classroom. To teach a class, whether you do it well or badly, is to achieve fifty minutes worth of self-forgetfulness. More even than the long summer vacations, it is the principal side-benefit that the profession offers.

Commencement was only a few weeks away. The seniors in my English class were still willing to go through the motions, but obviously they felt that the battle had already been either won or lost by then and in either case they were through battling. It was folly to try starting anything new with them at this point, but I had committed myself to it during an assault of winter energy and the books had arrived and been paid for. It was *King Lear*, and the only bright side of our ill-timed study was that it is the one Shakespearean tragedy I've never been able to read without a lump in my throat.

For various obscure scheduling reasons, the class met during one of the two lunchtime periods those last few weeks, and about half the students would come in with their trays and sit there eating Spanish rice and fruit jello while I tried to engage them in literary discussion. The day we started out on *Lear* there was gingerbread for dessert, and I can still remember the rosettes of ersatz whipped cream and the sound of the big electric mower working out on the playing field, the classroom smell of pencil shavings, floor cleaner and flatulence. Almost a week had gone by since Herman Redpath's funeral, and although there was still no word from Bebb and no lightening either of Sharon's dark mood or my springtime melancholia, I was able to forget all of this in my effort to interest twenty adolescents in what one of them launched our discussion of Act I, Scene 1, by describing as a boring fairy-tale. The one who made the crushing remark was Laura Fleischman, a girl as golden as one of Bebb's South Carolina peaches but still attached to the tree untouched, untasted, and to all appearances totally unaware that there was any danger of ending up by the roadside someday to go spoiled in the sun.

But later that afternoon, by way of compensation, there was a good turn-out for track practice. As coach I was there in my usual baggy sweat suit with grass stains at the knees and a whistle around my neck, and I got the names down on my clipboard as one by one they straggled out, my hurdlers and sprinters and broad jumpers, my shot-putters and javelin throwers. They were a pretty seedy looking crowd with nothing much in the way of ability, but they worked hard that spring and had done quite well in competition. The only real star among them was my sixteen year old nephew, Tony Blaine, and everybody knew it including Tony himself. The pole vault was his specialty, but he had versatility and endurance enough to do well in almost any event. I had to put him in as a miler once, and he broke the school record. He was a natural athlete and took it seriously. He took his body seriously—watching his diet, lifting his weights, getting enough sleep—but there was nothing grim in the way he went about it. He kept himself in shape the way a great lover might, as if he knew that the end he kept himself in shape for was in the last analysis not the most serious end a man could pursue or else so serious that, like the Joking Cousin, you didn't want to let on to the gods it was. He horsed around a lot. He was also very emotional—one of his bonds with Sharon was that they both cried at movies, even TV movies. He was also quick-tempered and in that way reminded me of his mother.

As I watched him jogging around the cinder track naked to the waist and barefoot like something straight off the Parthenon, I thought of the mystery of human generation. My sister Miriam with her poor broken bones already turning to dust in a Brooklyn grave; my ex-brother-in-law Charlie Blaine, that nap-taking valetudinarian trying to get through his life making as few waves as possible; and out of their almost unthinkable passion this boy who was both of them and neither of them, this cocky godling and larky shambles of a boy who himself at this moment carried in his belly the seed of unimaginable progeny. He came running over to me with his dark hair in his eyes and that panicky, inward-looking frown that comes with being out of breath and panted out, "I wish to God you'd tell Sharon not to hang around here in that get-up." I hadn't even seen her arrive.

She must have driven over straight from the swami's because she had on her black leotards as she lay there on one elbow in the grass. She had her hair tied back with a yellow scarf and was wearing hoop earrings. If she was aware of the stir she was causing among my sweaty charges, she gave no evidence of it. Shielding her eyes with one hand, she was squinting out to where beyond the track a solitary boy was practicing. He was running with a javelin at shoulder level, and the sun had turned the shaft of it to gold. She looked as though if she turned her thumb down, the boy would be thrown to the crocodiles, and as though she was thinking seriously about turning her thumb down.

Tony, his bare chest heaving. The smell of the freshly mowed field in the sun. The boy with the golden spear. Sharon reclining there like Sheba herself or some Coptic call-girl with every lazy hill and valley of her young flesh exposed to the gaze of the circumcised and uncircumcised both. To my steaming nephew I said, "She is black but comely, O ye daughters of Jerusalem. There's not an awful lot I can do about it," and after looking as though he might bite his thumb at me and spit on the ground, he tossed the hair out of his eyes and went on back to his laps.

That evening couldn't have started out more auspiciously. Sharon and I had a drink before supper, and she took out her guitar and played a few songs. She tried a setting Anita had taught her to "As ye came from the holy land of Walsingham" and "I know where I'm going" and Donovan's "Jennifer Juniper," and after a while Chris came padding downstairs to listen, and it wasn't long before Tony was there too. He had forgotten all about his earlier irritation and sat on the arm of her chair reading the words over her shoulder. Except for the way we were dressed, we presented a family scene of almost Victorian felicity with Sharon and Tony the brother and sister or young newlyweds and me the benign avuncular presence. Tony and I were in khakis and shirtsleeves and Sharon in blue jeans, but Chris, though he had taken off his jacket, sat there with his necktie on, his loafers polished, and a crease in his pants. He could have been some resident cousin or visiting parson. All we lacked was Bill clapping dimpled hands at the sunset through the bay window, but he was still in his crib upstairs napping. From the kitchen came the smell of supper, and every once in a while when there was quiet enough you could hear the peepers from the vacant lot across the street. We moved into the kitchen to eat.

It would be interesting to know how it happened. I suppose that when any group comes together, it is like a comic strip where in addition to the balloons where the words are, there are the clouds where the light bulbs and exclamation points and naked women are, and sometimes the clouds collide without anybody's being aware of it until all of a sudden there is a roll of thunder or in one corner of the room it starts to rain. At the level of the balloons nothing seemed to go wrong. I repeated some of what Bebb had told me about Joking Cousins. Chris got to laughing in his own curious style which involved not laughing *out* ha-ha but laughing *in* in an asthmatic way with his head tossing back and forth and his steel-rimmed glasses fogging up. Tony repeated some crude gossip about Laura Fleischman which was completely at odds with the impression she had given me that afternoon during the *Lear* class. I don't remember Sharon's saying anything in particular, but she gave no sign of taking offense at anything and seemed to join in whenever she felt like it. Then suddenly the first drops were starting to fall, heavy and cold. May had turned without warning into November.

It is Chris I see, his colorless face and his wiry, colorless hair that grew flat on his scalp like a cap. I see his father's pale, noncommittal eyes looking out through his glasses. He has tied his bow tie himself but it looks like the kind you clip on. There is a tendency to pinkness around the underside of his nostrils that makes you think he has a slight cold. It is the face that he uses for doing his personal business behind. It is impossible to tell what kind of personal business he is doing behind it as he sits there twisting his senior class ring around and around his finger and listens to Tony tell Sharon that she ought to start taking care of her own baby herself. Tony is very Italian, very like his mother, and keeps cutting backward with one hand while he speaks, as though there is a hornet trying to get at him from behind. His voice is rapid and rising in pitch like a sports announcer's.

She should wash the crap out of the baby's diapers herself, he says, and get up in the night when it cries. She should be the one to give it its bottle for Christ's sake. She should stop turning his brother into a goddamned nursemaid fairy.

A mist or ragged lower edge of cloud has come drifting down until all there is left to see of Chris's face is the lower part, the tiny pimples around the chin, the dry lips with the little film that seals them at the corners and then breaks as he parts them slightly to moisten them. The pussy-cat tie moves with his

Adam's apple. Tony's football-huddle arm is suddenly around his shoulder, and Chris's neck does an odd little sideways movement like a temple dancer's.

The rain, coming down heavier now, has for the moment washed all expression out of Sharon's face. Tony has caught her by surprise as for better or worse she and my namesake Tony are always catching each other by surprise. Her face is as perfect a blank as Eve's must have been at the moment of her creation. Anything can happen in that face. What happens is she picks up her glass and flips the water at Tony. The water hangs unfurled in the air for a moment like a split-second photograph. It misses Tony and soaks the front of Chris's white shirt. His flesh shows through.

Tony's chair-legs stutter noisily against the linoleum as he thrusts back hard. I bring the flat of my palm down slam on the table. We make a rain-dance beat. The wet wind has blown Sharon's hair across one cheek. She says, "You goddamn muscle-bound jock."

He says, "The way you come swinging your cock-tease tail around at practice every afternoon."

She says, "If I ever dreamed I'd have some little prick like you on my hands the rest of my life . . ."

Jock, cock, prick—the invective is exclusively phallic, a ritual copulation so that in the sky the gods will also copulate and the wet come streaming down to fertilize that kitchen where I stand up to defend my wife. I say it's a fine way to repay her for her friendship and interest. Month after month she comes, huddled in the empty bleachers at football time, standing in the cold mud for soccer, in the humid jungle haze of the swimming pool where wet boy voices echo like parrot cries from the tiled walls. I think of her leaning forward there with her chin in her hand.

A banana of all things is what she is shaking at him there by the red-topped counter where a bowl of them sits, our dessert, and where the hell does he think she can find time to take care of a baby or anything else when she has to spend the whole damn day picking up after him—his cruddy socks and underpants and that wreck of a room where she hates to open the door for fear of what she . . . For fear . . . opening the door.

At *fear* she stops and everything stops including the rain which becomes suddenly a slow, cold drizzle. We are all standing up now except for Chris, who is still sitting down at the table in silence. In the overhead light he is as white as his wet, white shirt. You can see one nipple through it. The corned beef hash has gone cold on his plate. Everything around him in the circle of light glistens from the drizzle, the rest of us shadowed. His eyes are pink. His voice comes cracked, plaintive through our silence which is soggy and soft as wet leaves.

He says, "Who says I'm a goddamned nursemaid fairy?"

For a moment or two we are all caught unfurled in the air like the water from Sharon's glass. Upstairs Bill has woken up from his nap and is crying.

After dark I went out to commune with my Thing. It looked bigger than I remembered it, hanging there in the light of the one bulb. Just a touch from my finger was enough to set it stirring on its chain. It felt very heavy. Shadows rose and fell and crisscrossed. The air smelled woody. I sat on the workbench and watched it a while. Raw pine. The parts where I'd sanded it were soft as skin. I noticed a part I'd missed inside the upper arc of one of the round holes cut out through a leg plank. Through the hole, I could see a piece on the other side begin to appear as the whole thing ponderously, almost imperceptibly, turned. As it turned, the piece seemed to come down across the hole like a wooden eyelid. Nothing is as fascinating as something you've made yourself. Just your own handwriting on an envelope, or a shelf you've put up, even a crap you've taken—they give you the feeling, if you look in a certain way, that they contain a secret and that if you could only get at the secret you'd find out that maybe it was the secret of your life. I must have sat out there a good half hour or more watching the thing before I was interrupted by Sharon.

She didn't come in but called to me through the window. She had a flashlight and in order not to shine it in my eyes, she shone it upwards so that all the shadows on her face went the wrong way and made her look like somebody else.

"Bip phoned," she said. "He's got his plans all made. He wants us to get moving and find a house for him and Luce. He doesn't care what kind of a house it is, but he wants it to have a barn or a garage that's big enough to start preaching Holy Love in. He talked a lot about the great whore and her abominations and fornications."

I said, "You've got to hand it to him."

Sharon said, "It could have been a whole lot

worse. He could have said they were coming to stay with us."

On the way back to the house, I asked her if everything was all right with her and the boys. I hadn't gone out to the shed until I'd thought it was, nobody shaking hands and making up or anything but Sharon being the one to go upstairs to see to the baby and Tony doing the dishes single-handed while she was gone. With November turning to May again, Chris and I had just wandered off like the swallows going back to Capistrano. I thought everything was probably all right, but I wanted to hear her say it.

"Poor old Chris," she said. "I felt so sorry for him I could have kissed him right there in the kitchen."

I said, "If you ever kiss one of them you better kiss the other one too."

She stopped right there in the dark. She said, "Hey *Antonio*. Are you kidding, Antonio?"

She didn't call people by their names very often and didn't have to. You could usually tell from the way she said a thing whom she was saying it to. It was more intimate than using names. But this time she used my name twice. It was as if I had slept through the alarm and she was trying to get me to wake up.

Five

WORDS WERE the least important part of what Lucille Bebb used when she was telling a story. She used long pauses. She used her lower jaw. She used her dark glasses and her eyebrows. But lots of clouds came dot, dot, dot out of her head with thoughts in them. Lucille's genius was to make these clouds somehow visible to her listener. You left her with the sense that she had described in detail events which as far as her words were concerned she had barely suggested.

Since Bebb had insisted that expense was no object, within a few days I was able to rent him a farmhouse about halfway between Sutton, where Sharon and I lived, and Stamford. The house belonged to a university couple who were away on a year's sabbatical and it came completely furnished so that Bebb was able to fly up from Houston with Lucille, sign the lease, and move in all within little more than a week of his original phone call. As Bebb had specified, the house came with a barn, and it was in the barn that Lucille gave me what turned out to be the first installment of an epic. Bebb had gone off to New York to see about having a sign made for his new church, and Lucille and I had our conversation alone. In setting down what she told me, I am giving perhaps ten times more than what she actually gave me, but this does not mean that I have taken liberty with the facts or embellished them unduly. It means simply that I have included the contents of the clouds.

She started off by telling me about elevators. She said there were elevators and elevators. There were the regular everyday elevators that you got into on the fifth floor or the sixth floor, say, and could ride on down to the ground floor. If you had business there, you could ride them down to the basement. There were some places where you could ride them clear on down to the sub-basement or whatever the bottom-most floor was called. But then there were also some other elevators, she told me, that you could ride farther down than that. There were elevators that went deeper than the bottom. Farther down than down. If I knew what she meant, she said, raising her eyebrows. I asked her where these elevators were supposed to take you. She paused for a while, then said, "Ask Bebb."

After a while she said there weren't too many elevators of this second kind. To your average person, they would look just like your average elevators. You had to be special yourself to know they were special, to know how to work them and where they went and why they went there. She happened to know there was one in Houston. She wasn't sure just where in Houston exactly, but she had an idea it was in one of the big department stores. And scattered over the country there were maybe ten or a dozen like it, mostly in big cities. There was one in Chicago, one in L.A., one in Seattle. There were more of them in the West than in the East for some reason. But there were supposed to be two of them in New York City.

She did not say anything for a while then, and part of what she did not say was that at that very moment, as we both knew, Bebb was in New York City himself. She just said there were two of these special elevators in New York City and let it go at that, let it go but on a rather long leash and for a rather long time. During this time one of the clouds rose up out of her head puff-puff like a child's picture of steam coming out of a steam engine.

In the cloud I saw Bebb. Bebb was standing alone in an elevator. He was wearing a raincoat buttoned up to his chin and his little Happy Hooligan hat planted squarely on top of his head. He had a very determined expression and was keeping track of the floors by watching the window in the elevator door. Down, down, the elevator went, and at each new floor a light flashed in through the window and lit up Bebb's face. The elevator went down to the ground floor, the basement, the sub-basement, and kept on going. Bebb's face was light and then dark again, light and then dark again. His arms hung stiff at his sides.

Lucille said, "They have their meetings down there."

I said, "Who have their meetings?"

The barn where we were standing was more or less empty. Hanging from one of the beams there was a knotted rope for climbing and from another a child's swing. There was a *Make Love Not War* poster on one of the walls. On the floor Bebb had marked in chalk where he wanted the altar table to go and the pulpit. He had ordered them already and expected them any day. Lucille was standing near another poster. It showed W. C. Fields in a beaver hat looking up furtively from a poker hand. I had not noticed before the resemblance to Bebb. Maybe it was just that they were both poker-faced.

Lucille said, "They come from way up, but they have their meetings way down."

It was only about eleven o'clock on a Saturday morning, but I said anyway, "You've been hitting the Tropicanas a little earlier than usual, haven't you?"

Lucille said, "You blame me?"

She had moved and was standing in front of one of the windows. With the light coming from behind, you could see how thin her hair was. You could see the curve of her scalp through it. She said, "You remember Mr. Golden, don't you?"

It took me a moment or two, but then I remembered. I said, "What about Mr. Golden, Luce?"

She dropped her lower jaw slightly. She said, "What about Mr. Golden yourself?" After a while she said, "Bebb told me once that to every one Golden there's maybe half a dozen Silvers."

I said, "Bebb talks to you about this kind of stuff?"

Lucille said, "Sometimes I can't worm a thing out of Bebb. Other times I can't hardly shut him off."

I said, "All he ever told me was he believed there were people around off of flying saucers and they were the same as what the Bible calls angels."

"That's what he tells people," Lucille said.

On again off again, on again off again, went the

light on Bebb's face as the elevator descended. Then the light came on to stay. The elevator had stopped and the door slid open. Bebb stepped out. There was an enormous circular room that looked like the U.N. Security Council or an operating amphitheater. It was brightly lit from the ceiling, and there were circular tiers of seats radiating out from the clear space in the middle. The clear space was heavily carpeted, and Bebb's footsteps made no sound as he walked across it. He climbed up into the seats and took an empty one about fifteen or twenty rows back. He took off his coat and hat and sat down. In the seat next to him was the man who had remained standing at Herman Redpath's funeral when everyone else got down to pray, or else it was the man's twin brother. He turned toward Bebb and welcomed him with the same gay and youthful smile. He had on a pair of earphones with an antenna sticking up over one ear. Bebb nodded back brusquely as he put on his own earphones.

There is such a thing, I am told, as a *folie à deux*, a state of things where a person's hallucination becomes so intense that he can give it to somebody else like measles and the two of them start hallucinating together. With Bebb away on his errand in New York City, Lucille had been hitting the Tropicanas earlier than usual that morning, and for a few moments out there in the barn, I, who hadn't touched a drop, was drunk as a monkey.

When Bebb's sign finally came, he asked Sharon and me and the boys to come over and see it. Like the Holy Love sign, it was a life-size cross made of opaque glass which could be lit up inside. Like the

Holy Love sign too, the two parts of the new church's name were written one on the horizontal member and one on the vertical member in such a way that they shared a common letter. OPEN was written on the crosspiece, and HEART came down through it where the E was. To make the lettering symmetrical there was a red heart after the N in OPEN. Bebb switched the light on for us, and we all stood in the spring dusk admiring it. It jutted out over the barn door so that it would be visible from the road.

Bebb said, "Revelations three twenty. 'Behold, I stand at the door and knock. If any man hear my voice and open the door, I will come in to him.' Boys, now you listen to that because it's dynamite. Jesus is cooling his heels right there at the door of your heart, and he's knocking. All you got to do is open up and he'll enter in and sup with you. Talk about your open heart surgery. Why, Jesus has got all the rest of them beat a mile. Once you open your heart up to him, I tell you it *stays* open. It stays open day and night and welcomes all who pass by with open arms—the widow, the orphan, the—boys, it even welcomes your enemy once Jesus gets it open wide enough."

Sharon was standing by the lilac bush. Bebb came over and put his arm around her shoulder. He pointed up at the sign and said, "Honey, how do you like that for the name of your old Bip's brand new church?"

Sharon said, "You've done it again, Bip."

Lucille said, "Bebb, find out what's everybody's pleasure and we'll all go back and have us something out on the verandah."

Bebb was still looking up at his sign. He said, "Starting tomorrow, I've got an ad that's going to run in all the local papers. It says, 'Have a Heart.' It says, 'Open your heart to Jesus. Open your heart to each other. Open your heart TODAY.' I've got my name on it just Leo Bebb, Evangelist. Nothing about Holy Love or Gospel Faith or any of the rest of it. That's ancient history now. Up here I'm starting out with a clean slate. I'm starting out fresh with nothing except Jesus."

A clean slate. A fresh start. The clothes he was booked in returned to him at the warden's office. His bus-fare home put in his pocket. But that was all. Except maybe Jesus. I thought of Bebb starting fresh back then, years before I knew him, after he'd finished doing his time for what they said he'd done in Miami. And here was Bebb starting fresh again now with Open Heart. I wanted to say, "Open your heart to us, Bip. Tell about Miami." I wanted to tell what little I knew about it myself. I wanted to tell Tony and Chris especially because it didn't seem fair for them not to know the full richness and roundness of the man which all of the rest of us standing with them under the life-size cross knew in essence if not in detail. It didn't even seem fair to Bebb for them not to know. I wanted to teach Bebb to them like school.

Bebb stood next to Sharon stuffed like a sausage into his dark suit with the lilacs turning to dusk behind him and his fat face full of secrets. I wanted to freeze him like a slide projected on a screen and give a lecture on him. With the end of a pointer I wanted to touch his mouth, touch under each eye, touch those curves of polished scalp and scrubbed cheek and where the extra flesh made his earlobes stick out.

I wanted to say, "This is Leo Bebb. He is full of beans and bounce. He is afraid of nothing except heights. I have seen him myself approach lions unarmed. He is a supersalesman for Jesus. He has done time. Exactly what it is he did time for and whether or not he was framed, I'm not sure. Only once in my presence did he refer to it directly. He said he had heard about as good singing behind bars as he'd ever heard anywhere."

I wanted to say, or didn't want to say, "Look at the way he's got his breastpocket handkerchief folded. Look how excited he is about his new sign and how he's put his arm around his daughter's shoulder. Could it be that those Miami children misunderstood some innocent gesture? There is no reason why he couldn't have just been taking a leak in the alley thinking he was alone and, when he heard their voices behind him, simply spun around in surprise."

Bebb stopped looking at the sign. He said, "What's your pleasure, folks?" and went around taking our orders.

I had never seen him angry before or speak a harsh word to anybody except Brownie, but after we'd been sitting on the porch for a while having our drinks, both happened.

Lucille was sitting tipped back in her rocker with her feet braced against the porch railing. It was getting dark, and for once she had taken off her black glasses and was staring vacantly out into the twilight when Tony returned with her glass which she had sent him out into the kitchen to refill. She took it out of his hand in a vague way and must have forgotten that it was full again because as she raised it to her lips to take her first deep sip, she slopped most of it down her front. The surprise made her push out with her feet against the railing, and before she could catch herself, she had tipped over backwards in her rocker. Her skirt was up around her waist, and her bony legs were sticking into the air. One arm was flung out to the side, and she was holding what was left in her glass miraculously unspilled. Her mouth was open in an odd, crooked way as though somebody had hit her in the jaw.

Bebb said, "Get up, Lucille. Get up this minute," and his voice was a frightening thing to hear. When Tony came forward to help her, Bebb barred his way with his arm. "Pick yourself up and go inside," he said.

I did not want to watch her pick herself up, but I watched her. Sharon helped get the chair out from under her, and then Lucille rolled over to one side and took hold of the railing. With this she managed to pull herself up to her knees and finally to a standing position. Her dress was hiked up in back and her thin hair sticking out in all directions. She brushed Sharon aside. With the dignity of a queen she moved off down the twilit porch taking what was left of her Tropicana and entering the house without a word or glance at any of us.

Almost as soon as she had gone, Bebb started talking about her. The anger had left his voice. There wasn't much light left, and such as there was was enough to see by only if you didn't try to see too much. As Bebb spoke, his face became almost indistinguishable from the blue dusk. He said, "First job I ever had was washing dishes in her father's restaurant in Spartanburg. She was a couple of years younger than me, and there was plenty of them after her. I never thought I stood a Chinaman's chance, but her father took a shine to me. It was him that helped me land a job selling Bibles. I wasn't even dry behind the ears yet and never got through high school because my father was laid up in bed a cripple all those years and I had to go to work early. But I knew Scripture backwards and frontwards—Mother, she'd seen to that—and soon I was making enough on commission to pop the question to Lucille. Nobody was more surprised than me when she told me yes. It was hard on her having me on the road most of the time. My territory reached from Louisville clear down to Birmingham, and there was times I didn't even get home weekends. It was hard on her not having a baby right off too. She lost three while she was still carrying them before one finally was born. Little thing didn't only live but a few months."

Tony was perched on the porch railing with his chin on his knee, Chris on the porch floor leaning up against the house. They looked as lulled as I felt lulled myself by the ebb and flow of Bebb's voice coming out of the dusk. He could have told them anything, and they would have hardly noticed. He could even have told them the way the baby had died, and the chances are the sense of what he said would have been lost in the sound. Or I could have told them myself.

Bebb is off somewhere selling Bibles, and Lucille is at home with their colicky first-born. For a week now she has been taking care of him by herself, picking him up, walking him, rocking him at all hours of day and night whenever the pains in his stomach set him howling until his lips turn blue. She is no longer sure whether it is night or day. She's not even sure which is doing the howling, the baby or she. She will be just about to doze off in her lonely bed for the ninth and tenth time maybe when the noise that is somewhere between a sewing machine and a chain-saw wakes her up, and several times she has dragged herself all the way across the room before noticing that she and the baby are making the noise together. On one occasion she finds a hand crawling up the side of her head like a spider and does not know how it got there until she realizes it's her own hand.

The baby is lying in the bathroom where she keeps the crib at night, Bebb's boy. She picks him up under the arms, his head lolling back until she cups it in one hand and holds him tight. She can feel his mouth against her throat, one fist the size of a golfball at her breast. From the bathroom to the bedroom, from the bedroom to the bathroom, until finally he is no longer tense and squirming but heavy and loose and warm and she lowers him carefully into his crib like a loaf and turns him over on his stomach. This time she has a hunch that he is down for what's left of the night and fixes herself a drink to celebrate, then another drink or possibly two, listening to some midnight dance band being broadcast from a hotel somewhere and wondering maybe where Bebb is now and what he is doing and who he is doing it with.

It is the eve of the Second World War, but there

in that bedroom in Knoxville, Tennessee, it is the eve of a good sleep and sweet dreams. She doesn't bother to undress, stretches out as she is. She closes her eyes. The bed starts to turn slowly like a display in a department-store window. She lowers one arm so that her fingers touch the floor, and this stops it. Her feet fill with helium and begin to bear her up into the sky. Higher and higher they bear her, her head trailing below through clouds. She is nearing the warm gravitational field of a dream.

She sees the marble counter of her father's restaurant. Down the counter someone is sliding along to her a hot fudge sundae with whipped cream and walnuts on top. The hot fudge starts to overflow, traveling slowly down her belly like fingers, like a voice whispering sweet, dark secrets. The baby is crying in short bursts with equal bursts of silence in between so that she can't tell whether the pattern is white on black or black on white or which is dream. With the corner of her mouth wet against the pillow, she strains to take in the secret of the dark and traveling fingers. Something infinitely sweet is being pulled just out of her reach down the smooth, veined surface.

Bebb's baby is howling. Bebb is off in some cheap hotel room full of Bibles. The dream, the secret, the sundae—it is gone now, the most precious thing she has ever lost although she can't remember just what it was any more as she gets up off her bed so fast and mad that for a moment she thinks she is going to faint. There is a humming in her ears that drowns out the baby, and she has to hold on to the bedpost to keep from falling down.

Then she bursts into the bathroom, slamming the door back against the tub. The ugly half-face in the crib, the smell of babyshit, the sight of her own face in the mirror. She grabs up the first thing that catches her eye. It is a long-handled toilet brush. What follows is a kind of Punch and Judy show.

Sharon had gone into the house to make sandwiches for us, and had turned some lights on inside. Bebb and Chris were talking. It was one of the miracles of the space age: Bebb, so round and firm and full of bounce, from Mars, and Chris from whichever one it is that's mainly just clouds of cosmic gas. Bebb was leaning against one of the pillars, a little of the dim, gold lamplight glinting in his eyes. Chris was cross-legged on the floor at Bebb's feet. He had his head tilted to the side and was smoking a cigarette. He was the only smoker among us, and Sharon, who on yoga principles would otherwise have objected strenuously, said he shouldn't give it up. She said Chris needed to smoke as an antidote to his own personality.

Chris was talking to Bebb about a job he hoped to get that summer with a repertory company that put on plays in a theater not far from us in Sutton. He would help with props and paint flats and do errands, and if things turned out as he hoped, he said, maybe they would let him have an occasional small part or walk-on. "I want to make the theater my life," I heard him say. It was the first I could remember having heard of it, this plan for his life, but I had a feeling that he might have made the same speech to me before and I simply hadn't been paying attention. You paid attention to Tony whether you wanted to or not. Just the bang of his footsteps on the stair or the way he left his clothes thrown around his room was vivid and memorable, but Chris was like an over-exposed photograph—indistinct, washed-out. "I want to make the theater my life," he said, this phrase out of *Mary Noble, Backstage Wife,* but no sooner did it slip from his mouth than it faded into the air with the smoke from his cigarette. He was talking about his life and his dreams for the future like a man conjugating verbs, and Bebb sat there listening as if it was the Sermon on the Mount, his expression intense and absorbed and the glow of the lamplight in his face.

Right after Bill was born and they let me in to see Sharon, a nurse came and placed both her hands flat on Sharon's lower stomach and pressed steadily down on it for a few seconds. I'm not sure what the purpose of it was, but she did it with such a measured and professional air that the image has stayed in my mind. I can see her still the way she leaned over the bed in her crisp white uniform and applied what you could tell was a good deal of pressure but not an ounce too much. She had her head turned away from Sharon so as not to breathe in her face, I suppose. She was looking at me. But it wasn't me she was seeing. She was seeing whatever it was that she was supposed to be doing to Sharon's insides down there under the covers. When Chris stopped talking about the job he hoped to get in summer stock—not with a period at the end but his usual semicolon or little row of dots—Bebb did something that brought that scene back to me uncannily. He leaned forward and put his hands down on Chris's shoulders, and although it happened to be me that his eyes fastened on, it wasn't me he was looking at. Bebb kept his hands on Chris that way until Sharon appeared in the doorway to tell us the sandwiches were ready.

Sharon stood looking out at us through the screen. Tony already had his hand on the doorknob to go in, and I could see her face over his shoulder. She opened her eyes as wide as they would go and opened her mouth. Very slowly she stuck her tongue out farther and farther until she looked as if she was trying to touch the floor with it and then she stuck it out a little farther still. She held it there for a while and then slowly withdrew it. At the same time she relaxed her eyes. I recognized it as something her swami called The Lion. It was supposed to be good for revitalizing the face and neck and also served to reduce tension.

Six

SOMEBODY left a rose in a hymnal at Open Heart. It was a tight-petaled, crimson rose that looked as if it had just been picked. The hymn that it marked was "Jerusalem the Golden," which was not one of the ones that had been sung that morning. Whoever left it, Bebb said, must have left it as a love offering, and he put it in a glass of water, eventually set it on the altar table with the other flowers and the cross.

The results of Bebb's "Have a Heart" ad were disappointing. He had set up chairs in the barn for a hundred and fifty, but not more than thirty or forty came. More than half of these were women, and more than half of the women were black. A lot of the rich people around Greenwich and New Canaan had black help, and the way Bebb figured it out, they must have felt homesick for the free-wheeling Pentecostal churches they had left behind them in the South and the ad had revived old memories. They were better dressed than most of the whites with their hats and straw purses and occasional white gloves, and Bebb began his service with a special word of welcome for them. He said in Christ there was no east or west and there wasn't any black or white either and Jesus knocked just as hard to get you to open up your heart if it was one color as he did if it was another color.

It was impossible to generalize about the whites who came. There were several young men dressed alike in black suits and black ties with their hair slicked down who Bebb said afterwards were Mormon missionaries who happened to be in the area. There was an elderly woman with hair the color of raw meat who brought some kind of small rodent-like animal in a cage with her and sat in the back row. There was an Italian couple I recognized as the proprietors of a vegetable stand we stopped at sometimes, and a blind man with a white cane and a white linen golf cap which he did not remove during the service. A bearded man who wore short pants and the kind of leather sandals that have thongs you wrap around your ankles came in a pickup truck with some children in back. There were one or two couples who might have been poor relations to the people with the black help. It was not a fashionable congregation. Except for Sharon, the blacks were the only women who had on hats, and of the men present I doubt that more than a handful were wearing neckties.

There had been some talk about Brownie's flying up all the way from Houston to help out at the opening Sunday, but apparently he had his hands full with Holy Love and called up to say that he couldn't make it. Bebb took the news in his stride, but it seemed to be a major disappointment to Lucille and may have helped account for her subsequent behavior that morning. Sharon and I were there, of course, and to my surprise the boys wanted to come too although neither of us had put any pressure on them. And at the last minute the boys' father, my ex-brother-in-law Charlie Blaine, also joined us with his housekeeper, Mrs. Kling.

We were on the point of leaving the house to go over to Bebb's church when they arrived. It was a fresh spring morning, but they had all the windows of Charlie's Buick shut tight and the air-conditioning on. Charlie felt that it was better for his allergies that way. Mrs. Kling was at the wheel. She was a tireless woman with big calves and a big bust who wore a lot of lipstick and always sounded as though she was trying to make herself heard through a closed door. Charlie was wearing an overcoat and a fedora and looked as if the bright sunlight hurt his eyes as he climbed out of the car to greet his sons. He still kissed them when he hadn't seen them for a while, and although Sharon said it gave her the creeps, I admired him for being able to do it so naturally. It has always seemed sad to me that about the only place where American males can embrace one another without incurring the darkest suspicions is on the athletic field. Charlie kissed Chris first, and it was like the meeting of apostles in a fresco, those two faded figures reaching out their arms toward each other in such a Giottoesque and dreamlike way. When it came Tony's turn, Tony gave him a bear hug that almost lifted him off his feet. Mrs. Kling stood nearby presiding over the reunion as though it was some new therapy that she had arranged for Charlie's gall-bladder condition, and when I explained to them that we were on our way to Bebb's inaugural service, she said that a little religion never hurt anybody and they would go right along with us. So the six of us ended up sitting with Lucille that first morning at Open Heart. Chris brought his tape recorder along and recorded Bebb's sermon with it.

Bebb took off from a phrase from Paul's letter to the Ephesians which went *I, Paul, the prisoner of Jesus Christ for you Gentiles.* He said, "You take a little child that's been—let's say he's being punished for something he never even did. They shove him into the closet and turn the lock on him. It's black as pitch in the closet, and there's none too much air to breathe. He stumbles around through the shoes and mothballs. Soft, hanging things strike him in the face, and he thinks there's creatures of darkness in there with him with buttons where their eyes ought to be and no arms inside their sleeves. He hammers his pitiful little fists on the door and begs and hollers for somebody to come let him out. But nobody comes. There's nobody even answers him.

"You take an animal in a cage. You take a royal Bengal tiger which is—why, Solomon in all his glory was not arrayed like a royal Bengal tiger in his black and gold suit. Up and down the cage he walks in his big velvet sandals, up and down and back and forth, year in and year out. Every time he comes to the end of his cage going one way, he shifts his head around so it'll still be facing out at the bars when he goes back the other way. He's a king, and he wants to look out where the freedom is. People come and throw peanuts at him.

"You take a man in jail. Jails aren't like they used to be—full of rats and bugs with everybody chained up and nothing except bread and water for dinner.

Jails are worse now. They're spic and span now, and they smell of creosote. Every week you get your clothes laundered in jail, and they give you soft slippers to put on your feet. The food's not half bad. If you keep your nose clean, you get to watch TV and go to bed most any time you want.

"But brothers and sisters in Jesus, it's *jail*. It's jail worse than jail ever was in the old days because it's like home. For lots of folks it's better than any home they ever knew. It's like home except for only just one thing. It's like that child in the closet. It's like the tiger in the cage. You can't get out.

"Through the windows you see somebody's wife hanging up the wash in the sun. Only you can't get out. From the vegetable garden out back, you can look across the highway to where the Howard Johnson's is. Easiest thing in the world just to drop in and have yourself a cone or some French fries. Only you can't get out. You can see the folks out driving places with their kids come walking through the swinging door with ice cream cones in their hands. Only you can't get out.

"Fellow sinners, you can take a look at the birds in the sky. You can watch the clouds change shape. You can watch the faces of the guards and think how when they go off duty, they'll drive home through the rain with the wipers going and maybe stop off on the way and pick up something special for dessert. You can tell how when they get home and open the door, they'll smell a smell isn't like any other smell in the world. It's the smell of their wife and kids. It's the smell of their dinner cooking. It's the smell of their own life. Only you can't get out. No, sir. Jail's what you can't get out of. Not for five years, ten years, twenty. Maybe you're never going to get out."

Bebb said, "Right here in Scripture, Saint Paul, he says, 'I am a prisoner for Jesus Christ.' I am in the dark closet. I am in the cage at the zoo. I am in jail. For Jesus' sake. I didn't have to be here. I chose to be here. I'm here for doing like Jesus said. I'm here for baring the naked truth. I'm here for showing my love to the brethren. I'm here for opening my heart. That's what Saint Paul says.

"What did Saint Paul do while he was in prison? Friends, I'm going to tell you what he did. Among his fellow prisoners there was mostly every kind of sinner you'd care to think of. There was murderers and thieves. There were child-beaters and rapists and sodomites. Before he was through, he had led many of them to accept Jesus Christ as their personal Lord and Savior. He had got them singing the songs of Zion. Many's the cell he washed down with the Blood of the Lamb before they finally let him out."

With their profiles overlapping, Charlie Blaine and Mrs. Kling looked like monarch and consort on a coronation medal only it was Mrs. Kling who was the monarch—some early world-conqueror with her heavy red lips and eyebrows penciled in thick and black—and Charlie the shadowy presence at her side. I remember the curve of Sharon's throat and the straw hat she wore with a wide, floppy brim. I remember Tony beside her, his upper lip moist and the muscles of his jaw appearing and disappearing like the spokes of a wheel. And it was at about this point that I first noticed Lucille acting strangely. She kept crossing and uncrossing her legs and rearranging her filmy skirt over her knee. She would open her mouth and put her hand over it as if to conceal a yawn or a belch. The barn was big and dim, and the only light was the small reading light on Bebb's lecturn. The pulpit didn't look big enough for him. He rose up out of it like a jack-in-the-box.

He said, "There's more than one way to skin a cat. To be a prisoner for Christ means more than just being a prisoner inside Comstock or Leavenworth or Soledad. Maybe Jesus calls some of us to be that type prisoner just like he called Saint Paul to. But there's another way he calls every last one of us to be a prisoner. He calls every last one of us to be a prisoner right inside our own skin. Why every last one of you sitting there listening to me knows exactly what I mean. There's a royal Bengal tiger in every single son of Adam and daughter of Eve and except you keep the cage door clapped right on him, he's going to get out and tear things to pieces. Tear himself to pieces too, likely as not.

" 'The spirit is willing but the flesh is weak' the Good Book says. That's another way of saying the flesh is strong. Brothers and sisters, the flesh is a mighty beast, and we've got to post guards day and night and put up electric alarm systems to make sure he don't get loose. We got to keep the beast locked up so we can feed Jesus' lambs for him and not feed *on* Jesus' sweet and tender lambs.

"Only listen to this now. We don't have to keep him in the lock-up forever. No, sir. It's not a ninety-nine year sentence. Because the day is coming when the locked up part of us is going to get washed in the saving blood of Jesus same as all the other parts.

Amen. The day is coming when the royal Bengal tiger in us will lie down with the lamb in us, and the lion shall eat straw like the ox, and they shall not hurt or destroy in all my holy mountain, saith the Lord."

Several amens were called out. I noticed the black faces especially. Many of them were smiling and nodding to themselves as if Bebb was showing them pictures of places they recognized from a long time back. Dressed up in their gloves and spring hats like their mistresses, they nodded yes, yes, that was how it used to be. The blind man sat with his white cane hooked around the back of his neck and his mouth ajar. Bebb blossomed out over the constricting sides of the pulpit like a great maroon rose. One stubby white hand thumped a counterpoint to his words.

He said, "Folks, Jesus was a prisoner too. I don't mean Jesus was a prisoner in prison though the Jews, they booked him there for a few days at the end. But I don't mean that kind of prisoner. And I don't mean Jesus was a prisoner inside his own skin like you and I, because Jesus was Rose of Sharon, brothers, he was Lily of the Valley. He was the royal Bengal tiger and the lamb without blemish both. There was no sin in him, nothing he had to jail up inside. He had the seat of honor in Heaven, and it was through him the earth was made. Only then he come down. He come down from Heaven. From *Heaven!* You ever stop to think what that means? You ever stop to think what it means to come down out of Heaven into this two-bit world?

"Up there in Heaven Scripture says the streets are of pure gold like unto clear glass and the twelve gates are twelve pearls and there is no Temple where people go to worship the Almighty because up there the Almighty is worshiped all over the place and day and night the angels sing praises at his throne. That's the place Jesus left to come here.

"He come down out of the heavenly place to this place. Down, down he come, and what did he find when he got here? He found a place where there's not enough food to stretch round. He found a place where every single night there's little children go to bed crying because that day it wasn't their turn to eat. He found a place where people are scared stiff of each other most of the time and hide from each other and sometimes come out of their hiding places to do hateful things to each other.

"You take your nine-year-old girl found beat-up and raped in the park. You take your woman shipped off to some cheap-jack nursing home to die of lonesomeness. Jesus found a place where even nature's gone bad. Where babies are born with little shriveled-up arms and young men with their whole life ahead of them get cancers, and there's droughts and floods, and peaches are piled up along the road going rotten to keep the price up when there's people don't have the price of a peach.

"Friends, Jesus come down to a place where every last man, woman and child is living on death row. You'd think the least thing we could do was draw close and comfort each other, but no. Except for a few loved ones, we close the doors of our hearts and bolt them tight on each other."

Bebb's voice grew quieter toward the end. He held on to the sides of his new pulpit with his shoulders hunched up. He said, "This world Jesus come down to, it's got good things in it too, praise God. It's got love in it and kindness in it and people doing brave and honest things, not just hateful things. It's got beauty in it. It's got the silver light of the moon by night and the golden beams of the sun by day. It's got the sound of the rain on the roof and the smell of the rain on the fresh-turned earth. It's got human forms and faces that are so beautiful they break your heart for yearning after them. But coming down from where he come down from, all the good things of the world must have just made Jesus homesick for the place he come down from. Brothers and sisters, the whole planet was a prison for Jesus. He got born here like the rest of us and did the work here he come to do, and he died here. But it was never like it was home to him.

"Same as creatures from some other part of the universe, Jesus was a stranger in this place, and that's another meaning to Saint Paul's words when he says, 'I am a prisoner for Christ.' Saint Paul means this whole planet's my prison because I don't belong to this planet. I'm down here just for your sake same as Jesus was. That's all. I belong to someplace else far, far away. Sometimes I get homesick for it something wicked."

Lucille was on her feet beside me. She had her hand up to her mouth as if she was going to be sick. She was wearing a gauzy dress with lots of pleats and folds that hung low on her skinny legs. She reminded me of photographs I've seen of Aimee Semple McPherson at the Angelus Temple. She wobbled back and forth on her spike heels for a minute and then like some kind of extinct butterfly started weaving her way back up the aisle toward the door.

Bebb could see what was happening, but he remained as cool as he had in the presence of the Joking Cousin at Herman Redpath's funeral. Nothing in his voice or manner changed as she opened the barn door noisily and went rattling out into the spring. I went after her as quietly as I could up the creaking aisle and many heads turned to watch me go, but such was the power of Bebb's oratory that by the time I reached the door, most of them had turned back to him again—those rapt black prisoners' faces looking up at Bebb from underneath their fancy, white-lady hats.

Lucille's heart. She did not open her heart to me when I caught her hurrying home across the lawn. She gave it to me instead and told me to open it for myself later. She pulled it out from somewhere inside the gauzy flaps and pennants and put it into my hand. It was a number of sheets of flowered stationery written on both sides right through the flowers and rolled up into a tube with a couple of rubber bands doubled up around it.

The sun was so bright that you could see her scalp through her thin hair like the curve of a wooded hillside when the leaves have fallen. She said, "Take it. Don't read it now. You'll know when to read it."

I said, "Are you sick? Is there anything I can do for you?"

She said, "Sometimes when he gets going like that, it scares the bejeezus out of me."

I said, "What is there to be scared about?"

Her dress was floating all over the place in the breeze. She had to brush away a bit of the wide collar that had fluttered across her mouth.

She said, "I'm scared he'll get telling too much."

I said, "About what?"

She said, "You name it."

She turned and managed to get up the porch steps in her high heels. At the top she paused, all her plumes stirring. She said, "I got to take something to steady my nerves. You go on back."

I offered to stay with her, but she wouldn't let me.

She said, "Keep it in a safe place and forget I ever gave it to you." At the screen door she paused again as if to say something else, but then she entered the house without a word.

I returned to the barn for what was left of the service as she had told me to, and when it was over, we all trooped back to the house to wait until Bebb had finished shaking hands with the last members of his congregation so we could say goodbye to him and tell him how well we thought everything had gone. Mrs. Kling insisted on being taken into the house to have a look at Lucille. God knows why, but we all went with her right into Lucille's bedroom. Mrs. Kling said, "It looks to me like you've picked yourself up some type of virus that's going the rounds. Your color's lousy. The last thing you should be tanking up on is all that orange juice. There's enough acid in that size glass to burn your radiator right out."

Lucille paid no attention to her or to Charlie either. I don't think she had the faintest idea who they were. She just lay stretched out on her bed with her shoes off and her dark glasses off and her eyes looking little and dried up. She reached out and took Chris by the hand and called him Tony. Poor Chris, he stood there trying to look as though the hand she was holding belonged to somebody else.

Lucille said, "Tony, I was just as good-looking as her once," indicating Sharon. "I weighed ninety-nine pounds, and I had sweet breath, and I could play *The Banks of the Wabash* right through without looking at the notes. I was a virgin up to the day I married Bebb, and that's more than I can say for some people. Sharon, that's some dress you're wearing, baby. If I was to tell everything I know, there's some of you'd say I was smashed. It's no wonder I got to take something to settle my nerves every chance. You hear him say open your heart? If I opened my heart, you'd tell me Lucille, shut it up again. Bebb, if he was to open his heart, you'd think you was dreaming. Ask him about Shaw Hill and Bertha Stredwig. Ask him was he his brother's keeper back in Poinsett days. Ask him what floor he gets off at someday. She's the apple of his eye. Sharon baby, you're the only apple of your daddy's eye that your daddy's got, baby."

She went rambling on for what seemed an endless time. Mrs. Kling tried to take her stockings off but got only one of them peeled halfway down when Lucille kicked out with her other foot and knocked Mrs. Kling's glasses off. If there was one thing in the world poor Charlie Blaine couldn't stand, it was a scene, but he stood through this one as if he was paralyzed. He had his fedora in one hand and the Vicks inhaler that helped him breathe through his allergies in the other, and a lot of the time I think he kept his eyes closed. Lucille kept holding on to Chris so he couldn't get away, but Tony and Sharon escaped into the living room where one of them must have switched the TV on to some Catholic program because Lucille's blurred syllables kept coming through all mixed up with fragments of the Latin mass.

By the time Bebb returned from his hand-shaking, she had dozed off and we were all milling around the porch in our Sunday clothes like relatives after a funeral. Bebb came bounding up the stairs with his maroon robe over his arm and showed us the rose that someone had left in the hymnal. He handed it to Tony, who smelled it and gave it to his father. Charlie took the stem between his thumb and forefinger and made it turn slowly around. Who could have left it? Why? The rose gave us something other than Lucille or the service to talk about for a few minutes. Then Mrs. Kling took it from Charlie and, after inhaling its perfume so vigorously that there seemed some danger of its disappearing up one of her nostrils, returned it to Bebb. We found ourselves suddenly immobilized by a silence as large and sprawling as a collapsed tent.

There was an unmistakable feeling of Sunday in the air. You could hear one of the departing members of the congregation racing his motor somewhere beyond the barn. A peabody bird sang his sad, unfinished song—Poor Sam Peabody, Peabody, Peabody . . .

Bebb broke in finally with a few cheerful remarks about the way things had gone at Open Heart. He was pleased that so many had come and that there were blacks and whites both. He expected more next time. The ads would keep right on appearing. The blind man had told him on the way out that he was a cousin of Harry Truman's.

As we left, I caught sight of him through the bedroom window. Lucille was lying flat on her back asleep among all those yards of Aimee Semple McPherson gauze. Bebb was sitting on the foot of her bed. He had her bare feet in his lap. I could not see either of their faces.

Seven

BOTH MY PARENTS were dead by the time my twin sister and I were twelve, and yet even so it always surprises me how few and faded my memories of them are. I have no memory of how one thing we did with them led to another thing, no sense of the time in between times—just a glimpse here and there. It's as if out of miles and miles of home movies the only thing left was a handful of disconnected scraps that had been edited out and preserved by accident. I remember waking up in a room full of green light that came through leaves growing over the window. I remember hearing my father's voice in the hall, and knowing it was my birthday. But of the birthday itself I remember nothing. I remember the door of our New York apartment opening and the bitter, wintry smell of my mother's furs. I remember the chill of her cheek against mine.

One of the fullest memories I have comes from when I must have been around nine or ten and was coming home on the school bus. We were just pulling out of Central Park when across Fifth Avenue I caught sight of my mother and Miriam. They were standing at the curb, and I made the bus driver let me out so I could run across to meet them. We took a taxi straight down Fifth Avenue to the Plaza, where we met my father and all went and had lunch together at Longchamps. I remember my father ordered rare roast beef for me because he said it was good for a growing boy. I remember the stiff breeze and the blue sky and the way the golden statue of General Sherman glittered in the sun with the pigeons fluttering around. I remember the promise of summer vacation in the air and F.A.O. Schwarz just across the way at Fifty-eighth Street. It is one of the best memories I have because it was such an unexpected thing to have happen, and I thought of it on the spring day, not long after Bebb's debut at Open Heart, when I unexpectedly picked Sharon up at her guitar lesson and we wasted the whole afternoon together. I hadn't planned to pick her up—she called and left word at the Principal's Office—and with a pile of papers to correct I certainly had no intention of wasting an afternoon with anybody. The happiest times are always, I suppose, by accident. And maybe the saddest times too.

The *Lear* class had gone better than usual. It was the third act that was up for grabs that day—Lear on the heath with Kent and the Fool, the storm coming up—and nothing could have seemed more remote from our condition, yet there was a moment or two when for some reason it worked, came alive almost, no thanks to me. There they all sat drowsy and full of lunch. There was a gym class going on outside. You could hear somebody calling out calisthenics, *one* and two, and *one* and two. There was a bumblebee softly bumping his way back and forth across the ceiling, but nobody was paying much attention to him. I sat on the window sill in my shirtsleeves asking some boring questions somebody had written in the margin of my copy and wondering idly who had written them there and when and not caring much whether anyone tried to answer them or not. "What evidence do you find in Act Three for a significant change in Lear's character?" was one of the questions I came to, and a fat boy named William Urquhart surprised me by answering it. He was sitting all bent over with his head in his arms on the desk, and I'd thought he was asleep. His voice came out muffled by his arm. He said, "He's gotten kinder."

I said, "What makes you think so?"

The second question coming so quick on the heels of the one he'd just answered was more than William Urquhart had bargained for, and he shifted his head to the other arm without saying anything. You could see where his cheek had gotten all moist and red where he'd been lying on it and there was the imprint of wrinkles from his sleeve.

The ball was picked up by a boy named Greg Dixon. He was the pimpliest member of the class and the least popular. He said, "Well when it starts to rain, he thinks about the Fool keeping dry too. He says it right here someplace. 'Come on, my boy. How dost, my boy?' Here it is. He says, 'Poor fool and knave, I have one part in my heart that's sorry yet for thee.' He's getting kinder to people like Urquhart said."

"Also, he says a prayer for people." It was Laura Fleischman who had spoken up this time. She always sat in the back row next to a good-looking basketball player named Carl West, who, in Tony's gallant phrase, was getting into her pants regularly. Usually she didn't speak at all or spoke with a kind of startled breathiness as if she was surprised herself that anything beside Carl could get a rise out of her.

Somebody horse-laughed not so much at what she'd said, I thought, as at the fact that it was she who'd said it. Carl West sat there beside her with his stocking feet stretched out as far as they could go and his head lolling back as if to watch the bee on the ceiling.

"Nobody says a prayer in my book," Greg Dixon said.

"Line thirty-five," Laura Fleischman said.

"That's no prayer," Greg Dixon said. "That's not like any prayer I ever heard of."

I said, "Go ahead and read it out loud, will you, Laura?"

Carl West sat humped way over sideways now as far from Laura Fleischman as he could get. He was staring down at his writing arm, tracing some scar on it over and over again with one finger.

In a small, half apologetic voice with the calisthenic count going on in the background, she read,

"Poor naked wretches, wheresoe'er you are,
That bide the pelting of this pitiless storm,
How shall your houseless heads and unfed sides,
Your looped and windowed raggedness, defend
you
From seasons such as these?"

Every person has one particular time in his life when he is more beautiful than he is every going to be again. For some it is at seven, for others at seventeen or seventy, and as Laura Fleischman read out loud from Shakespeare, I remember thinking that for her it was probably just then. Her long hair dividing over her bare shoulders, her lashes dark against her cheeks as she looked down at the page, she could go nowhere from this moment except away from it. She still had a long way to go before she left it behind for good, but I felt like Father Hopkins anyway as I watched her—*How to keep back beauty, keep it, beauty, beauty, beauty, from vanishing away . . .*

" 'Expose thyself to feel what wretches feel,' " she read, " 'That thou may'st shake the superflux to them, And show the heavens more just,' " and two, and *one* and two, the voice floated in through the open windows. Carl West had one hand up to his eyes as if to shield them from the sun, the other cupped at his crotch. The bee drifted heavily down from the ceiling and hit the blackboard with a little thud, then crawled drunkenly along the chalk tray.

I said, "Who are these poor naked wretches he's praying for, if she's right that he's praying?"

Greg Dixon said, "We are."

He said it to be funny—they were the poor wretches, presumably, to have to sit there and listen to Laura Fleischman read blank verse when they could be off somewhere having whatever Greg Dixon thought of as fun—but nobody laughed. Maybe I just ascribed my own thoughts to them, but it seemed to me that for a moment or two in that sleepy classroom they all felt some unintended truth in Greg Dixon's words.

Laura Fleischman in the fullness of her time. William Urquhart in his fatness. Greg Dixon with his pimples. Carl West handsome and bored with the knowledge that he could get into anybody's pants in that room that he felt like getting into. They were the poor naked wretches and at least for a moment they knew they were. The pitiless storm.

The *Lear* class worked, in other words. Only for a minute or two, to be sure, with no credit to either me or Shakespeare particularly. Something had worked anyway if only for me, and it was part of what I jogged out to the parking lot with, Sharon's message to meet her at Anita's in my pocket. The weather. The kids. The time of year. My poor dead sister and mother just happening to be waiting there at the curb when my bus came nosing out of Central Park.

I found Anita and Sharon out in Anita's back yard. Sharon was sitting on a canvas camp stool with Anita, gray and intense in her neat slacks and frilled shirt, leaning over her shoulder from behind. She had her hand on Sharon's hand showing her where her fingers should go. They both looked up as I appeared around the corner of the house, but Anita kept right on with the lesson. "Don't mind about him," she said. "That finger belongs on the fourth fret." That rapid, insistent little voice, the intelligent, prematurely wrinkled marmoset's face. Sharon winked at me.

Anita said, "Stretch! Stretch!" and brought her

other hand down to help arrange Sharon's fingers in the right position, her head, close-cropped and bullet-shaped, touching Sharon's. If the two of them had been alone, Anita would never have risked it—the touch of Sharon's hair against her puckered cheek, taking Sharon's fingers in hers that way and moving them around. Anita gave me her handsomest smile with wrinkles shooting out like tears from the corners of her eyes. She said, "If I'd just gotten my hands on her a few years earlier, we could have really gone places."

Sharon stood up a good head taller, holding the guitar by the neck in one hand and letting the other hand come to rest for a moment on Anita's crew cut. "So long, Shorty," Sharon said.

In the car she said, "Sometimes I wonder what it would really be like."

I said, "What what would really be like?"

She said, "She'd die grateful for one thing, and it mightn't be so bad either. Like a Swedish massage. Antonio," she said, letting her arm flop out the window as we took off down the Post Road. "Let's get the hell out of here for a while. Let's go spend a lot of money someplace."

I was still on a high from the *Lear* class and the smell of summer vacation in the air so when Sharon sat there with her arm out the window and made her suggestion, I fell like a ton of bricks. We got the hell out of Sutton and drove on to Greenwich because that was the direction we happened to be heading and spent money all over the place.

In the cheese shop we bought a wheel of brie, a Danish gjetost the color of Fels Naptha, a pound of

Stilton and two loaves of black pumpernickel. At Meade's, I lost my head in the stationery department—big pads and little pads, a half dozen different colored felt-tips, a vest-pocket adding machine and a self-erasing typewriter ribbon—and Sharon came out with a bag full of paperbacks including *The Yoga Way to Figure and Facial Beauty*, *You Are All Sanpaku* by Sakurazawa Nyoiti, a book about macrobiotic diets, a manual on vocabulary building, and *Sex and the Single Girl*. In a psychedelic place with huge paper flowers and inflated plastic liquor bottles in the window, we passed up the posters after a long inspection and settled instead on a transparent cylinder full of an oily blue liquid that curled and foamed like waves when you tilted it back and forth and reminded Sharon of the ocean near Armadillo. We wandered up and down the aisles of one of the biggest ten-cent stores I had ever seen and for a while we no more thought of buying anything than in the Louvre we would have thought of buying anything. We just touched things. We touched things made of rubber to look like centipedes and lizards and human eyes. We touched love beads and Tampax boxes, transistor radios, slippery pink piles of ladies' underwear, bags of M and M's like Jack in the Beanstalk beans, checker sets, bicycle lights and electric fans. We watched a clerk with a strawberry fall net a fantail goldfish, put him in a transparent sack with some water in the bottom and then blow it up with her breath and seal it off at the top like a balloon. Sharon said that Bebb's birthday was coming up soon and bought him a framed picture of Jesus like one that he used to have over the offering box at the first Holy Love. For Chris she bought a green eyeshade, like the kind poker players wear in movies, to use when he did his homework outside. For Tony she got a button the size of a butter plate that said Kiss a Toad Tonight. I wanted to find something for the baby, but she said there wasn't anything there a baby couldn't put in his mouth and choke on.

We ended up at a dress shop that smelled like the inside of a purse. It had thick wall-to-wall carpeting and salesgirls fresh out of Bennington or Smith who wore eye liner and lipstick the color of the insides of shells. Sharon tried on at least two of everything. She tried on a long white evening dress with lozenge-shaped holes cut out around the midriff that you could see her suntan through. She tried on a leather skirt and a dress made out of woven ribbons. She tried on a tweed coat that made her look very Round Hill and a suede coat that came to her ankles with some kind of kinky white fur at the collars and cuffs that made her look like a Russian whore. She sampled so many kinds of perfume that she finally ran out of parts of herself to sample them on and dabbed some on me. In the end, she bought herself a rain hat of shiny yellow plastic with ear flaps and a string to tie them under the chin.

It was almost like sex while it lasted. Without a thought in our heads, we were all fingers and eyes and heavy breathing, and when it was over, we drove down to the park where the roses and the duck pond are and sat against a tree in a kind of spent languor watching the ducks. We even dozed off for a few minutes, and I thought how it was too bad that sleeping together has come to mean making love together when it can also mean what it says, just making peace together. When we woke up, we found that the duck pond was full of pink clouds and the sun was starting to go down. I made Sharon drive home and sat beside her with my knees propped against the dashboard and my head pillowed against one of our softer packages. We hardly said a word all the way back.

I have a feeling it's the in-between times, the times that narratives like this leave out and that the memory in general loses track of, which are the times when souls are saved or lost.

When we got back we found Chris in the living room. He had Chopin on the stereo and was sitting on the couch reading. He'd spread a baby blanket out on the floor, and Bill was lying on it on his back playing with his feet. Through the window the sun was setting. The babysitter had had to go home for supper, he said, and Tony had left about the same time saying that a bunch of them were going off to a beach somewhere and not to wait supper for him. The sunset, the Chopin, Bill—it was a comforting scene to come back to after our Greenwich debauch, and Chris presided over it with such gravity that I felt callow and irresponsible in his presence. I wished Sharon had chosen another time to show him our purchases although he seemed pleased with the green eyeshade. He had taken some hamburger out of the freezer to thaw in case Sharon hadn't planned anything for supper. She hadn't.

After we'd eaten, I started correcting the papers

that I should have gotten to that afternoon, but by the time I was about a third of the way through I was so drowsy and so irritated at being kept up by them that I found myself filling the margins with angry red exclamation points and finally decided that in fairness to my students I'd better go to bed even if it meant not having their papers to hand back to them when I'd promised. It must have been around ten by then, and Tony hadn't come home yet. Sharon asked if he'd done his homework before he left, and Chris said he'd spent most of the afternoon outside in the sun reading *Playboy*. Sharon said, "He's some playboy all right," and I left them shaking their heads at each other in the living room and went upstairs to get undressed.

Hours later I woke up to a sound that in my dream had been caused by Anita Steen. I had been sitting in her studio where I was supposed to be taking some kind of lesson, but I had come unprepared and wasn't even sure what it was that she was supposed to be teaching me. I told her that I had forgotten to bring my instrument, hoping that her response might give some clues as to what the instrument was, but she just sat there looking at me in a solemn and expectant way. Without looking away, she reached behind her and from the shelves where she kept her collection of primitive noisemakers took down an African tom-tom which she clamped between her knees and started thumping with her flattened palms. Louder and louder she thumped as though it was some secret message that she was trying to drum into me literally. The whole building began to vibrate with it. When I woke up, I discovered that Sharon was not in bed beside me. The bedroom door was ajar, and there was a light on in the hall.

I found Sharon standing underneath the hall light in her nightdress. The thumping was still going on, and when I first stuck my head out of the room, she motioned me to be quiet as though, in some odd carry-over from my dream, she too was trying to decode a message and didn't want to miss a beat. The noise stopped for a few moments, and she said, "Guess what that's all about," and when whatever it was I mumbled didn't satisfy her, she said, "It's that half-assed nephew of yours, that's what it's all about." She said it as though I was the one she was mad at. When the thumping started again, she raised her voice to be heard over it. She said, "It's half past three if you want to know." Her face looked dark and dangerous. She said, "If he thinks anybody's going to let him in at this hour, he's nuts. Let him spend the night out there. It'll do him good."

A voice said, "You better let him in, Sharon. It's gotten a lot colder out, and he could catch pneumonia. All he's got on is his bathing suit."

It was the first time I'd noticed Chris. He was standing halfway down the stairs looking up at Sharon through the railing. He had some kind of white ointment smeared around his nose and chin. I couldn't make out whether he was on his way down or on his way up.

Sharon said, "I don't care if he freezes his balls off. Who does he think he is, tomcatting around till three A.M. and expecting us to snap shit when he comes home?"

Chris said, "You better let him in, Sharon. He's

got school tomorrow." He made no move to go either up or down but just stayed where he was, looking up through the banister and waiting for reason to prevail. The baby had started to cry.

I went to the window and looked down. I could see my nephew Tony standing there on the front step. He was barefoot and had nothing on except his bathing trunks and an unbuttoned shirt hanging down outside. His dark hair was plastered across his forehead, and in the moonlight his flesh looked silver. He stopped pounding again and leaned forward with his right arm flattened out against the house and his face buried in the crook of it. For the first time since I'd gotten up, there was silence both inside and outside except for the sound of Bill crying. Then Tony looked up at the window and saw me.

He said, "For Christ's sake, Tono. Open up, will you?" Even in the semi-dark with all that hair in his face I could tell he was close to tears.

I turned and said to Sharon, "I'm going down to let him in," and started down the steps toward Chris.

What I see in my mind as I look back on it is something that I couldn't possibly have seen in reality. I see Tony standing down there on the front step in his bathing trunks with his shirttail out. He is bare-legged and barefoot with the cleft down his chest a dark seam. His face is tipped up to me in the moonlight, the face of my sister's younger boy, who was named after me. At the same time, as though I could somehow have seen them both at once, I see Sharon standing up there in the hall in her night-dress. She is also bare-legged and barefoot. The light from the overhead bulb shines in her hair and on her bare shoulders, but her face is in shadow because it is tipped down to watch me descend past Chris. Tony is outside looking up, Sharon is inside looking down, and yet I see them simultaneously as though for a moment the walls had turned to glass.

Chris flattened himself against the wall to let me by, and Sharon said we could all go to hell. She went back into her bedroom and slammed the door. I don't know what happened to Chris. I suppose he went up and quieted the baby. I unlocked the door and let Tony in.

He was shivering with cold and exhausted, but I made him come into the living room and sit down. We sat side by side on the couch, and I told him that it didn't make sense to stay out half the night when he had practice the next day and was supposed to be getting in shape for track. I told him that he hadn't let anybody know what beach he was going to or whom he was going with. He could have been drowned for all we knew. He had woken up the whole house. I made the speech because I thought I ought to and because I was sure Sharon was upstairs expecting me to, but my heart wasn't in it. I couldn't help thinking that Chris could have said substantially the same things to Sharon and me when we came back that afternoon. And I was as eager to get to bed as he was. All the time I was speaking, he sat looking straight ahead of him, his shoulders hunched, his skin all gooseflesh, his lower jaw shaking.

When I finished, he said, "Honest to God, Tono, she's got it in for me. Anything I do, she's on my back for it. I was out there half an hour begging her to let me in, and she wouldn't do it just for spite. She'd have let me stay out there all night and freeze, Tono, honest to God she would."

I said, "She'd have let you in. You just have got to—" but he wasn't listening. He had his eyes fixed glassily on the rug in front of him, and he couldn't stop talking any more than he could stop his jaw from shaking.

He said, "I know I'm not perfect, but she's not so perfect either. She comes busting into my room just to see if there's anything she can chew me out for without even knocking. I've seen the way she leaves her own room, her clothes flung all over the place. And Jesus, she can be gross, Tono. I mean I've heard her say things that were so gross I wouldn't even say them myself and right in front of guys who hardly know her even. And some of the things she does like coming out to track in that yoga suit. I mean I don't see what she's—" but by this time I was the one who wasn't listening, or rather, I was listening the way I had listened to Anita thumping her tom-tom in my dream. It was the secret message I was listening for behind the thumping, and what surprises me is not that I had already by this time started to hear it but that it had taken me so long.

He wasn't telling me anything I hadn't heard a thousand times before, but at the same time he was trying to get ready to tell me something else, and even though I didn't know what it was yet, I knew how it must feel to be trying to tell it or not tell it and how it was going to feel to hear it if he ever managed to get it out. He was going on about how Chris oughtn't to have to be the one to take care of Bill, all that, and how hamburgers for supper week after week got to be monotonous, and although I still didn't know what he was leading up to, I already knew in some queer way that it was the saddest thing I'd ever heard, and I found myself responding to it before I knew what it was I was responding to. I reached out my arm and put it around his shoulder. He turned and buried his face against my chest. He was weeping. I was patting his shaggy, sea-smelling head like a child or a dog. Of all the words he went on to speak then, the only ones I can remember verbatim were, "I'm sorry, Tono. I'm sorry. I'm sorry." He must have said them a hundred times.

I suppose that I had known all along that he and Sharon were lovers. I had dreamed it and forgotten the dream. It was what Sharon and I had not talked about as we had driven home through the dusk from Greenwich with all the things we'd bought done up in parcels in the back seat. It was itself the done-up parcel that I'd tucked under my head to watch the pink clouds from. I had even planned to talk to my *Lear* class about it when we got to Act Four. "The wren goes to it," I would have read, "and the small gilded fly does lecher in my sight," and Laura Fleischman sitting in the back row next to Carl West would have no more realized what I was talking about than I would have realized it or would have realized just as much. "Let copulation thrive," I would have tossed out into that bee-buzzing room and would have tried to rouse them with it to some feeling for the terrible irony of the old man's fulminations. I would have talked about irony, about inner meaning and outer meaning. Several days later when we actually did come to Act Four, it was Lear's saying, "Give me an ounce of civet, good apothecary, to sweeten my imagination" that I dwelt upon, but by then I knew why.

There was nothing by then that I hadn't imagined. What Tony himself had told me was little enough, his words coming out half smothered against my chest, the few details he gave getting all confused somehow with the details of his giving them, with the salt smell of his hair, the chill, hard thrust of his shoulder against me. But what little he told me turned out to be more than enough, and the scene I constructed out of it was no less rich and full than it would have been if I'd actually been there to witness it.

It had been one afternoon that March apparently, the first warm day we'd had by then with some patches of snow still lying around in the shade like dirty laundry and the track team still doing most of its practicing inside, but there was a suspicion at least of spring in the air. Bill was out in his carriage with a babysitter. Chris and I had both stayed on after school—Chris was helping dismantle the *Julius Caesar* sets, and I had some scheduling changes to work out. Tony had come back to the house alone. He hadn't wanted to stand in line for a shower at the gym so he waited till he got home and took a long, hot one in the bathroom he and Chris shared. He hadn't bothered to shave that morning, so when he finished the shower he thought he might as well do that too, but he couldn't find his razor so he decided to borrow mine. To get to our bathroom he had to go through our bedroom, but it wasn't until the return trip that he saw Sharon was lying asleep on our bed. Or not asleep. What happened then was that they had simply taken each other by surprise again as for years they had been taking each other by surprise ever since he had been a short, fat twelve year old whose zipper was always coming unzipped at the top. They became lovers by accident rather than by design in this version. They were undesigning, accidental lovers.

"Tono, I'm sorry. I'm sorry." The queer feeling as I patted his head with my hand because I couldn't think of anything else to do. How nobody else's hair ever feels quite like hair. My nephew's hair was stiff from the ocean but soft underneath, springy, matted like a dog's coat.

It had happened in March. They had been alone in the house. They hadn't planned to be alone. Neither had known the other was there. Like comedians in a silent film, they had moved about the house always just missing each other. When he went up, she went down. When he entered by one door, she left by another. When she lay down to sleep, he stepped into the shower and turned the water on.

It wasn't he who came into her room. He was in his own room by himself lying on top of his bed after his shower. He was lying on his back with his knees drawn up. His eyes were closed and his head tipped back on the pillow. Awakened from her nap by sounds she possibly couldn't place, she tiptoed barefoot across the hall and pushed the door open on him. He opened his eyes. She came in. Give me an ounce of civet, good apothecary.

They had known all along what would happen as without knowing it I also had known. He as if for a shower, she as if for a nap, they had undressed in different rooms gravely and vaguely, letting the clothes lie on the floor wherever they happened to fall. In robes of air, they had approached each other slowly then, like royalty. It was no longer a house they knew, a time and place they had dreamed about and planned. It was a coronation.

All this I imagined later. With my lips touching his salt-stiff hair, I mumbled into his scalp, "That's all right. That's all right. Things happen, that's all." There in the living room at half past three A.M. I had all I could do just trying, absurdly, to comfort him.

Eight

THE NEXT DAY was a Saturday, and by midmorning I found myself on a train heading for New York. Bebb was with me. We had caught the express from Stamford. All the seats were full so we ended up in the aisle which was almost full itself by then. Bebb perched sidesaddle on the arm of a seat which was occupied by a little girl with leg braces, and I stood next to him. When the child told Bebb that it was all right for him to sit on the arm of her seat, he gave her one of his cards. It had a head-and-shoulders photograph of him looking straight at you with his eyes bugged out and his eyebrows raised as though he had just made a challenging pronouncement or, as Sharon said, as though somebody had shoved a thermometer up his ass. There were the Open Heart cross and slogans—Open your heart to Jesus. Open your heart TODAY—with *Leo Bebb, Evangelist*, printed in Gothic underneath plus the address and hours of services. The child showed the card to her mother who didn't seem interested but took a red crayon out of her purse and handed it to her. The child colored the heart and then started coloring Bebb red too. Bebb said, "Be careful you don't get it in my eyes, honey. I need those to see with."

I said, "Lucille told Sharon on the phone this morning that fellow Golden has turned up again."

Bebb looked up at me with an expression like the one on his card. He said, "She says she saw him snooping around the barn yesterday in a porkpie hat and windbreaker. She recognized him by his shape right off. She thinks he's the one left the rose in the hymnal Sunday stuck in at Jerusalem the Golden. She says it was his calling card."

I said, "You'd have noticed him, wouldn't you? He's not one to melt into a crowd."

Bebb said, "Antonio, if that man had've been there, everybody would have noticed him. You didn't notice him, did you?"

I shook my head.

Bebb said, "You can't always be sure what Lucille sees and what she just thinks she sees. When you come down to it, she's not always sure either."

I wanted to keep the conversation going, any conversation, because once it stopped, I started having silent conversations with myself, so I said, "What do you think yourself?"

Bebb said, "I'm not going to say she didn't see him, Antonio. She might have seen him."

I said, "Who do you think he is, Bip?"

The train gave a lurch, and Bebb stretched one arm along the back of the child's seat to steady himself. The sun was coming in through the milky window, and the air was thick with cigarette smoke.

He said, "Remember the fig tree, Antonio. 'When

his branch is yet tender and putteth forth leaves, ye know that summer is nigh.' "

"You'll have to explain," I said.

Bebb said, "Antonio, let me put it this way. I've been preaching the kingdom since you were in didies, and there's lots of times it's come out a weak and sickly thing. Why, you can feel it, Antonio. You stand up there in the pulpit and see No Sale written smack across every last face. But," he raised one cautionary finger, "there are other times too, praise God. There are times when your preaching shines out hot like the sun, and the congregation starts putting forth leaves. The young and tender shoots, Antonio. They feel summer is nigh, and they show it."

As Bebb shifted his position, I caught sight of the child's coloring. She had borne down hard on the crayon, but she had been careful about the eyes as he had told her. The face was a deep, waxy crimson, but the eyes were white. He looked badly burned.

I said, "Do you think Mr. Golden's one of your young and tender shoots then who's come north to follow the sun?"

"I'd admire to think that," Bebb said. He gazed at me thoughtfully a few moments, and his trick eyelid fluttered.

I said, "Lucille thinks he's from outer space."

Bebb said, "Antonio, when the kingdom's preached hot, there's no telling what's going to start sprouting. Life starts sprouting, new life. Maybe that means new worlds too. There's no talk about outer space in Scripture, Antonio, but there's angels and archangels. There's principalities and powers in the heavenly places."

"A power called Golden," I said, "a porkpie principality," and for the first time I found myself thinking about what our mouths were talking about—that wide, flat figure drifting through the high grass in Texas, that queer sub-paunch which for all I knew was where he folded out of sight his spangled wings or Martian appendages. I thought of Lucille's and my *folie à deux* and how Mr. Golden had been sitting there in the subterranean council chamber with his antenna sticking up as Bebb settled down beside him. I might even have asked Bebb about it then and there except that suddenly it was the way it is when you think you've gotten rid of a splitting headache and then you bend over to pick something up and there's a sickening thud behind your eyeballs again: suddenly my nephew was thumping on the door again with his sea-chilled fist, my wife standing under the hall light in her nightdress. I said, "Give me an ounce of civet, good apothecary," but Bebb didn't hear me, not expecting to hear such a thing. He had leaned closer and spoke in a confidential voice.

He said, "Of course I'm not kidding myself. He may just be from the IRS. They've been giving me nothing but trouble for years."

That night before when Tony finally pulled himself together and went upstairs to bed, I decided to go to bed myself right there on the couch. If Sharon asked me about it in the morning, I planned to say I just hadn't wanted to wake her up again climbing in beside her. The baby's blanket was still on the floor where Chris had put it, and I pulled it up over me and lay there for a while in the dark listening to Tony taking a shower upstairs. Whatever else you might want to say about him, I thought, you had to admit that at least he took plenty of showers. He took at least one a day and sometimes two, one at home and one at the gym. I don't think I ever actually went to sleep that night, but I wasn't wide awake the whole time either. I spent most of the night in no man's land and covered a lot of it while I was there.

One of the few things I retain from my Italian mother's sporadic attempts to bring up my sister and me as Catholics is a feeling that you're not supposed to pray for the dead, and I've always tended to avoid it the way I tend to avoid stepping on cracks. But more than once in my life, I've prayed *to* the dead which I suppose is a blacker heresy still. At least I've said things to them in my mind and tried to imagine what they might say back which is maybe what praying is all about anyway. That night, half asleep and half awake, I spoke to my twin sister Miriam.

I said, "What's supposed to happen next if you don't mind telling me?"

I said, "That roly-poly little wop you named after me, the one who told you the plot of *Abbott and Costello Meet Frankenstein and the Wolf Man* the time I brought them up to the hospital to say goodbye to you for the last time, well he's not a roly-poly little wop any more. He's Tarzan the Ape-man and Roger the Lodger rolled into one. He's not Costello any more. He's the Wolf Man. He's been sitting here in his bathing suit blubbering like a ten year old. He's antlered me in case you want to know. I'm a twelve point buck now. I am thirty-nine years old and my wife has been screwed by my nephew and my hairline is receding and for the first time in my life I can believe that someday I'm going to get old and die like you."

Conversations with the dead are never very satisfactory. The dead are not very interested in what you tell them and usually don't have much to say. Death is apparently as much of a rat race as life is, and they've got other things on their minds. I don't picture them sitting around in chairs like the cemetery scene in *Our Town* or cooling their heels in God's outer office singing Bach. As much as I can picture them at all, I picture them hurrying off someplace like the White Rabbit in *Alice*. They don't even stop when you speak to them, just look back at you over their shoulders maybe. I could dimly picture Miriam looking back at me as I spoke.

I said, "Say something, for God's sake." But all I could get her to say was, "I'm sorry, Tono." My nephew had already said that, and he'd sounded sorrier than she did.

I said, "What do I do, for Christ's sake? Do I tell her I know or pretend I don't? Do I send him back to Charlie? Do I ask for a divorce? Do I wait till I catch them in the act and take care of them both with one bullet? Do I play it like wop opera or like Noel Coward or don't I play it at all?"

"You're the boss," she said, moving on as if I was after a dime for a cup of coffee.

I said, "What the hell kind of answer is that? Have you forgotten he's your *son*?"

She said, "My son was a little butterball who could never keep his pants zipped."

I said, "That's just the trouble, he still can't," and

she didn't even smile, just kept plowing ahead as if she had a life to depend on it. There was moonlight on the rug like snow, the baby blanket up to my chin and my bare feet sticking out. I was boring my dead sister to death.

I said, "You died before you got to meet Sharon, but have you ever seen her from wherever you are? Can you see things from there?"

"Oh God, Tono," she said, "I suppose maybe I could."

"Then do me a favor and see her sometime," I said. "She's something to see, I can tell you. And see me. See him. Help us," I said, "Help us."

She said, "*Ciao*, Antonio." She had places to go.

I was almost asleep again, and couldn't keep up with her any more. "Help us. Help us," I said drowsily.

She said, "*Addio. Addio*, Antonio."

I couldn't keep her there any longer. From the Duchess's tea-party or whatever it was.

A few hours later I made it on stiff legs into the kitchen for coffee. Sharon was there already. She was sitting at the table with Bill in her lap feeding him his bottle and apparently enjoying it. She had her nose and upper lip drawn down a little in a way that made me think of the Virgin in Michelangelo's Pietà. She didn't look up as I came in, holding the bottle tilted down to Bill's mouth with one finger against his fat cheek to tickle him with if he started going to sleep on her. Her legs were crossed, one bare foot in midair throbbing slightly with her pulse. I could see down her neck to where the tan ended and the pale, freckly part began. "The Instant's by the toaster," she said, still too busy with Bill to look up, and it occurred to me that this was the first time I'd seen all of her or at least more of her than I'd ever seen before, or wanted to see. Or this was the first time that it was all of me that was doing the seeing. She was looking down at the baby drowsing in the crook of her arm. One way or the other it was the first time we had met fully.

I thought at the time that it was the turning point of my life, that all our four destinies, Sharon's and Bill's and Tony's and mine, hung on whatever I said next or didn't say right there in that kitchen with the steam from the kettle turning to cumulus in the morning sun. Looking back, I see it as a medieval painting, our three figures motionless in gold-leaf, the words coming out of my mouth like a streamer—*Benedicta tu in mulieribus*. My question at the time was what words would they be, what fatal, sad annunciation? What urbane evasion or Pagliaccian tirade? *Ne timeas, Maria*. We were frozen in the golden air, waiting.

What I said was, "I spent the night on the couch so I wouldn't wake you up." She glanced at me then, her eyes more green than brown in the sunlight. She frowned slightly. The sound of my voice made Bill turn his head. The nipple was still half in his mouth. There was a trickle of yellowy milk on his chin.

It seemed a turning point at the time, but I'm not so sure now. When you think you've reached a turning point, the chances are you've already passed it. It was probably sometime during the night that I'd decided without knowing it that the injuries I'd sustained were critical but that the bleeding was all internal and was going to stay that way. I would see to it that from the outside nobody noticed a thing. Unless Sharon noticed. She hitched the baby over to her other arm so she could re-cross her legs, and the nipple came out of his mouth with a little rubbery pop. Her smile caught me off guard the way it more or less always did, that hang-dog, Rastus flash of teeth and eyes. Tony had said he was sorry. Miriam had said it. For all I knew maybe Sharon's smile was saying she was sorry too—sorry about my night on the couch, sorry she'd made me believe I was going to get old and die someday—but you couldn't be sure. The rubbery pop of Bill's nipple had a vaguely indecent sound. Maybe she was just smiling at that.

When Tony came down in his Saturday uniform of spectacularly faded jeans and decaying loafers held together with adhesive tape, I watched eagle-eyed from the toaster to see what would pass between then. He said, "What's for breakfast, Shar?" She said, "Cow flops." That's what passed between them.

The rage and tears I'd witnessed that night had happened before, and they would happen again, and I suppose they both enjoyed in one way the time when they were happening and in another way the time when they weren't happening. There was no furtive glance of guilty lovers either, no secret touch as he passed by her, the sole of one loafer flapping loose against the linoleum. Whatever they had been once, and for all I knew might become anytime again, they were not lovers then. Any fool could see it. The furtiveness and the guilt were all mine.

My antlers glittered as I turned my eyes back to the smoking toaster and my enflamed visions. Sharon was tan except where she was pale and freckled like thrushes' eggs. Tony was advancing on her with the jouncing buffoon of his own flesh straining forward to point his way. Every detail complete with close-ups and tricky angle shots ran through my mind like a stag movie as I stood there scraping the black off my toast into the sink. I was the only one of the three of us with something to hide.

Sharon told me Lucille had called to ask if we'd drive Bip to the station because their car was being fixed. He had errands to do in New York, Lucille had said. Also Mr. Golden had turned up again. Tony was sitting between us with his chin in a bowl of shredded wheat and bananas. His manner with me was all Tom Swift. He didn't show even the faintest trace of discomfort or remorse. He'd succeeded in unloading all that on me the night before so that now I was the one who had a hard time looking *him* in the eye.

"Do you mind driving him, Big Bopper?" Sharon said. "This is my Evelyn Wood morning."

As I glanced up at her, I knew that I had to get away that day—their fresh-faced guilt was too great a reproach to my shifty-eyed innocence—and almost before I knew what I was about, I heard myself saying that I had some errands to do myself in New York and might as well keep Bebb company on the train. Maybe I wanted Sharon to ask me not to go. I don't know. She didn't. She took Bill and put him over her shoulder, making circles on his back with the flat of her hand until he produced a small, wet rattle.

Nine

WHEN THE TRAIN got to Grand Central, Bebb and I went our separate ways. I left him at a freight elevator. He said it would take him down to where the subways were. He stood in it looking grim and preoccupied, I thought, a trussed, bulky package of a man. I watched the doors slide shut on him. The arrow on the button panel lit up red. The arrow pointed down. How far down was anybody's guess.

I had no errands in New York, of course, and had been too busy dreaming on the train to dream up any, so when the doors snapped shut on Bebb, I found myself with no idea where to go next. For a moment I considered taking the next train back. I would return unexpectedly to the house and surprise them in the act. Or I would return unexpectedly to the house and purposely not surprise them in the act. They would find me sitting downstairs and know that I knew what they were up to without having to surprise them. But this was nonsense, of course, because they couldn't be up to anything what with Chris and the baby at home. Only instead of being relieved by that thought, I was depressed by it. It was as if I had gone away with Bebb and left them there not for my sake but for their sakes, and the fact that like me they weren't up to anything only added to my sense of emptiness and loss.

With no goal in mind, I could just as plausibly have walked east from Grand Central or south, but instead I headed north up Park. My sense of the color and character of New York geography dates back to my childhood there, and I think still in terms of my childhood frontiers. South of Forty-second Street is still the old Aquarium at the Battery with its tank full of horseshoe crabs and the statue of George Washington in front of the Treasury Building and a store called Shackman's where you could get the best favors and false faces in the city. West of Fifth is the Natural History museum and the old Met and Riverside Drive, especially the part up around Grant's Tomb, but otherwise it's no man's land. As a child I never knew anybody who lived west of Fifth, and I'd have to think hard to remember one now. East from Fifth is shops, the romance diminishing as you move from Tiffany's and Schwarz's on Fifth itself to Brooks on Madison, to cigar stores and delicatessens on Lexington. East of Lexington is drunks asleep in doorways and the old El. Park is the lights left on in the Grand Central Building at Christmas-time in the shape of a cross, is apartment building awnings either Rolls Royce maroon or ping-pong table green sheltering doormen in white gloves with whistles and black umbrellas in case of rain. Park Avenue is the rainiest part of the city. And going north on Park is still going home. It hadn't actually been home for thirty years, but north on Park was the way I went that morning of the day when I first woke up to the knowledge that my wife had taken as her lover a child who was named after me.

In the spring, a young man's fancy lightly turns to thoughts of love, the old poem goes, and in a different key maybe, but nonetheless, my thirty-nine-year-old fancy turned the same way. Heading north up Park toward the home we'd shared as children, I thought of my sister Miriam, whom I'd loved. I thought of how I hadn't been able to get much out of her that sleepless night on the couch when I'd tried to tell her ghost what was going on, and I wondered what I would have gotten out of her if she'd still been alive somehow. She would probably have been furious in some predictably Italian way though whether more furious at Sharon for being the seducer (this would have been her inevitable choice among my various versions as I suppose it was also mine) or at Tony for letting himself be seduced or at me for not smelling the rat before it was served up cold at three o'clock in the morning, I could not say. I thought of how year after year one nurse or another in rubber-soled white Oxfords had taken us off to the Park where she conferred with her buddies while Miriam and I roller-skated or drew on the sidewalk with pieces of hard, flat chalk that looked like marble chips or yelled at each other in those vaulted brick tunnels to hear the echo bounce. I thought of how she was all by herself when she died in that awful A-shaped cast with most of her bones broken, but of how Charlie and her two boys and I had all been at the cemetery when she was buried on Christmas Eve day. It was when I realized that I hadn't been back to the cemetery since then that I found the errand I'd been looking for. I would go out to Brooklyn and check in at Miriam's grave, and I would do it not just because I had nothing better to do but because it seemed the right time to do it. But I'd have lunch first. At Forty-ninth Street I thought of the United Nations and my old friend Ellie Pierce, who as far as I knew still did volunteer work at the information desk. My lovely, pre-Raphaelite Ellie with her brocade slipper pumping up and down on the soft pedal as she played Mozart for me or Satie. Ellie, that indefatigable collector of causes, so Vassar and Urban League and Bergdorf's.

A man who has been cuckolded by his nephew is in a uniquely vulnerable state, especially if it happens to take place in the spring when he's vulnerable enough anyway, and the thought of seeing Ellie again gave me a sense of might-have-been as strong as heartburn as I pictured us ambling for an hour or two down some little stretch of the road we had not taken. But when I got to the U.N. they told me at the information desk that she didn't work there any more. They thought she might still come in from time to time to do some filing upstairs, but nobody had seen her for weeks. One of them thought she'd been in the hospital that winter. Maybe she was still there. It was all vague and doubtful, and I'd about decided to give up and have a sandwich by myself when somebody came up behind and tapped me on the shoulder. When I turned around, there was Ellie.

She looked older and more chic than the last time I'd seen her, less pre-Raphaelite and flowing than Edwardian and a little angular. But she looked well too. She had some gray in her hair and was wearing a gray suit with a yellow silk blouse and a yellow rosebud pinned to her lapel. She said, "Tono, I couldn't believe my eyes," and when we kissed each other on the cheek, she smelled, as she always had, of shampoo. I said, "You look terrific. They've been trying to tell me you were in the hospital," and she said, "Oh, that was just for a little repair work." She blushed slightly, I thought, and I wondered if what she meant was a hysterectomy—that most unhysterical of wombs, which had never known any action, out of action at last. "Tell me," she said, with just the slightest hesitation as she found the right name, "where's Sharon?"

I said, "She's home learning how to read."

"Tono, Tono," Ellie said.

I said, "Nobody calls me Tono any more. Sharon says it's too close to her baby word for number two." When was the last time I'd called it number two?

"Well, you can't blame her for that," Ellie said. Then, "What *was* her baby word," which was the last thing in the world she wanted to know but it gave her time to look me over. Did I look older to her, I wondered. My hair had no gray in it, but there was less of it. I wished I'd put on a clean shirt.

"No-no," I said. "She used to call it no-no for some obscure reason."

"Tono Parr," she said, smiling and shaking her head at the same time as though I had dropped something and broken it.

We had lunch together in a French restaurant, my old friend and I. Ellie was the one who knew about it. You had to walk down stairs to get into it, and it was small and smelled of garlic and household ammonia. I had a martini first, Ellie a Cinzano, and she told the waiter what she wanted to eat in her lovely Vassar French. Then she said, "Now tell me what you've been up to, Tono—I can't help calling you Tono anyway. I want to hear everything," and before she was through, she very nearly did.

"Open your heart to Jesus," Bebb's ad said. "Open your heart TODAY," and I wanted to open my heart there to Ellie Pierce not so much so she could see what was inside but so I could. I used to think that to talk about the things that go on in your heart is to take a lot of the bloom off them, and it's true that it does. But it's true too that unless you talk about them, you can't be sure that anything's going on there at all. I said, "Well, we've got this baby for one thing. He's not getting any younger, and he's still bald as an egg." Bill was the last thing I would have expected to tell her about first. Ellie made me tell her more about him, and I wondered again about the hysterectomy and if she still had a womb and what would ever become of it if she did.

I told her about how I was teaching English again and about the wooden thing I had hanging out in the shed. She seemed pleased about the wooden thing because I used to make smaller scrap-iron things during the years we'd known each other. She said she was glad I was still working with my hands by which I suppose she meant she was glad there was still some tangible connection between whoever I had been then and whoever I was now. She said, "Is it supposed to *be* anything, Tono?" She had always liked things to be something.

I told her I didn't think so, and when she asked me to describe it, I was reduced to trying to draw it on the tablecloth with my butter knife.

"It looks like a big A," she said, and she was right. I hadn't noticed before, but it did. Was it Miriam's A-shaped cast, I wondered, or A for Antonio which, the way things were happening, might turn out to be a brand new name for number two? "It's the scarlet letter," I said.

She said, "You don't change, Tono."

She looked so understanding sitting there behind her *artichaut vinaigrette*, so handsome and resourceful in her gray suit with the yellow rosebud. She looked as though there wasn't anything I could tell her that she wouldn't find the right place for in her file, nothing she couldn't cross-index so the connections between things would come clear at last—the sea-smell of my nephew's hair, Bebb's face burned crimson where the crippled child had crayoned it, Laura Fleischman's reading "poor naked wretches" out loud in class. I had opened my heart far enough to show Ellie my bald son and the contents of my woodshed. The question now was would I open it far enough to show her the rest. Would I treat her to a glimpse of Lucille wobbling down the aisle of Open Heart in her French heels and Aimee Semple McPherson peignoir? Would I raise for her the apparition of Leo Bebb at this very moment for all I could prove to the contrary meeting in full subterranean council with God only knew what? Would I run off for her the reel of Sharon and my nephew that afternoon in March? Ellie was asking me something about the drug situation at Sutton High School as I reached across the table and took her hand in mine.

It was like when the furnace and the deep freeze happen to come on at the same time so that the lights go dim for a second or two and the TV fades. Ellie hardly hesitated in whatever she was saying, her face barely flickered, and then she was back running normally again. But the risk of overloading the circuits was clear. I gave her hand a comradely squeeze, withdrawing mine to my empty martini glass. I said, "How about telling me about you for a change?" And she did.

She told me how she'd organized a group of tenants in Manhattan House to protest what she felt were discriminatory rental policies. She told me about a museum tour of Greece she had taken. She talked about Mayor Lindsay and the subway strike. She used "we" more than "I" most of the time, but I got the impression it was something more like a committee than a twosome. I kept wondering if I'd been right about the repair work, whether that was what she'd really have liked to be opening her heart about—how it felt to be empty inside, a dead end street. But if she opened her heart to Jesus on the subject, she didn't even take the chair out from under the doorknob for me. We agreed we wouldn't let years go by again till the next time. I would bring Sharon in, and we'd all have dinner and go to the theater. I asked her if I could get her a cab, and she said no, she needed the exercise. We touched cheeks once more out on the sidewalk where the sun nearly blinded us after our dim lunch and then headed off in different directions.

Ellie never found out what was in my heart, and I never found out what was in hers, and maybe it was for the best. Just our failure to was a familiar failure, and it was the familiar I needed that day, not open-heart surgery. My only regret after we parted was that I hadn't asked her about my old cat Tom. I'd like to have heard how he was getting on at Manhattan House.

I would also like to have been able to weep a little at Miriam's grave—it would have been a kind of purge for me, and I knew Miriam would have enjoyed it—but it didn't work that way. I've never been much good at tears on demand. At Miriam's death-bed and funeral both, I remained dry-eyed. I cry best when I expect to least. I remember, for instance, when I took Sharon and the boys to see the movie of *Hello Dolly*, which is not what you'd ordinarily think of as a tear-jerker. It was during the big restaurant scene when Barbra Streisand comes sweeping down the grand staircase in her satin and feathers, and everybody starts singing "Hello Dolly" and then the next thing you know, there is Louis Armstrong singing it, Satchmo himself sweating and grinning with his lips wobbling, that face that was turned out back in the days before black was beautiful, just black, and all of a sudden the tears were streaming down my cheeks and I had to stuff popcorn in my mouth. The other time I remember was at a swimming meet between Sutton and Portchester. It was a relay race, and by the time the last relay of swimmers had grabbed the batons and dived in, the noise bouncing back and forth from the tiled walls became so pure and intense that you could hear right down to a kind of distilled silence at the heart of it, and once again I found myself blinded. But there at my sister's grave, I didn't even get a lump in my throat.

At the cemetery entrance they had given me a map with the way I was to go marked out on it, but I missed a turn somewhere and wandered most of an hour down one avenue after another of mausoleums and cenotaphs, old rugged crosses and obelisks and monoliths of every size and shape with just single names cut into them. GALLAGHER, KURTZ, CRUCETTI—with no first names or dates to get in the way they looked like final pronouncements or the presidents of banks. By the time I located the small marker with PARR on it, my first feeling was just relief that I'd finally made it. My parents shared a stone between them, but Miriam had one all to herself. Charlie had picked it out, I think, and it looked rather like him, a faded, canned-salmon-colored granite with the carving of her name still pale and unweathered. Miriam herself would probably have preferred something more on the order of the grieving angel who knelt nearby with a face that reminded me of Liberace. I noticed that though my parents were smooth and level, Miriam had sunk a little, and I decided to speak to the people at the gate about putting in some more sod. It looked forlorn that way, like a fallen soufflé.

I stood there and thought about her and thought about how maybe after a little, a tear might come to make us both feel better, but no tear came. I could not seem to think her into anything much like reality. Even her name the way Charlie had had it carved didn't really seem hers. Miriam Parr Blaine. It made some kind of a career woman out of her, like Helen Gahagan Douglas or Grace Livingston Hill. Then my mind started wandering, and it wasn't long before I wasn't thinking about my sister or about anything else in particular, just staring down at the grass so hard I didn't see it, without a thought in my head.

It's not an easy business to stop thinking, and although according to Sharon it's the whole point of yoga and can be achieved by anybody who works at it, I find it hard to imagine how that can be so. It seems to me that to work at not thinking must be to *think* about not thinking. As I stood there at my sister's grave, my mind was empty not because I'd worked at emptying it but because it had just happened that way, which seems to be how it is with most good things. Despite my mother's efforts to make me a Catholic, I'm afraid that in this regard anyway I turned out Protestant. If there's any such thing as salvation, I suspect it's not through works that we come by it but through grace.

Something else happened there in Brooklyn that afternoon that may have been through grace too although at the time I wouldn't have said so probably. I was still standing there in this kind of empty-headed trance, and then it was like what happens when, just as you're about to go to sleep at night, you seem to trip over something and can feel the whole bed shake under you. I came to, I suppose you would say. Some stirring in the air or quick movement of squirrel or bird brought me back to myself, and just at that instant of being brought back to myself I knew that the self I'd been brought back to was some fine day going to be as dead as Miriam. I knew it not just in the usual sense of knowing but knew it in almost the Biblical sense of having sex with it. I knew I didn't just *have* a body. I *was* a body. It was like walking into a closed door at night. The thud of it jolted me down to the roots of my hair.

The body I was was going to be dead. Through Sharon and Tony I'd finally come to believe it, but through grace alone I banged right into it—not a lesson this time, a collision. You might say that there at my sister's grave I finally lost my virtue, saw the unveiling of middle-age's last and most intimate secret. There in Brooklyn I was screwed by my own death.

I'd taken a subway out, but I felt I needed a taxi going back, and when I got to Grand Central again with forty minutes till the next train, I dropped into a bar and ordered myself a double martini. Standing.

The bar had one of those beach-ball-sized, sequin-covered, revolving globes that scatters light all over the place like snowflakes, and I was sitting there watching it when for the second time that day somebody came up from behind and tapped me on the back. It was Laura Fleischman. "I just happened to look through the window," she said, "and there you were." The momentum of her surprise had gotten her just as far as that, then stranded her there, speechless, in the flurry of light.

I called her by name, knew perfectly well who she was, but it was as if there was something absurdly elementary that I didn't know like who I was myself or whether it was our native language I was speaking; and then "Carl West," I said, of all inanities. "Have you got Carl West with you?" Fitch–Abercrombie, battery–assault, it was the crudest kind of free association, and the moment it was out, I regretted it.

What happened in her face didn't take more than a second or two to happen, but I saw it all. She left her face and retreated to wherever it was she kept Carl West, and while she was inside there with him, the face she'd left behind was totally unguarded.

I've heard it explained that when you sneeze, your soul leaves your body and people say God bless you to keep the devil from slipping into you and taking your soul's place. My impulse was to say something like God bless you to Laura Fleischman for fear that if I didn't, I'd have that face on my conscience for the rest of my life. But then her soul got back on its own somehow. She smiled, and said, "No," by which I took her to mean not just that Carl West wasn't there at Grand Central but that at least for the moment he wasn't there inside with her any more either.

"I've been to the orthodontist," she said, and when I made some fatuous remark about how there didn't seem to be anything wrong with her smile as far as I could see, she said, "It's a molar that's coming in crooked."

It turned out she was waiting for the same train I was, so I made her take the stool next to mine and asked her if she'd have something to drink with me. She said she'd like a 7-Up, which made me feel like a child molester, but by the time the bartender brought it to her with a slice of lemon and a cherry, together with another martini for me, the feeling was past. I was her English teacher again, at least had been once on some other planet.

Sharon sitting in the kitchen that morning with Bill in her lap. My old friend Ellie telling me over lunch about rental policies at Manhattan House.

Miriam off there in Brooklyn where I'd forgotten on the way out to say she needed more sod and where the poor echo of her death had been drowned out by the thud of my own (was it really Tony I had heard thumping at the door that night Sharon wouldn't go down and open it?). It had been Ladies' Day for me so far, and each of them I'd sought out to give me God knows what only to come away from them if not empty-handed, at least with nothing in my hands like whatever it was I'd expected. And now Laura Fleischman, whom I hadn't sought out at all, and as we sat side by side on our leopard-skin stools with the light from the globe swarming around us, I thought of that loveliest of all French phrases, A *l'ombre des jeunes filles en fleur*, which Scott Moncrieff renders as "Within a budding grove" when even a plodding literalism would come closer to the loveliness of it—"in the shade of young girls' flowering." John Skelton's "Merry Margaret/As midsummer flower,/ Gentle as falcon of hawk in the tower" comes as close to it in spirit as anything I know in English.

In any case, what we talked about was the chances Sutton had of beating Stamford in track and whether seniors ought to be allowed to cut gym in the spring to get ready for finals, but it wasn't small talk. It was big talk because all that we both of us were was in it, and there was nothing left over of either of us to think about anything else while we were talking. And that is how we missed our train.

Laura noticed first. She picked up my hand to get a look at my wrist watch, and I bent forward to get a look at it too, and when our foreheads touched for a second, I noticed it less in my forehead than in my stomach where it felt like when the express elevator freefalls the first twenty floors.

Two things could have happened then of which just one, needless to say, actually did, but to report that one only would be to report less than the truth. A thing can't be both itself and not itself, logicians say, but they must have been thinking of logic rather than reality when they said it, human reality anyway. What we live through in our dreams is no less a part of who we are than what we live through when we're not dreaming, and the events of one leave marks no less deep than the events of the other. Who is to say that what actually happens in a man's life is all that more important to him than what happens not to happen? We missed our train, Laura Fleischman and I. It was an event as much a part of history as Sharon's telling my nephew there were cow flops for breakfast. There were no two ways about it. But two ways branched out from it. The exigencies of narrative force me to set them side by side. It would be more accurate to present them as a double exposure. The way we took and the way we didn't take.

One way was this. I said, "So we've missed it, so now what?" Laura Fleischman sucked the last of her 7-Up through the straw, rattling the ice. "I've got a timetable here somewhere," she said and started burrowing into a large straw pocketbook that looked as if it might have been her mother's. I saw what she was after before she did and reached in after her to get it out before she buried it again, and there in her mother's straw pocketbook, our hands touched. I might have gotten my hand the hell out of there and used it for smoothing the timetable down on the bar top. Might have. The past subjunctive. That ultimate grammatical sublety. That capsulized metaphysics. It was the point where the two ways branched.

Let us say I might have but I did not get my hand the hell out of Mrs. Fleischman's pocketbook. I had had two martinis not counting the one I'd had with Ellie at lunch. The revolving globe had made it the last act of Peter Pan where they're up in the tree at night and the fireflies are out. I had run into my own death in Brooklyn and had lived to tell the tale if I felt like telling it. Laura Fleischman hadn't moved her hand. So I folded her hand up in mine and shut my eyes and said, "It takes me back to dancing school."

She said, "What does?" Even if you hadn't happened to be holding her hand yourself, you could have told from her face that somebody was. I had seen her look that way in class when I'd asked her a question she didn't know the answer to.

"Your hand does," I said. "It's damp. Like a dancing-school hand." When you hold a girl's hand and talk to her about holding it, you are holding more than a hand.

She said, "I know. I know what you mean," as though I had explained something that had needed explaining more than anything else in the world. The bartender put a saucer of potato chips between us. When I let her hand go, she moved the potato chips to the side with it and spread out the timetable.

"Like which one can we take," she said, running her finger down the column.

"I'll tell you what Bodhidharma would do," I said. I emptied the potato chips onto the timetable and picking it up with a hand at each side offered it to her. "Take one of these," I said.

She took a big one and broke part of it off with her teeth.

I said, "Now you don't have to take one at all. You've already taken it."

"I've got to be home for supper," she said.

I looked at my watch. I said, "Whoever heard of getting home for supper at quarter of four?"

"Bodhidharma maybe?" she said.

It was in Cocteau's *Beauty and the Beast*, I think, where there was a scene of the beast in a long cape with a high, stiff collar walking down a corridor in his palace. Every time he approached a pair of gilded doors at the end of the corridor, they would swing open and there would be still more of the corridor beyond them, all paneled and mirrored like Versailles, and then another pair of doors. On and on. So it was with Laura Fleischman and me that spring afternoon after we left the station according to this one of the two ways. Doors opened onto doors and they in turn opened onto other doors until finally we came to the last pair of doors, and they opened too.

I tell her I've thought of people I ought to see in the city the next day and have decided I might as well spend the night there rather than go home and have to come back again the next morning, so Laura Fleischman goes with me to the Gotham maybe or the Plaza and sits off in a corner somewhere looking at *Cue* or at a Van Cleef and Arpels showcase while I register, and going up in the elevator we speak like strangers, which we are, about how the best time in New York is summertime because it's not so crowded then, just the backs of our hands touching, our knuckles, and the way her hair falls, I can see the nape of her neck and the top of her spine and with her eyes lowered she looks like a girl being lectured by a nun. She has a nun's face herself almost, a slow smile she doesn't use any more than she has to and high, calm cheeks I can see framed in starched linen, embarrassed eyes. It is a white room, and when I open the window, the air has New York in it and springtime and carbon monoxide, and if when I am an old man somebody gives me some of that air to smell, it will either make me young again or kill me sure. A curtain balloons into the room. The sky is a dingy mauve, lights coming on. Laura Fleischman pushes her hair back off her bare shoulders and holds it behind her with one hand. We talk about something at the open window, and this time there is none of either of us in what we are talking about because we are both of us waiting, and what we are waiting for is not just what is going to happen in that room but something farther off than that.

A *l'ombre des jeunes filles en fleur*. In that flowering shade, I can't make out clearly by what sequence of events we have come here. I can't imagine, and I have tried hard to imagine, the things that were said, the doors that had to open around us and inside us to bring us through that final door. I suppose the corridor of the afternoon must have just kept extending before us, and we followed along without ever thinking farther ahead than the next turning. But there at the end there is nothing I can't see. I see the Beast, of course—the moist, imploring eyes, the hairy, furrowed brow and glistening snout, the stiff and arching horn. Beauty is by him. Gentle as falcon or hawk in the tower. Beauty is the shade he rests in and the cool flowering where he gets lost. Somewhere between her pity and her love, within that cleft and confluence, he rises up a prince.

The other way was this. I reached into Mrs. Fleischman's straw pocketbook and took the timetable out. We had just time to pay the check and get down to the track before the next train left. We couldn't find a seat together, but I got one directly in front of hers and talked to her for a while over the back until my neck began to cramp. Then she settled down to a creased paperback of *Great Issues in American History* and I looked out of the window and watched as far as 125th Street and a little beyond until the martinis began to take their effect together with the rockabye jouncing of the New Haven roadbed and I fell asleep. Laura woke me when we got to Stamford, "Mr. Parr," she said, "we're here, Mr. Parr," and opening my eyes to her face bending over me, I couldn't be sure which of the two ways was the one we'd followed and the moment was both itself and not itself, whatever logicians may say. I dropped her off at her house on my way home, and we shook hands in the car as she thanked me for the lift and the 7-Up I'd bought her at the station.

It was dusk when I got home myself. Sharon met me in the hall. She said, "Listen. When Bip got back from the city, Luce was gone, and she isn't back yet. That was a couple of hours ago. She never goes out by herself and their car's busted anyhow. Bip's in a sweat."

She had on her black leotards with some kind of

wrap-around skirt over them. It seemed weeks since the last time I'd seen her, and I was about to kiss her hello when I stopped myself and then in a split second stopped myself from stopping myself and kissed her. She said, "I'm glad *you're* back anyway." At Miriam's grave I hadn't been able to make a lump in my throat happen. Here, it was no trouble at all.

Ten

BEBB DEPLOYED us like troops. Although it wasn't raining, he had on his black raincoat that pulled under the arms and his narrow-brimmed hat. He was carrying a flashlight as long as a nightstick and arrived unannounced while we were having our Saturday night supper. Tony had gone upstairs to get ready for some kind of date he had lined up, and Sharon and Chris and I were having our coffee.

Bebb said, "I'm going to be honest with you, I don't like it. If it was anybody else, you might think she went off to a picture or someplace and just didn't leave word she'd be late. Not Luce. Besides, the car's on the fritz, and she was never one to go in for walking any more than she had to, can't anybody blame her for that. Why Sharon, you know what her balance is like even when she's—Why, in *flat* heels, she's not all that steady," he said, bringing the butt of his flashlight down on the table, "and on those spikes of hers she hasn't got a chance. She took off on wheels, that's for sure. What we've got to find out is where she took off for and why she took off."

He gave each of us an assignment. Sharon was to

stay home with the baby in case anybody called. Bebb and Chris and I were to make the rounds of railway stations, bus depots, and taxi stands to see if we could find out anything there. "There's no use calling," he said. "I tried that. Right off they think you're out to make trouble for somebody and clam up." On our way we were to drop Tony off at Bebb's house so if Lucille came back while we were away, she wouldn't find the place empty. He didn't say that of the two boys, Tony was Lucille's favorite, but all of us knew it. When Sharon explained that Tony had a date, Bebb yelled up the stairs to him, and he came down in his undershorts with a towel around his neck and his hair standing up in the air from having just been washed. Bebb said, "Tony, I'm asking you to give up your pleasure tonight and help me find my wife because my soul is exceeding sorrowful, and I need you. Will you do it?" and Tony said, "Yes, sir." I had never heard him call anybody sir before. Then Bebb said, "Now we're all going to bow our heads," and none of us was quick enough to grasp what he'd said until he'd bowed his own head and started praying. His bald scalp glistened in the kitchen light. He had his eyes clamped shut and his face screwed up tight.

He said, "Oh dear friend Jesus, who art the hope of sinners and the mender of the broken-hearted, we need thee bad this night. Jesus, thou art the good shepherd of the sheep, and we are here to tell you one of thy sheep is lost. We don't know where to start looking. We don't even know whether she was in her right mind when she wandered off or whether her vexed and troubled spirit had led her to seek comfort in the bottle where she's used to finding it. We don't even know whether she went off on her own or somebody come and took her off by force or guile. There's nobody here knows better than you she's a sinner like the rest of us, but life hasn't been a bed of roses for her either. Please put your love around her like a warm coat so nothing hurtful can get at her wherever she is. And help us go forth now and do our best to find her. We ask it for her sake and our sake, both. And for thy mercy's sake too. Amen." He pronounced amen with a long a.

Bebb's prayer had frozen us all in our tracks like a witch's spell: Tony in his underpants with his feathery hair floating over his head like a black cloud; Chris caught halfway between the table and the sink with his thumb and forefinger in a pair of milky glasses; Sharon holding her face in the V of her hands so her eyes were pulled sideways. I was the only one with open eyes, and when Bebb raised his head from his praying, he looked into them and said, "Antonio, there is more rejoicing in heaven over the one lost one that's found than over the whole ninety and nine that never got lost in the first place."

We left Tony and Sharon in the two different houses each near a telephone and with however many miles there were of night between them. I hadn't arranged things that way. Bebb had. I caught a glimpse of Chris sitting there beside me with just a little glow from the dashboard lighting him up around his father's lashless eyes, and I wondered if he knew about his brother and Sharon and what he thought about it if he did. I decided that whatever he thought about it, he probably didn't think about it as much as he thought about lots of other things, and maybe that was just as well for him or maybe it wasn't. When we got to Sutton, I let him and Bebb out at the bus station, and I drove on down to the railroad.

The ticket window was closed and I couldn't locate anybody in the waiting room or the freight office, but across the tracks I saw what looked as if it might be a porter sitting on a bench under a light bulb. Climbing the moldering stairs of the overpass, I crossed over and described Lucille to him. Skinny with black glasses, I said, pushing sixty, maybe a little unsteady on her feet. Through my description, she emerged as stark as the last name on one of those Brooklyn monuments. CRUCETTI. The man turned out to be a taxi driver. He shook his head and said he'd been there only a few minutes. Then he pointed back across the tracks and said, "Try him."

There was a large man leaning up against the wall under a sign that had MEN on it with an arrow underneath, and when he saw us both turn to look at him at the same time, he raised one arm to us. He had on a porkpie hat and a windbreaker, and his pants hung loose and baggy on him like sails. I recognized him right away as Mr. Golden.

Just supposing the impossible to be possible, I thought, how did you approach a Principality or a Power or even a man from Mars? With tears in your eyes and excuses on your lips? The way a missionary approaches a Fiji Islander? Did you approach him at all? That one arm raised in salutation—was it raised across the littered tracks only, across the candy wrappers, fruit peels, toilet paper dried and soaked and dried again until it had turned to divinity, seafoam? Or was it raised across light-years, was it raised maybe even across whatever it is (if anything) that separates what is holy from what people throw out of train windows and flush down cans? This side of getting back in the car and telling Bebb I couldn't find anybody to ask, I suppose the prudent thing would have been just to wait there and let Mr. Golden approach me if he felt like it. But curiosity led me on. I mounted once again that dingy Bridge of Sighs, walked a second time past FUCK YOU in lipstick and a place where somebody had tossed his cookies, and wondered if maybe to reach the high angels this was the kind of route you always had to take. Mr. Golden hadn't moved from his place under the sign that said MEN. He smiled as I approached. His teeth were strong and white but you could see that all the back ones were missing. "Mr. Golden?" I said, extending my hand, and he said, "Who he?"

He was dressed as if for work—he could have been a foreman of some kind or a nightwatchman—and his presence at the station suggested that he had some professional reason for being there; but as soon as he started talking, I had the feeling that the clothes he had on were play clothes and his being there at the station was just part of a game he was playing—not a cat-and-mouse game but something like ring-around-the-rosy or flying a kite. A surburban railroad station at nine or ten o'clock on a Saturday night isn't the place you'd normally think of going just for the hell of it, but I had a hunch that this was why Mr. Golden had gone there. He was having fun.

I said, "Haven't I seen you someplace before?" and he said, "If a man keeps his eyes open, there's no telling what he'll see in this world. Think what it would be like to be blind this time of year." With his thumbs in his armpits, he took a deep breath. He said, "I'm crazy about the spring," said it as though he was confessing to some amiable quirk, his eyes sparkling like a girl's. "Just breathing the air gives me the biggest kick. I wouldn't miss it for anything." His voice was on the high side, like a taut rubber band when you pluck it.

I said, "You're the mystery man of the year. Nobody knows who you are or what you're after. What's the story anyway?"

He said, "Can you name me anybody who isn't a mystery man? When you come right down to it, what does anybody know about who anybody is or what anybody's after?"

I said, "Does the name Leo Bebb mean anything to you?"

"Lifesaver?" he said. He had taken them out of his windbreaker pocket and offered me one which I accepted. Spearmint. He didn't take one himself but put the pack back in his pocket. "Does the name such-and-such mean anything to you," he said, almost imitating my voice but not quite. "I don't even know if you mean anything to me yourself yet."

I said, "First you turn up at the funeral of Herman Redpath. Then you turn up in Connecticut and are seen hanging around Open Heart. Now you turn up here." He was listening to me attentively, I thought, his lips slightly pursed, but he wasn't looking at me. He was looking up at the sky where way up, too high to hear, a plane was slowly passing over blinking a red light. I said, "Is it any wonder we'd like to know what you're up to?"

He had a lean, fine-featured face, sallow and creased without the faintest trace of whiskers. He had a smallish head and a stringy neck and then this body that looked about six sizes too big for him and this heavy garland of flesh swelling out around his loins as though inside his clothes he had started to roll down some cumbersome undergarment. He could have weighed three hundred pounds, I thought, and yet there was something about the way his pants hung that made me wonder if he weighed anything at all.

He said, "I don't want to keep on giving you smart answers, but do I have to be up to something? Do I have to be some kind of crook or crank or queerie?"

I said, "There's no law that says you've got to tell me anything you don't want to."

He said, "There's laws about everything else."

I said, "If the tables were turned, you'd want to know about me."

"There's no need to turn the tables," he said. "I want to know about you with the tables just like they are now. Tell me about yourself."

Possibly he was an undercover agent for the I.R.S., Bebb had said. Possibly when Bebb preached the Kingdom, he was somebody the Kingdom had taken root in like a mustard seed and who wanted to stay near where the seed had come from, as Bebb had also said. Possibly, as Lucille and Bebb had both said, he was from outer space. "Silvers you might see most anytime if you keep your eyes open and look for the ones has hair and faces the same color," Bebb had told me once, "but goldens are scarce as hen's teeth." Possibly he was a hen's tooth. Whichever he was, I thought, assuming he was any of them, he would have a reason for wanting me to tell him about myself, and for a moment or two, standing there in the night, I almost considered telling him except that I wouldn't have known where to start or where to stop either, so I just said, "Lucille Bebb's missing. We don't know where she's gone."

It was the first time I'd caught him looking directly at me, and all the life there was in him seemed to rise up into those young eyes of his as though seeing was only a small part of what eyes were for.

He said, "Yes. Well, that's how things happen. It's just not the biggest surprise in the world, that's all. She's had to carry that pitiful little death around Jesus only knows how long, and she wasn't exactly a tower of strength to start with. I'm sorry she's lost," he said, and as he said it, the main part of the life drained back down into his face again. His eyes were looking at me now in the normal way of eyes as if to judge how sorry I was myself that Lucille was lost, and I realized that up till now I hadn't been sorry at all much, just interested how we were going to end up finding her—passed out in a corner somewhere or wobbling off into the woods, maybe some friend taking her off on a bender while Bebb was away in the city. I said, "You haven't seen her then?"

He shook his head.

"But you know her by sight?" I said, "You know Bebb."

He said, "Look, do I know this?" He had taken a pinch of his cheek between his thumb and forefinger and gave it a little tug as though to loosen his face, take it off even. "Do I know these?" he said and extended both his hands in front of him, turning them first palms up and then palms down.

"You're old pals," I said, wondering why Bebb had lied, had said maybe the man was this that or the other. All the time Bebb had spent speculating about who or what Mr. Golden might be, inside his shirt he'd probably been wearing a locket with a lock of Mr. Golden's hair in it.

He said, "Pals is your word. I didn't say pals," and I thought Oh Bip, you have been given back to me unstained. He wasn't Bebb's pal, he was just a soul Bebb had saved without their being introduced first, and there he was in his porkpie hat looking at me through those lovely eyes as though he knew he'd given me something back I hadn't wanted to part with.

I said, "You mean all this time you've just admired him from a distance."

"Oh sweetheart!" he said. "You want to know the distance?" He put his hands in his pockets, and rocking back on one heel all three hundred or zero pounds of him, he swung the other foot forward and took a carefully measured stride. Then he took two more just like it. I thought the fourth stride was going to be the same, but he cut it about in half, scraping a little at the concrete platform with the toe of his sneaker as though to mark an exact spot.

"The front pew?" I said.

His strides had landed him about ten feet away from me beyond the range of the overhead light so I couldn't see his face any more. On the far track a train came through fast without stopping. The draft of it set his pants flapping, and the racing lights lit him up from behind like a statue. All through the train's noisy passage he was evidently talking, gesturing, and when the last car shot by, he kept right on into the soft and sudden wake of silence. It was like the reading you do in dreams—word for word what he said made sense enough, but I couldn't quite make out what it was all about.

"Time and space," he was saying. "You've got all the time in the world and not enough space to swing a cat. Month after month, week in week out," he was saying there in the dark, "all the doo-dah day. Well, you get so after a stretch you know his face better than you know your own face. There's not a point in the world trying to hide anything from each other." he said. "What's the point? The cat's out of the bag anyway. If the cat wasn't out of the bag, you wouldn't be there in the first place. Hide what?" He said, "I set it down as an eternal rule of life that what works just fine on the inside doesn't work a hoot on the outside. Say all you want or mostly want anyway is to chew the fat about the old days, just shake hands again, why not? But the brushoff's what you're like to get. The cold shoulder." He was holding one palm out toward me vertically like a traffic cop, the rails behind him glinting in the moonlight. "Soon as they spot you coming down the pike, they think it's bound to be gimme or else. It's two different worlds," he said. "One of them you're, oh, Peg o' My Heart. The other you're poison. Bad news." He said, "It's one world in and it's another world out." Stepping a few feet forward into the light again with the sweetest, saddest smile, all those back teeth missing or not in yet, he said, "In just a single life there's so many worlds that a man's days stretch out like the Milky Way." He pushed the porkpie up off his golden brow so I could see that what little hair he had, flat and mashed, was silver. "Worlds," he said. "They leave you old and limp all the worlds you live in before your number comes up."

He had his head cocked to one side and hitched at his belt with one thumb. I was ready for anything by now, ready to see the belt hitched loose, the bolster around his crotch turning out to be folded wings unfolding. They folded out and up in origami folds and pleats and counterfolds the colors of stained glass. They were bigger than he was, and he was big enough. He said, "Tell Leo not to be afraid. It'll all come out in the wash anyhow."

I said, "Why not tell him yourself? I'll be picking him up in a minute."

He said, "I told him already. This afternoon I said, 'Look, Leo. Don't be afraid.' "

I said, "This afternoon he didn't even know Lucille was missing."

A breeze threatened to blow his hat off and he grabbed one side of the brim and held it in close to his wrinkled cheek. He said, "I meant don't be afraid of me."

Ne timeas. I saw him in his windbreaker with a lily in his hand, saw Bebb's startled, fat face looking up at him. Still holding the porkpie, he ducked his head shyly. "You'll have to excuse me. I've got bladder trouble." He started to move off in the direction the arrow pointed.

I said, "Just one more thing. Is Golden right?"

He paused and glanced back. Closer to the light, his face looked paler, more withery, like a soaked hand. He smiled. "As right as any of them," he said. "I've had so many handles in my day." The two stringy tendons at the back of his neck as he walked away, that huge, flat butt.

I suppose I didn't get who he was then because I didn't want to get it. He'd said it straight enough in his own way. Who wouldn't believe in angels if he thought he could swing it, or visitors anyway from older, wiser worlds? Silvers and goldens. I tried to swing it. I didn't even want to accept bladder trouble at that point. If he had a bladder, I wanted it to be only the kind of bladder you float on, fly with: Mr. Golden drifting along over the rooftops of Sutton calling down *Don't be afraid*.

It was obvious Bebb knew who Mr. Golden was and knew God knew what-all else besides, but I had no intention of asking him about it. Let him keep Mr. Golden under his Happy Hooligan hat along with all the rest he kept there. I didn't even mention the meeting when I picked him and Chris up as they walked down the hill from the bus depot. They'd had no more luck gathering clues about Lucille than I had. We drove on to Stamford and Greenwich and had no luck there either.

On our way back to Bebb's house to drop Bebb off and pick up Tony, Chris said, "Maybe the thing you ought to do now is notify the police."

Bebb said, "Chris, I've thought about that. I may have to turn to the police before I'm through, but not yet. Sometimes the medicine's worse than the bellyache."

I said, "Where do you think she's gone, Bip?"

He said, "By this time maybe she's gone home, and she'll be waiting there for us when we pull in."

Chris said, "I have a hunch she's not."

There was a silence as we rolled on down the dark road in the heavy, quiet way cars have at night. I was driving slowly, half thinking we might find Lucille walking along in the ditch. I kept picturing her suddenly looming up in the glare of the headlights in her French heels and gossamer.

Bebb said, "Chris, do you belive in E.S.P.?"

Chris said, "Yes. Do you believe in it?"

Bebb said, "I believe in it, and I have a feeling she's not home either."

I said, "Can you put yourself in her shoes and figure out someplace she might have wanted to go specially?"

Bebb said, "There was one time years ago the place I found her in was a tree. Sharon and her, they'd had them some kind of a fuss, and she'd got herself up there somehow. She was in a tree reading *Silver Screen*. It was like getting a cat off a telephone pole."

"*Silver Screen*," Chris said.

Bebb said, "There was a time you couldn't keep her out of the pictures. I've known her to take in two double features in a day. There was a place in West Palm she found that showed triples."

"Maybe she's gone to the pictures," Chris said.

Bebb said, "Not any more. Those black glasses she wears, they're because the light hurts her eyes. Even pictures hurt her eyes. She's got so she can't stand light any more."

Chris said, "Who can?" He said it not to be witty but in a dreamy kind of way, wedged in there between Bebb and me in the dark.

Bebb said, "Boys, I'm not going to kid you. I'm worried. I've been worried for many years." He said *boys*, but he was talking to himself and neither of us tried to say anything. I took my eyes off the white line just long enough to glance at him. That face that had looked on Golden plain. That face that had many times gazed down on Herman Redpath while he laid his hands on the old brave's wispy scalp and conjured the sap to rise. That pop-goes-the-weasel, jack-in-the-box face that at any time might spring open or shut on anything. It seemed to have settled, like an old house. The lower jaw had slipped forward. The cheeks hung. The eyes looked loose in their sockets. It was the color of the moon. The next thing he said was, "Chris, what's your opinion of Anna May Wong?"

That Bip, as Sharon was apt to say with a mixture of resignation and awe whenever he did something particularly Bip-like. He worked his plump arm free and slid it around the shoulders of my nephew Chris, that movie fan and Shakespeare buff who dreamed of making the theater his life. With the moon in his face and God knows what in his heart, Bebb talked to him the rest of the way back about Anna May Wong and Leonore Ulric and Erich von Stroheim; and Chris, that ectoplasmic boy, took from it the shape and substance of something like life. We were squeezed together in the front seat, and I could literally feel it happening in him. That Bip.

We found Tony asleep on the couch in Bebb's living room, and when we woke him up, he messed up his hair and threw his shoulders around to loosen them up. He said that nobody had either come or called. Bebb phoned Sharon then at our house, and you could see from his face that she was telling him the same thing.

On my way home with Tony and Chris, we passed Laura Fleischman's house. It was around midnight, and there was only one light on. The light was upstairs, and I wondered if it was Laura's. I tried to picture her in bed there reading *Great Issues in American History*. I tried to picture her hair on the pillow, her nun's face. It was hard to believe that only a few hours had gone by since I bought her the 7-Up. Maybe I had just dreamed it. Maybe I was just dreaming Mr. Golden. It may have been the longest day of my life, and it was hard to believe that I hadn't dreamed the whole thing.

Eleven

THE NEXT AFTERNOON Charlie Blaine and Mrs. Kling turned up for the second Sunday in a row. Spotting them from an upstairs window, Sharon went off like a burglar alarm. Bebb was phoning every hour on the hour to see if Lucille had turned up, which she hadn't, and Sharon said I'd have to take care of my relations by myself, so in desperation I ran downstairs and headed them off before they got into the house. In desperation I took them out to the shed to see my monument. Mrs. Kling gave it a look and said, "It looks anemic. If I was you, I'd paint it."

There it was, turning ponderously on its chain from Mrs. Kling's poke, an iceberg, a theology, whatever it was. The fall of the Roman Empire. Parts of it seemed to turn faster than other parts, little clusters of discs, dowels, knobs, crisscrossing. Ellie had been right. It was basically an A-shape with the pierced crosspiece in the middle that the tongues curved down through. It was the honest, pale color of raw pine, and I liked it that way. I said, "What shade would you suggest?"

She stepped back on one bulging calf, a fist on her

hip. She squinnied at it. "Bright ones," she said, as if addressing somebody in the next room. "Bright ones and plenty of them." She turned and stared at me—those heavy mink eyebrows, that tomato-colored mouth. Beside her, Charlie was the color of smoke in his gray spring overcoat that hung below his knees, a pearl gray fedora. She gave me a push on one shoulder. "Live it up a little," she said.

I said, "My God, maybe you've got something," which was the last thing I'd expected to say, but I saw it suddenly painted like a toy in paint-box colors—putting-green greens and sunflower yellows, fire-chief reds, laid on thick and glossy. Why not?

She said, "How about it, Charlie?" wheeling on him.

Charlie slipped his hand softly down one satiny flank of it. He said, "Well, it might just make it come alive."

And he was right. It might just make it come alive, I thought, and at the idea of painting it I could feel myself coming a little alive—a good brush to get up into those star shapes and crescent shapes, floating the colors down smooth and heavy along the flat surfaces, working them up into the angles of joints and the insides of curves. I said, "It would jazz it up all right, Charlie, that's for sure."

He smiled.

It was one of the better moments my ex-brother-in-law and I ever had together, and we had Mrs. Kling to thank for it.

When I couldn't think of any way to stall them further, I finally brought them into the house. Chris and Tony were off someplace, but Sharon came down after a while, barefoot, with an opaque look in her eye. The first thing she did was tell Charlie he didn't look up to snuff to her. It was the worst thing you could ever tell Charlie, and she knew it. He wouldn't let the subject drop. She said, "I don't know, Charlie. You look a little . . . *winded.*" What followed was one of my worst moments with my ex-brother-in-law, for which in this case I suppose I had Sharon to thank.

He turned to Mrs. Kling as though they were alone in an emergency ward and said, "There, Billie. It's what I've been telling you."

Mrs. Kling said, "There's nothing wrong with your wind, Charlie. You've been all through that with Fletcher, and Fletcher's tops."

Charlie said, "I don't mean shortness of breath. I mean the feeling I get when I breathe in."

Sharon said, "You mean like there's an iron band around your chest?" I managed to give her the eye as she said it, and what her eye gave me back was *shove it*, which was not the most significant exchange we ever had, but what was significant about it was that it was the first time since I'd found out about her and Tony that I'd let our eyes exchange so much as the time of day.

Charlie said, "Oh God, no" with his left thumb creeping up under his left armpit and his fingers starting to work at his wishbone. "It's in my throat. Way back."

Mrs. Kling said, "OK, Charlie. Tell it like it is."

"Physical symptoms aren't the easiest things in the world to verbalize," he said, "but I'll give it another try. When I breathe in, it's as if the air is hitting something it never used to hit before. There's a kind of dry, *cold* sensation. It's like there is something back there the air's hitting against."

"Like a lump?" Sharon said,

"Not a lump," Charlie said, swallowing. "I don't think that's what it is. It's more like a sensation than an actual obstruction."

Mrs. Kling said, "Open up, Charlie, and hold your tongue down." She took his lower jaw in her hand and pushed it in toward his Adam's apple. His eyes were fixed glassily on the ceiling. "I'll tell you one thing," she said, peering in. "You had onions for lunch. And maybe a little cat mess. There's no lump, Charlie."

Charlie touched the corners of his mouth with a handkerchief. He said, "It would be too far back to see anyway."

Mrs. Kling said, "All rightsy, if that's how you want it." She said it with ominous heartiness and swung abruptly around to me. "Give me a flashlight," she said. She held her hand straight out like a statue till I found one in the desk drawer and gave it to her. "Roger," she said. "Have you got a closet big enough to hold three of us?"

"What are you up to, Billie?" Charlie said.

"You're what I'm up to," she said.

I took them to the hall closet. Sharon wanted to come in too, but there wasn't room for four, and of the two of us, Mrs. Kling wanted me. "He won't listen to another woman," she said.

Sharon shut the door on us, and Mrs. Kling and Charlie Blaine and I stood there for a few seconds in total darkness. Then Mrs. Kling switched on the flashlight. She told Charlie to put it into his mouth. She said, "Close your lips around it tight, Charlie, like you're sucking a pickle."

The closet smelled of raincoats and shoes and Charlie's onions, and Charlie was lit up inside like a pumpkin. His cheeks glowed the color of fingers cupped around a flame. There was a religious sheen on the underside of his nose. Mrs. Kling's glasses glinted as she leaned toward him.

I wondered what a stranger would have thought, what I would have thought myself if some fortune-teller had foretold the scene. Mrs. Kling and I in that closet with Charlie. Given the people we were, I suppose you could say it was inevitable. Everything was. I found the thought comforting.

Mrs. Kling pushed me with her elbow. She said, "Look at there." Her finger was black against Charlie's translucent beauty. She said, "Boy, is that ever plugged up. See that shadowy part?" Her black finger was moving in the vicinity of his cheekbone. I said I saw it. "Tell *him*," she said. "He thinks I'm giving him a snow-job."

I said, "It looks like you're plugged up all right, Charlie." Charlie tried to say something, but with the flashlight in his mouth it was unintelligible.

Mrs. Kling said, "It's those lousy sinuses. You've got yourself an old-fashioned case of post-nasal drip, Charlie. What you feel in your throat is snot."

Later I found myself sitting on the foot of our bed trying to make conversation with Charlie through the open bathroom door. Mrs. Kling had prescribed a salt solution to be inhaled through the nose and spat out through the mouth. Charlie was doing it. Strapped as

I was for something to talk about, I decided against bringing up Lucille's disappearance. Neither Sharon nor I had mentioned it so far. It would only have raised questions that I couldn't answer, plus others that I could. I might have tried talking about the boys, but whenever I did that, he would steer the conversation around to how much a month it cost Sharon and me to keep them, and then whether I actually told him how much or less than how much or brushed the question aside, I always ended up sounding as though I was asking for more. Then Charlie would look nervous and hurt. If I had been made of sterner stuff I suppose I might have talked to him about the boys and sex. I might have told him that it seemed to me sex for Tony was a hydroelectric dam that for the time being was being used for weight-lifting and broad-jumping and hanging African violets around in his jockstrap, not to mention all those showers, but that potentially it could supply the whole town of Sutton with light and heat or blow it off the map and himself with it, not to mention what it had blown off the map already. Or onto the map. I might have told him how it seemed to me that sex for Chris was a shadowy presence in the wings which was maybe why he wanted to make the stage his life. The only shadows on the stage were the shadows you knew about, and the roles were fixed there. Nothing could happen on the stage that wasn't in the script. You didn't have to worry about the wings. But I couldn't talk to Charlie about sex either.

He was bending over the washbasin in his shirtsleeves. In between rinsings, he would straighten up, and we would find ourselves facing each other in the mirror. His eyes looked dimly expectant, and what I found myself coming out with finally was the information that I'd gone out to Brooklyn the day before and taken a look at Miriam's grave.

"Oh my God," he said, and then he was bending over again, cupping the salt solution in his palm and snuffing it up through his nostrils. Here was the man who had married my sister, I thought, whose name she had died with, died of maybe—Miriam on her wedding day with her black hair braided around her head in a wreath, Charlie in his Navy whites with a peeling sunburn on his nose and forehead. I could hear him spitting out into the sink, this man my sister had gone to bed with, as far as I knew the only man. I wondered if he had ever gone to bed with Mrs. Kling and hoped I would never have to hear about it if he had.

"I don't think I could take it," he said. "I'd rather just think about how she was when she was alive."

"Not me," I said. "I like to think about how she is now she's dead."

He said, "What makes you go and say a thing like that for, Tono?"

Maybe because he was the only man my sister ever got a chance to go to bed with. Maybe because Tony was his son. "I don't know," I said. "Do you ever think about being dead someday yourself, Charlie?"

"I guess I do," he said. "I guess everybody thinks about it sometimes."

Some of the solution must have gotten trapped in his lousy sinuses and started to run out unexpectedly because he suddenly doubled over. When his face reappeared in the mirror, I said, "What do you think about when you think about being dead?" Poor Charlie.

"I don't know," he said. "I try not to think about it any more than I have to."

I said, "You should think about it."

"That's morbid," he said. "Do you think about it much yourself?"

I said, "I thought about it when we were all in the closet looking at your head lit up from the inside. I thought about it when what's-her-name told me I ought to paint my masterpiece out there."

"Why did you think about it then?" Charlie said.

"Because I decided maybe she was right," I said. "Maybe I ought to paint it for the same reason they put lipstick on a corpse."

"What's the matter with you?" Charlie said. "You're not even as old as I am. What are you anyway?"

"I'm thirty-nine," I said.

"That's nothing," Charlie said.

I said, "I didn't used to think it was."

"It isn't," Charlie said. "I'm going on forty-seven. Thirty-nine isn't anything."

"It isn't sweet sixteen," I said. "It isn't Tony," at which I stood once again on the threshold of the door that Bebb urged the faithful to open. Charlie was rolling his sleeves back down again, having finished with his sinuses for the time being and also, I'm sure he hoped, with our conversation. I could hear Mrs. Kling downstairs talking as if over long distance to Sharon and the sound of Bill crying. She'd probably picked him up and was holding him clamped to her bust like a football. *Tony* I'd said, naming his name. I might have said Sharon wasn't the only one in that house he'd screwed and then stood back and watched it start his sinuses running again. He'd screwed me too, screwed me royally and maybe for keeps. I might have said I was planning to nail his balls to the wall.

Charlie said, "There is a book called *The Middle Age Crisis* that's all about what you're going through, Tono. You ought to take a look at it. It's quite an eye-opener." He was standing in the bathroom door putting on his jacket.

I said, "I'm sure it is, Charlie, but right now I'm up to my ears in *The Call of the Wild.*"

"That's Jack London, isn't it?" Charlie said.

I said, "Sigmund Freud."

Charlie's lips were slightly parted, and his eyes had gone blank. He was testing to see if he could still feel the dry, cool spot at the back of his throat when he breathed in.

"You ought to give *The Middle Age Crisis* a look-see," he said. "I think it would do you good."

When Tony and Chris came drifting back, Charlie took them out to an early supper with Mrs. Kling. He asked Sharon and me to go too, but we used Bebb's prayer meeting as an excuse. Poor Bebb. The attendance at his morning services hadn't picked up as he had predicted, and he thought if he added an old-fashioned prayer meeting at a different hour, he might attract a different crowd. Even if Charlie and Mrs. Kling hadn't been there to spur us on, Sharon and I would probably have gone anyway just to swell the ranks. At the last one only about seven or eight had shown up including the woman with hair the color of raw meat who ever since the opening service had been one of his most faithful followers, She always brought Mickey with her. Mickey was the gerbil she carried around in a cage. He spent most of his time at church in the exercise wheel. It needed oiling.

Sharon and I arrived early to find Bebb and a policeman about to sit down in the living room. We told Bebb we'd wait on the porch, but he asked us to stay.

The policeman asked the following questions.

Full name: Lucille Yancey Bebb.

Age: 57.

Place of birth: Spartanburg, South Carolina.

Hair: Brown, Bebb said, changing it then to auburn.

Eyes: Bebb hesitated. I wondered if like me he'd seen them so seldom because of black glasses that he couldn't remember for sure. Hazel, he said.

Any identifying marks: Bebb said no, then changed it to yes. It was his third slip in a row. The policeman looked up from his yellow pad. Bebb was sitting bolt upright facing him, and his trick eyelid chose this moment to do its trick. Sharon and I exchanged the second glance I'd risked without words to use in case of an emergency. Bebb covered his face with his hands for a moment so that just the tip of his nose stuck out between them. Lucille had some scars on her wrists, he said, reappearing. He said it without a flicker.

Had anybody noticed her indulging in peculiar behavior lately, the policeman asked. *Indulging* was a policeman's word, I thought: peculiarity was indulgence. Bebb's eyelid alone was worth at least a friendly warning. Bebb said he hadn't noticed anything peculiar. He turned to Sharon and asked her. Sharon said, "Have you told him about the Tropicanas, Bip?" She was sitting on the sofa beside him, and when she said it, I noticed her slip her little finger over his little finger on the cushion between them. Bip said, "My daughter here means sometimes when Mrs. Bebb's low in her mind, she takes a little too much."

Alcohol? the policeman asked, and Bebb said she mixed it with orange juice. Sharon said, "Don't give out the recipe, Bip." It didn't seem to help Bip much.

When the policeman asked what he meant she was low in her mind, Bebb said, "We're Southerners, officer. We're a long ways from home."

It was one of his classical utterances, like *All things are lawful for me* and *I believe everything*. "We're Southerners," he said; all three of them were. It was like a line of great poetry—not that I hadn't always known the truth it contained but that this was the first time I'd ever heard it put into words. There seemed to be nothing it didn't explain: the poor attendance at Open Heart, the grim look on his face as the door of the freight elevator closed on him at Grand Central, all Sharon's lessons. Maybe even Sharon and . . . but I had begun to develop a safety mechanism by then. As soon as my thoughts gave signs of turning the wrong way, it cut them off automatically. They were Southerners. They were a long ways from home. The policeman said he would let them know if anything turned up.

The prayer meeting that followed was less than a success. Only about a dozen showed up including the red-haired woman and the blind man who had said he was a cousin of Harry Truman's. The gerbil's exercise wheel made it hard to concentrate on the praying, and it was obvious Bebb's mind wasn't on it either. The blind man asked us to pray for his sight to be restored. First we all prayed silently together. Then Bebb prayed out loud by himself. When it was over, the blind man jumped up and said, "Praise the Lord! Hallelujah!" but he ended up knocking down several empty chairs and tripped over his white cane. I don't think Harry Truman would have been impressed.

After the service we asked Bebb to come back with us, but he thought he'd better stay home in case anybody called. Sharon said she would stay with him. I could pick her up later. I left them sitting side by side on the porch steps. Sharon had her head on his shoulder. The sun was getting ready to set and had turned both their faces gold.

Twelve

WHEN I got home, I went straight to my desk and took out the rolled-up sheets of flowered stationery that Lucille had given me. They had apparently been written over a period of several months in different colored felt-tips. In some places they were quite difficult to read, and the flowers scattered all over the working part of the paper didn't make it any easier. *Les très riches heures de* Lucille Bebb:

Today I got bread, butter, bacon, baloney, beets. Brownie and Bebb. We should be living in Baton Rouge, Birmingham, Baltimore, Boca Raton, Buenos Aires, or Bethlehem, anyplace where they don't have Indians. I never minded nigger smell too much. It's a lot of it just lemon juice. Indian smell is hair grease and dirty drawers. Bebb says Herman Redpath isn't long for this world but he doesn't look that bad to me. Bea Trionka says half the kids he says are his aren't. They just let on they are to make him feel good. She says that part of him doesn't even work any more, and she ought to know. Bebb must be slipping when it comes to laying on hands.

Bebb went off to a meeting (guess where) and I sat by the fan and watched TV with the sound off. There was an old woman and a young woman sitting in a restaurant talking. The old woman was doing most of it, and you could tell she was making the young one mad the way she kept twisting up her napkin. Finally the young one couldn't take it any more. She got in a couple of cracks and flounced out. The old woman didn't want to let her see she'd made her cry, but soon as she left she got a handkerchief out of her bag and had a good one all by herself at the table. Sometimes it's hard to know what people are talking about even when you can hear every damn word they say.

Maybe Bebb was right. Herman Redpath was hanging his legs into the pool. They looked like sticks of wood. He's gone all yellow [hollow?]. *He looks like Papa did when it got into his glands and spread clear through him. I asked Bebb what does he think happens to people after they're dead, and he said as many kind of things happen one side of the grave as the other, just like he knows. I told him when Herman Redpath's time comes be sure to tell me what happens to him and he says it's not always given us to know but if it is he'll let me know too. At supper he ate just the one frank and a bitty piece of lettuce. He's worried what's going to happen after Herman Redpath's gone, will we still have a roof over our heads and stuff and stuff. Who cares?*

After Sharon come he never [touched?] *me again except once in a while when it was like he couldn't help himself and wanted to get it over with as quick as he could for both our sakes like puking. They all of them got to get rid of it someplace. God knows where he did all those years. I guess it kept building up in him all those years till the cork finally popped in Miami. When I asked him about it through the cage he told me what he . . . right in the eye . . . whispered like he never . . .* [At this crucial point the writing became indecipherable except for a few phrases because Lucille had scratched out most of it and there was also a bunch of violets in the way]. *One little girl put . . . he was having* [hating?] *the first . . . restaurant . . . lonesome . . . burning his hand* [husband?] *like fire* [fury?] . . . *Sharon . . . face himself again as long as . . . nobody ever . . . cellmate* [urinate? ultimate? The rest of the paragraph was blocked out entirely.] *I never saw him bare but only a few times in my whole life.*

He says you got to have something to hold onto. Here are the things I've got to hold onto. I've got every doorknob in the whole place, the draw handles, the flusher handle, the stair rail, the TV with green fuzz down one side of everybody's face, and the Barca-lounger and the Digest and my own teeth mostly and the ice box and the bed post when the room starts turning and my sun specs and Brownie's hand that's got hair on the back of it and soft inside like a powderpuff. And a closet full of junk and stuff and stuff. Shoes. He says store not up for thyself treasure where moth and rust and so forth.

He says I've got my good memories. Here are my good memories. I remember a Jack Horner pie made out of a hatbox and crape paper with different color strings coming out so when you pulled them it shot the pie all to hell but you ended up with a comb and lipstick set or a ring. I remember Sundays when we closed down Papa let me jerk any flavor I wanted so long as I didn't make myself sick and cleaned up the mess. I remember waking up to the noon whistle and there was a letter from Sammy Jackson set on my water glass addressed just Little Miss Brighteyes, Clover Street. I remember Cora Bates's fancy-dress. I remember Gloria Swanson, Doug Fairbanks, Norma Shearer, and Mickey Mouse. I remember the piano. I remember Sammy J. I remember Tweetybird.

He says count your blessings. When I stopped getting the period, one. When we got out of Knoxville, two. When we got out of Armadillo, three.

He says you got to have faith. Faith Murphy had the worst breath in school and ate nosepick. Talk about faith, when I saw the little weasened thing wasn't moving any more I prayed I would be struck dead if that would make it move.

They called him Blinky Bebb. He says he doesn't have any control over that eye to this day or even knows when its cutting up and everybody has parts like that they don't have any control over such as heartbeat, breathing, dreaming and so on and so forth. It's all in the hands of God Almighty he says. I asked him did that mean his eye was in the hands of God Almighty and he said that was a way of putting it. So its God Almighty winks Bebbs eye sometime and if so why? If all those parts are in God's hands I asked him what do we have left over we can call our very own. He said sin right off. Just when he said it his eye cut up. I told him right then when you said sin your eye cut up. He said I know, can you blame it?

Dear Jesus,

I am writing you this just in case. How come they called you Jesus of all the other names in Scripture? They could of called you Matthew, Mark, Luke or John, they are names with some spunk to them. Jeeezzzus sounds like it had vaseline on it to make it slip in easy. I never liked my own name either. I use to say my name was Ellicul and I came from Grubnatraps. I was a virgin up to the day I married Bebb and for a spell afterwards just like Mary your mother. Later on I killed my own baby, his name was Herman. Sometime I go for days without once thinking about it. Bebb went and got him a swingset even tho he wasn't but a few months old the day he died and when we moved to Armadillo that swingset went with us. Bebb set it up in the yard. Sometimes the breeze clanked the swing around. Once I put my finger in the crack of the door where the hinges are. What happened was the fingernail turned black and after a while it dropped off. I told Bebb it was a accident.

Bebb says underneath are the everlasting arms.

He says surely he hath born our griefs and carried our sorrows.

He says we are all washed clean in the Blood of the Lamb and so on and so forth.

One time what I said to him was Bebb, the only thing I've been washed in is the shit of the horse.

You know what he did? He took the very same finger the nail fell off of only that was years before and I told him it was a accident, and he kissed it. That was when I first thought maybe he was from Outer Space.

Mr. Jesus, is that where you are from too?

Love,
Ellicul of Grubnatraps

P.S. *I haven't said one single thing I wanted to.*
P.P.S. *Who is the fat man keeps hanging around Holy Love?*

They wouldn't let the undertaker take Herman Redpath tho Bebb says theirs a law. They must of got around it somehow. They did it all themselves. Bea Trionka wasn't there, just the men, but Johnson Badger told her what they did. Some of it anyway. They put salt on his tongue and up his nostrils and ears and up his rear end. They painted red and blue designs on his chest, red for the earth and blue for the sky. They buttered his legs. They put moccasins on his feet. They hung an apron on him to cover his private parts. The apron was black to remind him he wasn't to use anything down there till he got where he was going. After they had him in his brown suit they put in his pockets: a box of Sun Maid Raisins, a jacknife, leather bootlaces, a deerskin pouch, some strings of beads, a whistle, a birds wing and ten bran new ten dollar bills. I said to her Bea what do you Indians believe about after a persons dead? She said we don't have to believe anything because what you folks have to believe, we know. She's like all the rest of them.

Its supposed to be a big honor to keep the flies off

Herman Redpath. I guess for flies its a big honor to lay your eggs on him. I said I can't do it because Antonio is here and we got to have heap big family powwow. Bebb tries to make out like he doesn't mind Sharon isn't here too.

I woke up and there was Bebb setting in the rocker by the window rocking in the moonlight, he hadn't even taken his tie and jacket off. When he saw I was awake he started talking. I never saw him so wound up, he must have talked half the night. Part of the time I listened and part of the time I dropped off. It didn't make a partical of difference to him which because he wasn't talking to me so much as he was talking to himself or Jesus or whoever he talks to in the night. He talked about the funeral and the hundred thousand and where we're going to go to next and the big things we're going to do when we get there. He talked about Holy Love what's going to happen to it and can Brownie handle things by himself and so on and so forth. After a while I must have dropped off again because the next thing I knew he was talking about something different and he was talking in a different way, slower, like he was reading fine print or telling something he was watching happen out the window while he was telling it but couldn't see too good. He was telling what happened to Herman Redpath after he was dead.

To Whom It May Concern. This is a true account of what Leo Bebb told on the night after Herman Redpath's funeral. He was cold sober and I was sober too it being something like three o'clock A.M. *As near as I can remember them, these are the words of Leo Bebb.*

Herman Redpath took off his brown suit and set it down beside him where an eagle come and carried it off in his beak to make stars out of it in the sky like the Big Dipper but not stars that will be visible from this planet for a long time to come if ever. Before he took his suit off Herman Redpath put the things he had in the pockets into the deerskin pouch and hung it around his neck with one of the bootlaces. It was cold but the butter on his legs helped keep him warm. The moccasins helped too. Nobody is sure how old Herman Redpath was when he died but he must have taken off a few years when he took off his brown suit because if he wasn't a young man yet he wasn't an old man anymore either. The flesh didn't hang on him like laundry. He didn't have liver spots or breathe through his teeth. He could dogtrot.

He dogtrotted against the wind because that was the direction the eagle flew off in and the place where he dogtrotted was a big wide prairie stretching on and on as far as the eye could see and flat and hard as a paving stone. It wasn't day and it wasn't night and the color of the sky wasn't all that different from the color of the ground which was nothing but scrub and rocks. He could hear his moccasins pounding on it chunk chunk except on the pebbly parts chicka chicka like a rattle, it was the only sounds he could hear because it was all there was, not a snake or a bird or a four-footed creature. He was alone. Till he come up to a big bolder the size of a phonebooth.

Out from behind that bolder raging and screaming there suddenly jumped out a creature was part snake, part bird, part four footed creature and then some. It had its face where its hindparts should have been and it had its hindparts where its face should have been and when it opened any part of itself up you couldn't tell what part it was opening or what it might take a notion to do with it when it was opened. It come tearing full speed at Herman Redpath flapping all the things it had would flap and making the kind of noise a bird would make if it was a snake. Its eyes were rolling around under its tail something wicked and it was hung all over with damp whiskery things where its eyes ought to been. It howled like a coyote would howl if it was a blackwidow spider, and when it saw Herman Redpath wasn't going to cut loose and run it lept on him. It lept on him the way a Royal Bengal Tiger would leap if it was a swarm of maggots. It knocked him to the ground.

Herman Redpath could feel there was something hot and feathery tightning up around his throat from one direction and something icecold and scaley tightning up around it from another direction and down from above something was coming right for him that looked like a concertina and smelled like sewer gas. The mouth of Herman Redpath was chock full of tongue. His eyes were shooting out on stems. He hadn't but only one hope left in all the world. That hope was his deerskin pouch.

The deerskin pouch had got tore off his neck in the scuffle and was laying next him on the ground, the way his neck was twisted he could just see it. Between his hand and the pouch was maybe about 6 inches. The only transportation the hand had was three fingers, two of them having got broke in the fight already, so that hand started in to crawling after the pouch on its three fingers like a roach thats been part stepped on. Somehow that hand made it. Somehow those fingers wrapped themselves around that jacknife and got it open. No clock could measure the kind of time it took, but finally Herman Redpath got so he had raised the jacknife high enough to where it was pointing right down over something the like of a poach egg that grew between what you might have called the creatures sholderblades if it had've had sholders. Not a moment too soon Herman Redpath used up the last ounce of strength he had left and struck him a good hard one smack into the middle of the poach egg. The sound it made was the sound a blownup balloon makes when you let it go without tying the end off.

Herman Redpath got up. He fixed the deerskin pouch around his neck with another bootlace and took off again. The ground begun to rise after a while and soon he was dogtrotting up hill. The higher up hill he went, the colder it got. The wind blew harder. He was glad for the butter on his legs. Even the small black apron was some comfort. The wind kept blowing it up against his stomack and when he reached down to see could he make it stay put, he accidently touched something he hadn't touched anything like for many a year. It wasn't an old dishmop hanging there anymore. It was a bunch of Concord grapes.

By and by he come to a teepee. There was smoke coming out of a hole in the top and the flap was pinned open. He thought if he could just warm himself in there for a little, he would be able to keep going up to the top of the mountain. He crawled in through the opening, and up near the fire laying on a pile of soft animal skins he saw a woman. She was a young woman with black braids down far as her knees. Like King Solomon said about the Queen of Sheba, her lips were like a thread of scarlet and her breasts like two young roes which feed among the lillys and her belly a heap of wheat.

This woman she welcomed Herman Redpath and told him to come sit down where it was nice and warm. She made a poltice of herbs and dressed the wounds the creature had left on him. She bound up his broken fingers. She offered him meat and drink only he didn't take any of it because something told him he better not. When all this was done, she reached up her arms and showed him how he was to lay down side of her there on the animal skins. She undid the deerskin pouch he had round his neck, and she was fixing to undo the black apron too but before she could undo it, Herman Redpath saw if he was once to lay down with her there next the fire, he would never get up again and he would never make it to the place where he was going. So he reached down into the pouch and pulled out the strings of beads instead. She put one string around her neck and wound the other string into her black hair. Then she commenced making signs at him made him know for sure if he stayed he was a goner. So he took the crisp new ten dollar bills he had in the pouch and handed them over to her too. While she was busy spreading them out by the fire to see how many of them there was he'd gave her, he tied the pouch back on his neck again and took off out of there like greased lightning.

It was a long way to the top of the mountain. He wished he hadn't been so careful about not touching the food the woman had offered him but he put the Sun Maid raisins into his mouth and they took some of the edge off. There was times he thought he heard the voice of the woman hollering sentimental things after him, but he didn't look back once. It might have been the wind. His feet felt heavier and heavier as the ground got steeper. The poltice the woman rubbed on his sore places had set in to itching and burning some. But finally he got to the top and when he got there it seemed like maybe this was the place he was going to settle down and spend the rest of forever in.

Why everything Herman Redpath had ever wanted and hadn't got was there. Everything he'd ever lost and thought he'd never find again was there. All the good times he'd ever had was happening there at the same time and some of the good times he'd never gotten around to having, they were happening there too. There wasn't a person he'd ever given a hoot about that wasn't some way there to make him feel at home. To welcome him back. To set a extra place for him at the table. To laugh and cry with him. To bear his children. To put up with his cussedness. To remember back with him like they'd been there themselves all the best things he could remember out of his whole life clear back to Betty Shortleg with her breath that smelled of apples how she squirted sassparilla at him through the gap in her teeth, back to his greatgrandad showing him the way it was Tecumseh had stood up better than 7 foot tall at Fort Meig with his arms stretched out like eaglewings. All these things and then some were on top of the mountain with Herman Redpath. They were in his ears the way the sound of the sea is in seashells. They were in his eyes the way seashells are at the bottom of the sea. These things were happening alright except the place they were happening in was no place except right there inside Herman Redpath's own head. Herman Redpath was alone.

Herman Redpath stood on top of the mountains on his shiny legs with the black apron to cover his nakedness and the deerskin pouch tied around his neck, and there wasn't a solitary thing you could say was truely happening anywhere nearer than a million miles except what was happening on the inside of Herman Redpath. But he had a hunch if he just hung around there awhile, it would all start happening truely on the outside too, all the good dreams of his life coming true together and every last one of the best times he could remember out of his life coming back to life again. He squatted down on his heels with his knuckles on the ground in front of him. He started in taking deep breaths. Then he felt something bumping him on the chest. It was the deerskin pouch.

He opened it up to find out what was in it to make it bump so, and out flew the birds wing. It spun around over his head three times like it was tied to a cowboy rope. Then it took off down into the canyon ahead. Herman Redpath knew he had to follow. He knew even was he to spend the rest of forever on that mountain the only thing he'd ever find there was ghosts.

This was the worst time yet. The mountain face was steep something cruel on the far side. It was so steep when the stones gave way under his feet he'd slip and slide with the mussles in his legs tensing up in a shaky way that made him feel foolish and ashamed. It wasn't getting darker but the air was getting thicker and harder to see through. He couldn't see the horizon anymore. Soon he couldn't see the ground underneath his own feet even, and the only way he knew it was so steep was from slipping and sliding. It got warmer as he went down. After a bit the temperature of the air got to be exactly the same as the temperature of his body and stopped right there. From the time that happened he couldn't feel his skin anymore. It was like either he didn't have skin anymore, or the air was his skin.

Down at the bottom of the canyon the ground stopped being hard. It felt like he was walking in cake flour. He couldn't hear his feet anymore or hardly feel them. He couldn't feel or hear anything else anymore either. Plus he couldn't see anything the air being so thick and tepid. It seemed like because he didn't have any skin anymore he didn't have any shape either or any boundaries. He had a feeling his legs were still working but he wasn't sure he was moving. He could have been just hanging in the air on the end of a string.

Herman Redpath knew the place he was was noplace. He knew the place where he was going was nowhere. And he knew even if there was a way to get from noplace to nowhere there wasn't hardly anything left of him solid enough to get there with. He couldn't think of anything left in the deerskin pouch could help him now, and he was just as glad. It wasn't all that bad being without shape or boundaries. One way of looking at it you weren't anyplace in particular. The other way of looking at it you were everyplace in general. Both ways had there good points. He couldn't even have told you his name if you'd asked him, and he didn't care a pin. He didn't care if he never got to the place he was supposed to get and if you'd have told him there wasn't any such place, he wouldn't have cared a pin about that either. It was very restful.

Then Herman Redpath smelled something. It was a smell half way between peanuts and seaweed. It was a private, historical kind of smell. He couldn't hear or see or feel anything, and there wasn't anything around to know if he could taste it or not. But he could smell. And he figured out what he smelled must be his own smell because there wasn't so much as the ghost of anything else it could be the smell of. By smelling it he got his nose back. It was a start anyhow.

Then he knew what the smell was. It was a smell left over from the time the Joking Cousin had taken a leak on him. There wasn't a doubt in the world but what the smell he was smelling deep down in that canyon was the smell of John Turtle's piss.

Herman Redpath grabbed ahold of that piss smell and pulled himself back into his skin with it like it was a rope. He pulled himself back into a boundary and shape with it. He pulled himself up the other side of the miserable canyon with it. By the time he got up there he could feel the ground solid under his feet again. He could hear the chunk-chunk of his moccasins. It wasn't anything in his deerskin pouch that had saved him this time. It was the piss of that crazy John Turtle. He thought well you never know, and thanked John Turtle in his heart. The air had thinned out so he could see again. The only trouble was the thing he saw wasn't encouraging.

There was a wall in front of him like the wall of a oldtime stockade. It was a wall made of upright peeled logs pegged together so tight there wasn't a crack you could have squeezed so much as the queen of spades through. It was high as the Houston Astrodome and it stretched out to right and left as far as the eye could see. There was just one small doorway through it. In the middle of the doorway there was an old man squatting on his hunkers. His hair was white and hung down his front in two braids. His face was cracked and rutted like a 8 week drought. It took him a few minutes before Herman Redpath recognized the old man was his own greatgrandad the same that had shown him how Tecumseh held his arms out at Fort Meig. This greatgrandad had also been a friend of Tecumseh's brother Tensquatawa the Shawnee Prophet.

Herman Redpath raised his right hand to the old man and the old man raised his. The old man said You smell like you been dawbing yourself all over with peanuts and seaweed, son. So Herman Redpath explained it all out to him about John Turtle. He squatted down on his hunkers like his greatgrandad and they stayed face to face that way chewing the fat for a long time. Herman Redpath did most of the talking but the talk come out with breaks in between the different parts of it for his greatgrandad to get in his 2¢ worth if he felt like it, and there wasn't half as much cussing and shameful language in it as there was toward the end of his days on earth when he was too old and wore out to care what folks thought. When they finished chewing the fat Herman Redpath stood up and raised his right hand again but this time the old man didn't raise his right hand back. He didn't show any sign of moving out of the doorway to let Herman Redpath through either.

Herman Redpath could guess what would happen if he tried tangling there with his own greatgrandad who had Tecumseh and Tensquatawa both for a friend so he asked him polite as you please would he mind moving off to one side to let him pass on through. The old man stood up. There was a lot of rattling, jingling noises when he did it because he was hung all over with wampum and teeth and dried up things that probably he was the only one could give a name to. He was a good head higher than Herman Redpath, and never mind how old his face looked, he had the build of a man in his prime. When he was up, he filled the doorway. When he spread his legs and put his hands out to the sides, he filled it some more.

The old man said to Herman Redpath, Son, before I can let you pass on through you got to tell me two words, one for the earth and one for the sky. It's the rule of the place.

The only thing Herman Redpath had that was left in his deerskin pouch was the whistle so he took it out and gave two loud whistles on it. The old man didn't budge an inch. He just scrunched up his sholders a little like the sound of the whistle made his ears hurt. So Herman Redpath tried some pairs of words on him. First he would try a word for the earth and then he would try a word for the sky just like his greatgrandad told him.

He tried Fire and Water. He tried Here and There. He tried Bad and Good. He tried Wolf and Eagle and Thick and Thin. He made up some names like

Om-pom-poo and Forp and tried them. When Death and Life didn't work he turned it around and tried Life and Death. He tried some long Indian words he hadn't thought of for years like She-who-lies-with-her-ten-toes-up-and-smiles-like-a-planted-field and He-who-lies-with-his-ten-toes-down-and-falls-like-the-rain. But after the first few pairs of words, the old man didn't even bother to shake his head anymore.

Poor Herman Redpath. He had come such a long way. He had run into so many kinds of danger and was still so sore in most of the places where the creature had mawled him. He thought of the kind of thing he might have been doing now if only he'd layed down on the animal skins like the woman had invited him to. He thought of the top of the mountain and Betty Shortleg and all the lost things he would of gotten such a kick out of finding again even if all they were was ghosts. He thought how peaceful it was in that canyon where the air was warm as his own spit and it was like he didn't have any skin. And now his greatgrandad wouldn't let him through the wall.

It made him so mad he thought of trying some bad words just for the spite of it. He thought of trying words like Shit and Fuck and Turd and Fart only he just didn't have the energy. He felt that helpless, all he could do was hang his head and look at the ground. He looked at his moccasins. He looked at his buttery shins. He looked at the black apron. He looked at his belly that didn't sag anymore like an awning full of rainwater but was flat and hard as a washboard. Next thing he looked at was his chest where there was painted on it some red and blue designs, red for the earth and blue for the sky.

The red design was the Indian way of setting down the word for the earth, and the blue design that curled in and out of it like a snake was the Indian way of setting down the word for the sky. The words themselves were too powerful to say outloud so Herman Redpath did them in sign language instead.

The sign for the word for the earth was to get down on your hands and knees and press your two lips on the packed yellow dirt where he and his greatgrandad had been squatting while they chewed the fat. So he got down on his hands and knees and did that.

The sign for the word for the sky was to uncover your nakedness, throw back your head and reach your arms up as high as they would reach and then a little higher. So he took off the black apron that was tied around him and did that.

The old man winked one eye and stepped aside.

*Just for a split second when the old man winked his one eye, Herman Redpath thought of a person he had known back on earth in the old days. He didn't think of him by name because he'd forgotten his name and he didn't think of him by looks or by any feeling he used to have about him in the days when they knew each other because he'd forgotten all that too. The only way he could think of him was by two words which he'd seen written up someplace crisscross with one O in the middle to make do for them both—*HOLY *stretched out crossways and* LOVE *running straight down through it. He thought if ever he run into that person again someday where he was going, as didn't seem likely, he would tell him that the word* HOLY *was a moth-eaten pale-face way of saying the sign for the* *earth, and the word* LOVE *was a flea-bitten pale-face way of saying the sign for the sky.*

It took Herman Redpath less than a second and a half to think all this. Then he bust out through that door in the wall like nobody's business. He was naked as the day he was born. If his greatgrandad hadn't moved out of the way in time, the old man would have been skewered.

So that's how it was Herman Redpath come to the Happy Hunting Ground. What it was like when he got there and what he saw and what he did, all those things aren't given us to know for now. The only thing that is known about what happened beyond the door in the wall is that it wasn't for years that Herman Redpath found out what the whistle was for. In the meanwhile he kept it hanging around his neck on a leather bootlace so he'd have it ready when the time came.

I believe Leo Bebb truly saw all this with his own eyes. It may be he was seeing it right then while he was rocking in his chair in the moonlight telling me about it. I believe Leo Bebb knows more than he lets on about many many things like for instance about Mr. Fatass Golden. I believe Leo Bebb is from outer space.

Am I crazy, Mr. Jesus?

At the bottom of the last page, one word in each of the five petals of a daisy, Lucille had written in tiny letters MY ONLY FRIEND IS BROWNIE.

Thirteen

THE MESSAGE of the daisy petals led me to put in a long-distance call to Brownie immediately. As soon as he answered, I told him about Lucille. I told him she'd left no clues behind and that so far the police hadn't turned up any. I told him I was calling in hopes that maybe she had gotten in touch with him. Maybe he could give us a lead. I didn't mention *Les très riches heures*.

Brownie said, "These are the times that try men's souls, dear. I just don't know what to say. I wish there was something I could do to help."

I said, "Brownie, did she ever let anything drop to you that might give us a clue where she's gone? Has she called you up or written you the last couple of weeks?"

Brownie said, "She and I have known each other a good many years now and we've been through thick and thin together, but we've never been the kind of friends that exchange phone calls and letters. We were never close in that way."

I said, "I happen to know she considered you one of her best friends, Brownie. *Considers* you."

"That is correct, dear," Brownie said. "There's no call to use the past tense. I am sure wherever she's gone and whatever reason she had for going there, she's alive and well. You've got to have faith."

I said, "I'm afraid Bip's desperate."

Brownie said, "He wouldn't ever have gone to the police if he wasn't desperate. You're going to have to help him, dear."

"I wish I could," I said.

Brownie said, "You can help him by telling him you know she's all right."

I said, "I don't know she's all right, Brownie."

Brownie said, "Tell him thou shalt not be afraid for the terror by night nor for the arrow that flieth by day because thou hast made the Lord thy habitation."

I said, "I don't think even Scripture would cut much ice with him at this point."

Brownie said, "Then tell him Brownie says he hasn't got anything to be worried about."

I couldn't be sure it wasn't my imagination, but it seemed to me that Brownie had lowered his voice slightly.

I said, "Do you know something you're not letting on, Brownie?"

There was a silence at Brownie's end. Generally I can't stand telephone silences and will babble any inanity to end them, but I gritted my teeth and made myself sit this one out in the hope that it would eventually force Brownie into giving some kind of answer.

Finally he said, "We are all of us seeking a homeland, dear, even though we have only seen and embraced it from afar. We are all of us strangers and pilgrims on the earth."

I said, "That's not answering my question, Brownie."

"I wish I could lend you a helping hand," Brownie said. "Bear ye one another's burdens—that's what we're all put here for."

More and more it was like talking to a book of Biblical quotations, but I decided to try once more. I said, "For Christ sake, Brownie, is Lucille down there with you or what? Let's cut out Scripture."

Again Brownie paused. Then he said, "Maybe you'd think better of Scripture if you'd read it clear through to the end. The end of Scripture is Revelation, dear."

"Revelation," I said.

"And the most important part of Revelation," Brownie said, "is the last part."

"The very last part?" I said.

Brownie said, "Give or take a few words, dear."

"I will be sure to look it up," I said.

Brownie said, "You be sure to do that," and with a sigh of relief that was audible all the way from Texas, he said goodbye and hung up.

It was not the first time in my experience that Brownie had tried to communicate with me in Biblical cipher, and I lost no time looking up his reference to Revelation. I was primarily interested, of course, in whatever Brownie was trying to tell me but I was interested too in finding out how the Bible ended. My sporadic readings had never happened to include the last page. It was the first time I'd ever thought of the Bible's actually having a last page, of there being after all those thousands of words one final word.

The Bible I found was a Gideon that must have been in the house when we first moved in. The black binding had gone rusty and was starting to wear thin around the corners. *Placed in this Hotel by the* GIDEONS was stamped on the front cover, and below it there was a circular stain. I pictured some drummer in stocking feet using it as a coaster. Inside, the text was littered with letters of the alphabet to mark footnotes. There were hyphens and diacritical marks to indicate the pronunciation of proper names. Every once in a while an innocuous word like *and* or *is* or *the* would be printed in italics. Reading it was like listening to somebody with a bad stutter. "The grace of our Lord Jē′-ṣŭs Chrīst *be* with you all. Ā-mĕn′" was the last verse, but Brownie's "Give or take a few words, dear" led me back to the next to last. Twitching and stammering, it went "He which testifieth these things saith, ¶Surely I come quickly. [r]Ā-mĕn′. [s]Even so, come, Lord Jē-ṣŭs."

There could be no mistaking Brownie's message, I thought. He must know something he couldn't say over the phone. Maybe Lucille herself had been in the room as he spoke. Maybe he had promised not to give her whereabouts away. Maybe he thought the operator was listening. In any case, whatever Brownie knew, it could apparently be found out only by going to Texas to find it. There was no time to lose. *Come* was obviously what Brownie was saying. *Come quickly. Come, dear—come* whoever cared enough to find out the truth. Bebb. Me.

But the name in the book was Jē′-ṣŭs, Saint John

the Divine or whoever it was that wrote Revelations getting stuck on that first syllable so that with his eyes rolled up and his chin bobbing it kept coming out Jē′, Jē′, Jē′, until finally the blessed relief of ṣūs. Come, Lord Jē′-ṣūs. Maybe that was Brownie's message too, I thought: that the only one whose coming would make any difference in the long run was Jē′-ṣūs. Jē′-ṣūs hopping the plane to Houston. Jē′-ṣūs at the Red Path Ranch. Jē′-ṣūs knocking at the door to have Brownie open it or Harry Hocktaw or Mrs. Trionka. Maybe Lucille herself. She and Jē′-ṣūs would sit down over a couple of Tropicanas, her life-blood. Drink up. She would tell Jē′-ṣūs she never cared for his name. Jē′-ṣūs would tell her to take off her black glasses.

I had made the call upstairs in our bedroom, and when I hung up, I sat there on our bed with the Gideon Bible open on my knees. I'd told Sharon I'd come back and pick her up at Bebb's. I had Brownie's message to deliver. It was getting late. But I couldn't move for some reason, just sat there staring at the dreary, double-columned page as though exhausted already by the long journey I knew would begin the moment I sat up and started downstairs. *Come quickly.* It was the urgency of the thing that paralyzed me.

I knew I should do something right away, but I couldn't get going. I felt like lying down on the bed—Sharon's and my bed. And Sharon's and Tony's bed too likely enough. That was something else I should probably do something about, I thought, though God only knew what. Talk it out with one of them maybe, maybe with both of them—work it through, work it off. Teach school with it. Lear's lines drifted through my mind, "We two alone will sing like birds i' the cage./When thou dost ask me blessing, I'll kneel down/And ask of thee forgiveness." All three of us kneeling down somewhere, asking of each other something. Come quickly. But for the time being it was more than I could swing. I might even have actually lain down there, shut my eyes on the whole clamoring snarl of things, but then I heard a car drive in. I heard the unmistakable voice of Mrs. Kling. She and Charlie were bringing the boys back from supper. I beat it down the back stairs.

I rolled out of the driveway as quietly as I could with the headlights off and drove straight to Bebb's. Bebb and Sharon were sitting in the dark living room watching TV, their faces the color of moonlight. I didn't tell them about Lucille's *très riches heures*. I didn't ask Bebb if it was true that he'd told her the story of how Herman Redpath reached the Happy Hunting Ground and if so, how he'd come to know about it. I just reported my conversation with Brownie and quoted from memory the next to last verse of the Book of Revelation.

Bebb said, "Antonio, there isn't a doubt in my mind but what she's back in Houston and Brownie's telling us to get our tails down there pronto. He couldn't say it straight out for fear she'd get wind of it."

Sharon said, "Why did she go, Bip?"

On the TV screen there was a short man in a tuxedo and a fat woman in a sequined evening dress standing in front of a microphone. Somebody came in pushing a wheelbarrow. The laughter crackled like a bonfire, and Bebb got up and turned down the volume.

Bebb said, "Maybe she went to see would we come after her."

"Are you?" Sharon said.

Bebb said, "Honey, I don't just know what I'm going to do." He was still standing by the TV. The fat woman had turned her back to the short man in the tuxedo. He unzipped her dress and helped her pull it off over her head. Underneath she was wearing overalls.

Bebb said, "For many years Lucille hasn't what you might say *moved*. She has set around watching TV and drinking Tropicanas. She has been there when you went out, and when you come back in later, she was right there still. I don't mean she hasn't kept moving in her own way. There's no telling how many miles a day a woman travels just doing her chores. I mean she hasn't moved inside herself. She hasn't gotten anywheres or even wanted to. For a long time Lucille Yancey Bebb has been stuck."

He was talking to himself, the nutcracker jaw cracking the words out one by one. He was staring down at the carpet, his eyes catching the silvery light of the TV like soap bubbles, pearls. He could have been seeing Lucille herself as he talked about her just the way he could have been seeing Herman Redpath that night as he talked to Lucille about him: Herman Redpath jogging along with the deerskin pouch around his neck; Lucille stuck year after year behind those black glasses or Lucille wherever she was now, moving wherever she was moving. Behind Bebb I could see that the fat woman in the overalls had gotten the short man into the wheelbarrow and was wheeling him in it across the stage.

Bebb said, "Well, at last she's taken off. It could be a good thing or a bad thing, depending. Say she's gone back to Houston. Then why'd she go there? To get away from something here? To find something there? Brownie maybe. She always took to Brownie. It might be a good thing to chase after her and bring her back. On the other hand it might be just the wrong thing."

I said, "There didn't seem to be any doubt in Brownie's mind anyway."

Bebb said, "Antonio, Brownie's an old woman. Always was and always will be. He'd say you don't take chances no matter what. Brownie'd say as long as Lucille stays put, at least you know where she's at. That's playing it safe. You take Brownie himself. He's played it so safe all his life he's never lived. He's slid his life in under his tail and sat on it. The man's got spiritual hemorrhoids."

Bebb was working one arm up and down as he spoke. He said, "Because thou art lukewarm and neither cold nor hot I will spew thee out of my mouth. Antonio, life is a gamble. If you don't take chances, you're not alive. I promised Lucille Yancey to honor and keep her as long as we both should live. Maybe that means I should go down and fetch her back now before she goes off the deep end. But maybe not. Maybe I honor her most by leaving her go."

Sharon said, "You better do like Brownie says and bring her back, Bip. If anything happens to her, you'll never forgive yourself."

Bebb said, "Suppose nothing happens to her ever again. Can I forgive myself that?"

Bebb switched on the overhead lights and turned off the TV. A young woman holding a different type of denture cleanser in each hand was sucked up into a small bright hole in the middle of the screen and then disappeared.

On the plane to Houston the next morning, Bebb the great gambler, the great believer, was sick. He did it neatly into a paper cup. When he was finished, I could see the tears rolling down his cheeks. He said, "Every time I puke, I cry. I can't help it. Antonio, I've been that way ever since I was a kid."

Fourteen

WE DIDN'T LET Brownie know we were coming for fear that if Lucille was down there with him as we suspected and got wind we were on our way, she might clear out before we arrived. We took a taxi from the Houston airport and had it let us off at Holy Love, where Brownie's office was.

The church was open, but we couldn't find Brownie or anybody else. The office looked much as it had when it was Bebb's except that on the wall behind the desk Brownie had hung a much enlarged photograph of Bebb and Herman Redpath that must have been taken not long before Herman Redpath's death. It showed Herman Redpath sitting in a wicker armchair on the lawn in front of Holy Love looking a good deal like John D. Rockefeller in his old age. His bony hands hung down over the ends of the chair-arms as if somebody else had arranged them there. The toes of his high-button shoes pointed slightly in toward each other. He was in his shirtsleeves and wearing a string tie. Bebb was standing behind him in his preaching robe with his hands on the old man's shoulders. His head was directly above Herman Redpath's head, and they were both staring into the camera. They looked like some kind of totem pole.

We had already let the taxi go, so after failing to find Brownie and not wanting to spread word of our arrival by a phone call, we decided to head off for the residential compound on foot. Holy Love was on the fringes of the ranch, so there were several miles of flat, dusty road ahead of us. We had brought a single overnight bag between us which I carried. Bebb had loosened his collar and tie and knotted a handkerchief around his neck to catch the sweat. To keep the sun off his bald head, he put on a Mexican sombrero which he'd found hanging in the corridor outside Brownie's office. It made him look like part of a nightclub act.

When we came in sight of the stables, some barefoot children ran down to the fence to watch us pass by, but Bebb's sombrero apparently kept them from recognizing him, and he made no attempt to identify himself. I'm not sure he even noticed them. His face looked grim and pale under the jouncing straw brim as he trudged along. He had fastened the drawstring to keep the sombrero on, and the string-ends hung down in a tassel from his knob of a chin. The only time he spoke was when we passed a low cinderblock building where there was a flagpole out front with a flag at half-mast. Bebb pointed to it and said, "Herman Redpath is gone, Antonio, but he is not forgotten."

Except for the children we saw no signs of life until we got as far as the greenhouse. A pickup truck was just pulling out of the drive with pails of cut flowers in the back—white iris, white carnations, long-stemmed roses, and some shaggy yellow species that I didn't recognize. The truck stopped under a tree, and from the shadows of the cab a bare arm shot out and waved at us. A voice called, "Hiya, good-lookin'." Pushing the sombrero back off his forehead, Bebb stopped to watch the driver get out and run across the road to us. I recognized him immediately as John Turtle. He threw his arms around Bebb and hugged him.

He said, "Oh Leo, we been missing you real bad down here. Things aren't the same with you gone anyhow."

Bebb said, "I've had spells of missing you too, John Turtle."

"That's real good," John Turtle said, "the way we both been missing each other, me and you."

"That's friendship for you," Bebb said.

John Turtle was looking at Bebb, but he reached out sideways and poked me in the stomach with his finger. He said, "How you doing, Friendship? Gettin' much lately?" His gold-framed teeth glinted in the Texas sun.

I said, "How about yourself, John Turtle?"

"You hear me complaining?" John Turtle said.

Bebb said, "Boys, if I don't get out of this sun for a minute, you're going to find yourself talking with a pool of grease." Sweat was running down from under the sombrero and had soaked through the armpits of his Palm Beach cloth suit.

John Turtle said, "Come on over to the truck and take a load off your feet. Tell me all the things that's been happening anyhow."

"You too," Bebb said. "Tell me what's going on down here, John Turtle."

John Turtle had parked his pickup in the shade. He lowered the tailgate, and the three of us sat down on it with John Turtle in the middle and our feet dangling just off the ground. I have never smelled a body-smell to equal John Turtle's. It was a fourth presence there on the tailgate. If it had been music, it would have taken the Houston Symphony to do it justice.

"So tell me what's new, John Turtle," Bebb said. He didn't say. "Tell me if my wife's here," didn't even mention her. John Turtle didn't mention her either. They neither of them spoke Lucille's name as we sat there on the tailgate with all those flowers, and yet I had the feeling that it was Lucille they were speaking about the whole time anyway. Their conversation was like one of those trick pictures in which, once you look at it the right way, you discover that the empty space among the trees is really a human face.

John Turtle told Bebb what was new with a number of Indians. He said, "That oldest boy of Harry Hocktaw's, he got caught in the sauna bath playing ring-around-the-rosy with Louemma Pole. I'm telling you there was some awful boo-hoo when all them Poles and Hocktaws got together on it after. I come too. Oh my yes. We work it all out, don't you worry. Harry Hocktaw's boy gonna have him a nice little wife anyhow. He's gonna have sweet-potato any time he feel like it. Louemma Pole, she gonna have a snake in her grass to the end of her born days."

He said, "The day old Maudie Redpath turned a hundred and six, they had some big hoopla. They had a barbecue. They had Lizard Shoptall's hot jazz combo. There was champagne and prizes and balloons. They set Maudie's chair up on a old buckboard and pulled her all over the place. She did a dance on top of there like there wasn't one other soul left alive in the world to remember how you dance it. If you dance it right, you suppose to turn into a blackbird anyhow. That blouse she always wears you can see through, there's some says they could see where her old titties started to come out all over black feathers. Then she had an attack and come near to swallowing her tongue. She say she feel much better afterwards. Live another hundred six years easy."

John Turtle put his arm around Bebb's far shoulder and let his cheek come to rest on the near shoulder. He said, "Lily Trionka lose the baby she was carrying eating too much cherry-vanilla ice cream on a day like this and then riding the exercycle thirteen miles to work it off. You can just guess who she say was the daddy, him in his grave with the butter on his legs not knowing one thing about it. Well, if she's true, then what she was carrying around inside till she went and lost it was her own uncle."

Here John Turtle sang a song that he seemed to be making up as he went along. It had no tune to speak of. With his cheek on Bebb's shoulder still, he could have been singing it to Bebb or to Lily Trionka's lost child or to nobody in particular. It went,

> *"Baby baby don't you cry*
> *All us folks we got to die*
> *Do no good to sob and sigh*
> *Have yourself some cherry pie*
> *Look for eagle in the sky*
> *See what's up there winks his eye."*

Then he said, "Johnson Badger been having bad luck right straight through. That crazy nephew Buck try horsing around with the Electrolux and got stuck so bad they had to take him down to Doc's in town with that thing hanging off him like a gas pump. Johnson's wife Donna she run her golf-cart into a stump and broke the bone in her eye."

When John Turtle showed signs of stopping, Bebb asked him about several other Indians who had been left out. After he had finished hearing the news about them, Bebb told John Turtle the news about himself.

Bebb said, "John Turtle, I'm going to be open with you, you being the Joking Cousin and all. Things haven't gone just like I hoped they would up North. Things I'd as soon not have had happen, some of them have been happening, and things I hoped was going to happen, to be honest with you they're the ones mostly haven't happened—haven't happened *yet*," Bebb said, holding up one finger. His damp face was mottled by the leaf-shadows. " 'Fear not for I am with thee, saith the Lord. Yea, I will uphold thee with thy right hand.' I believe that, John Turtle. I've got to believe that. In the meanwhile my soul waiteth for the Lord more than they that watch for morning. More than they that watch for morning, John Turtle."

Bebb untied the handkerchief from around his neck and used it to mop around under his jaw and at the back of his head. He said, "I was born and bred in the South. I had me a baby boy was born and died here, and when my time comes, I'm fixing to be laid to rest right next to his little grave in Knoxville, Tennessee. I've had bitter times down here same as

I've had good times. I've made many bad mistakes here, I'm not denying it for one minute, and I've paid dear for every last one of them. But the South's home, John Turtle. Thanks to the great generosity of Herman Redpath, who was the givingest man it has ever been my privilege to know, I have comforts up North I never had anywheres else. I have a house with four bathrooms. I drive a car with air-conditioning and stereo. When I soil my clothes, there's people will come pick them up at the door and have them back spotless inside twenty-four hours. But there's a woman comes to worship with a sorrowful-looking kind of possum in a cage. There's a wheel in the cage to do its exercise on. That's how I feel up North. It's where I've been called to preach the Cross of Jesus. And I've been going at it hard. I will keep going at it hard. But how long, John Turtle, how long? Until the cities lie wasted and without inhabitants, saith the Lord? Until the land be utterly desolate?"

We sat there over his question in silence, the three of us. Across the road there was a bird on the power line. It made a noise that sounded like tightly packed coins chinking in a sack. I decided that since nobody else was going to say it, I would have to say it myself.

I said, "Tell us what's new with Lucille." The remark could have been meant for either of them. That way, I thought, if she wasn't at the ranch, I wouldn't be giving it away to John Turtle that she was missing. He would think I was just asking Bebb to tell him, John Turtle, what was new with Lucille. If Lucille *was* at the ranch, John Turtle would assume that she was there with her family's full knowledge and consent and that we just wanted him to tell us how she'd been getting on since she came.

Bebb, of course, didn't say anything. I could hear the silence he was making not saying anything. John Turtle also didn't say anything. Just the bird on the power line: *chink, chink*. Every once in a while a lovely whiff from the flowers made it through the smell of John Turtle's body. I decided that either Lucille wasn't there or John Turtle wasn't going to let on that she was, and I was just about to say something else when John Turtle finally spoke.

He said, "She didn't look too good anyhow."

Bebb said, "When didn't she look too good?"

John Turtle said, "This morning when I seen her she didn't."

I said, "Where did you see her?"

John Turtle was swinging his legs back and forth letting the heels strike together each time on the backward swing. He was wearing a pair of scuffed black cowboy boots with built-up heels and pointed toes.

He said, "She was over to Brownie's when I seen her the last time. I'll give you a lift."

Bebb said, "Is she at Brownie's right now?"

John Turtle said, "She's not at Brownie's right now, see. She didn't look so hot this morning."

John Turtle was looking down at what he was doing with his feet, and Bebb was leaning forward to see up into his face. Bebb's face as he was looking up at John Turtle was not just expressionless. There was hardly anything left in it to make an expression with.

Bebb said, "How do you mean she didn't look so hot, John Turtle?"

John Turtle said, "I mean she looked kind of cold. She's not over there at Brownie's anyhow. She moved."

Bebb said, "John Turtle, I want you to take us where she moved to right this second. Antonio and me, we're planning to surprise her."

"That's going to be a surprise," John Turtle said. With the toe of one boot, he managed to loosen the other boot at the heel until he could pull it off. He reached down and scratched the sole of his foot, his eyes narrowed in a grimace of relief, his cuff-link teeth showing.

He said, "Lucille, she's kind of dead anyhow."

In connection with her yoga lessons, Sharon once brought home a book about macrobiotic dieting. The book explained that Occidentals need macrobiotics more than other people because they are all *sanpaku*. When a man is *sanpaku*, the whites of his eyes show underneath his irises. That is a very bad sign. It means that you are susceptible to all kinds of diseases both physical and mental. It means that you are apt to come to a sudden and tragic end. It means that you should waste no time taking up macrobiotic diet number seven which consists of eating nothing but brown rice for ten consecutive days.

I had never seen anybody look as *sanpaku* as my father-in-law, Leo Bebb, did at that moment sitting on the tailgate of John Turtle's truck with the pails full of white flowers behind him and the bird on the power line making noises like tightly packed coins in a sack. You could see the whites not only underneath his irises but above them too. This side of hell, they were about as *sanpaku* as eyes can get. I don't think even diet number seven would have helped much.

"You look like somebody shoved a lighted cigar up your ass," the Joking Cousin said. This time he had both arms around Bebb's shoulders.

Fifteen

THAT EVENING Bebb, Brownie and I stood shoulder to shoulder in a Houston funeral parlor. Parlor was the word for it—wall-to-wall carpeting, comfortable chairs, pictures. A schooner in full sail. An autumn wood. In one wall there was an alcove. In the alcove there was a box tilted toward us lengthwise like a display of fruit in a grocer's window. Lucille was in it. They had done a pretty good job on her except for the mouth. It was hard to say what they'd done wrong with the mouth except that it wasn't quite what Lucille would have done with it herself.

Bebb said, "They haven't got the mouth right."

Brownie said, "Just remember, dear, what you're looking at is only mortal clay. Mrs. Bebb herself is with her Father in heaven."

"The mouth isn't right," Bebb said. "They've got the wrong dress on her. I never saw that dress before in all my life."

Brownie said, "Donna Badger contributed that dress. They both of them wore the same size."

Bebb said, "They should have used her own dress. That one doesn't look right on her."

Brownie said, "Her own dress wasn't in a state they could use it, dear."

Bebb said, "It was real nice of Donna Badger to make a contribution of that dress, but . . . Why that dress no more looks like a dress Lucille would ever have wore!" He said, "Antonio, you remind me to express my appreciation to Donna Badger for contributing that dress, hear?"

I said, "Take it easy, Bip."

Brownie said, "Let us bow our heads and say together the Lord's Prayer."

I bowed my head, but I did not shut my eyes. I looked at Bebb's feet. One of his shoes was untied. It was a black shoe, and it was still dusty from our walk that afternoon from Holy Love. It must have been untied for some time because the laces had worked loose over the instep so that there wasn't enough of the ends left sticking out to tie. He would have had to start pulling them tight from the bottom holes up in order to have enough at the top to make a bow with. The whole time we were saying the Lord's Prayer together, I was tying Bebb's shoe with my eyes.

When the prayer was over, Brownie said, "Maybe we better go now. John Turtle is waiting in the car."

"Brownie," Bebb said, "you and Antonio go if you want. I'll be along in a few minutes. It's the last time I'll get to see her, and I don't want to rush it."

Brownie said, "It's not the last time. She'll be there on the other side waiting when you get there. She is there right now, dear."

"No, she's not," Bebb said.

"Where is she, Bip?" I said it before I knew I was

going to, and it was only as I said it that I realized that I expected Bebb to *know*.

"Tell him where she is," Brownie said. Poor Brownie. I see his face turned to Bebb, his eyes gone all dreamy and pale behind his glasses, his store teeth parted to take in whatever sweet words he thought Bebb was about to throw our way.

Bebb turned on him with his face nearly as red as the child's crayoning on the train. It seemed to swell bigger and bigger like an inner tube through a split tire. He said, "I'll tell him where she is. There's where she is. She's in that box with her mouth on crooked and that miserable dress. She's there with her insides pumped out and something else pumped in. All is left of Lucille Yancey's that poor shell that used to hold a life in it. She's in that box if you want to know where she is. She's a empty box inside that box."

Bebb said, "Brownie, you miserable pissant, why didn't you wait till I come before you let the undertaker have her? Without he'd gone and used his needles and chemicals on her poor flesh, I might have raised her."

He paused for a moment, his face red and his shoe untied. Then as if maybe it wasn't too late after all, he turned to Lucille and said, "*Talitha cumi!*" He said it in the same tone of voice he'd used the time she tipped over backwards in the porch rocker.

For the first time whatever they had done wrong with her mouth seemed to come right. It was the kind of lopsided thing she might have done with it herself if she had had ears to hear what Bebb had just said to her. He said it again, "*Talitha cumi*. Damsel, I say unto thee arise."

For a moment I was certain I could see her flat chest in that borrowed dress start to breathe. The bottom half of the lid was closed over her from the waist down, and I watched for her to start pulling herself out from under it like somebody getting out of a kayak. For a moment it seemed the reason she was so absolutely still was that she was pulling herself together to move. The three of us stood there watching her.

"Brownie, you poor old woman," Bebb said finally, "it might have worked if you only hadn't gone and jumped the gun. Just like it worked when you were laid out there in Knoxville, Tennessee, the color of cement in your underdrawers till the Lord in his mercy gave you back your pitiful life again. She might have rose up the same as you did. Now there's not enough of her left to raise spit."

There were tears coming down from underneath Brownie's glasses, but all his teeth would do was smile.

Bebb said, "Never mind." The inner tube had burst. He was resting on his rims now.

He said, "She just picked up and went where she felt like she had to go. She's got plenty to keep her busy now without me trying to drag her back against her will. Who knows? Maybe Herman Redpath will give her a hand on the way."

Brownie said, "The communion of saints, dear." He had taken his glasses off to wipe his eyes. When Brownie took his glasses off, you felt you shouldn't look at him.

I said, "Maybe Herman Redpath will give her the word for the earth and the word for the sky."

Bebb said, "She tell you about that?" He was facing Lucille in her alcove with his eyes closed. He said, "One night back there she couldn't get to sleep. I wasn't asleep either. We commenced to talk in the dark. She wanted me to tell her what it is is supposed to happen on the other side and all that. I suppose she might have been thinking about things even back then. Like she wanted to make sure where she'd end up if that was where she decided to go. Of course I didn't suspect anything at the time. I thought she just wanted to find out about Herman Redpath, him having just passed on. So I spun her that yarn to help her go to sleep with. I made it up as I went on, like a bedtime story. The places he went and the things that happened. The things he had to do. It was a kind of lullaby. She went to sleep by and by."

I said, "I think she believed it, Bip. I think she thought it all happened just the way you said."

Bebb opened his eyes and turned to me. For a second I thought his eyelid was going to do its trick, but there was only the faintest tremor. Then it recovered. He said, "Who says it didn't?"

Through the crook of his arm I could see Lucille's forehead with the hair growing out of it. I remembered reading somewhere that your hair goes on growing for a while after you're dead and wondered if Lucille's was. Bebb placed both his hands on the edge of her box. He said, "Good-bye, dear heart." He didn't say it in an emotional way. He said it as if the time had simply come to say it.

When we got back to the car, he told John Turtle

we would wait if he wanted to go in and pay his last respects. I wondered if he hoped maybe John Turtle would take a leak on her just in case the going got tough later on.

According to Brownie, what had happened was this. The same Saturday that Bebb and I had taken the train to New York together, Lucille had arrived at the ranch. She had not told Brownie she was coming, just phoned him from the airport when she got in and told him to come get her. She had no luggage and wasn't even wearing a hat and coat. She said when they moved north, she had left a lot of things behind at the ranch that she needed now and nobody would know where to lay their hands on them except herself. Brownie said she kept coming back so many times to this expression of laying her hands on things that it sounded as though that was what she was really there to do—not so much to find the things she needed and take them home with her but just literally, to lay her hands on them again. He said she talked in a somewhat jumbled way, but it wasn't the first time he'd heard her talk like that and he had an idea she'd probably taken a little something on the flight down. He said when he asked her where Bebb was, she told him to tell *her*. She said wherever Bebb was, he was spending more and more of his time out there and the less said about it the better. When reporting this to Bebb, Brownie said, "She meant outer space, dear. You know how that was always her joke," and Bebb sat there listening to him with his face done up so tight he couldn't have flickered so much as an eyelash.

Brownie said that when he suggested to Lucille

that they ought to give Bebb a ring and let him know she'd arrived safely, she didn't offer any explanation but just told him she didn't want anybody to know she was there. She made Brownie promise he wouldn't give her away. Brownie said, "It was the valley of decision, dear. I knew I ought to call you, but she seemed so set on nobody knowing. It was like her whole life depended on it. You at least had Sharon and Antonio. You had your faith, dear. But all she had right then was me. So I promised. When Antonio phoned the next day, I was stretched nearly to the breaking point."

Brownie said, "That was Sunday evening you called. Most of Sunday she spent laying her hands on things just like she said. She hadn't left all that much behind when you moved, but what there was was right where she left it. Nobody's moved in there since you went north. Bea Trionka went over and visited with her a while. Bea says there were only a few drawers had anything in them, but she'd take it out what little there was and sort through it and put it all back again. Some old belts and shoes and some underthings that needed mending, worn out things like what you'd leave behind and never give another thought to. That's mostly all there was, dear. There was a shoebox full of old snapshots and a few keepsakes, but Bea says she didn't make any special feature out of them. She just showed Bea a couple of things she had in there and then put them back. Bea felt like what she wanted to do most was just see her own place again. I guess there wasn't a thing in it she didn't get around to laying her hands on before she was done."

Brownie told Bebb and me all this before we went to the funeral parlor. We were sitting in the big, high-ceilinged room where Herman Redpath's pipe organ was. There was something museum-like about it with just the three of us sitting there. I felt there should have been velvet ropes across all the chairs.

Brownie said, "We had supper together Sunday night, just her and I. I mixed her up a Tropicana first. I had the orange juice on hand, and the gin I got off of Lizard Shoptall. I thought if she wanted to unburden herself of anything that was on her heart, this would be the time. Sometimes it's easier to say things to an outsider, dear. But you know how she always was. She let me do most of the talking. Just once in a while she'd come out with one of her salty comments. I remember I said Sharon's boy must be a lot to handle these days, and she said something about how he wasn't the only boy Sharon was handling these days. It was just the way she had, and down in her heart there never was a kinder soul. She said Mr. Golden had turned up again up North. I asked her could anybody find out what he was up to, and she gave me one of her long looks when you wished you could see behind the dark glasses, and finally she come out and said, 'It's not what he's up to. It's what he's *down* to.' I remember she said, 'Going down, please. Everybody watch your step.' Dear, she didn't say anything different than the kind of thing she always said. She didn't give a clue what must have been in her mind the whole time. She even mentioned something about when she'd be getting home. How could I guess what she meant by home? I'm not sure now what she meant even.

Maybe all she meant when she said home was what I thought she meant then. Maybe what happened come as much of a surprise to her as it did to me."

Brownie was wearing his powder-blue suit with the silvery clip-on bow tie which was his usual costume for Sundays. I suppose he had put it on special that Monday for the trip to the funeral parlor. The lenses of his glasses were pink because the pink sky was reflected in them through the window. His aftershave seemed unusually fragrant. Dear Brownie. In many ways he was a breath of spring in that museum of a room.

He said, "After we got the dishes done up, we went and sat out on the porch. It was a lovely, warm night. There was just a little breeze and a new moon. I remember I looked up, and I said, 'When I consider the heavens, the work of thy fingers, the moon and the stars, which thou has ordained . . . What is man that thou art mindful of him?' It is a question I often ask myself, dear. Next thing Lucille, she said, 'Read me some parts out of Scripture, Brownie.'

"You see it was Sunday, and I'd left my Bible out there on the table when I come back from church so it was right there beside me, and there was light enough from the window to read by. Now it wasn't like her to ask to have Scripture read out loud to her. In her heart she was a Christian woman, but nobody that knew her would have expected she'd ask a thing like that, and I should have seen right then something was wrong. But I didn't see it, not even then. I'd just quoted from the Psalmist, and she'd probably seen the Bible laying there on the table. It just seemed natural as could be at that time, and I asked her if there was anything special she'd like me to read. She told me to just let the book fall open in my lap and start reading from the first place my finger touched. So I did like she told me, and the book fell open to Second Kings, the tenth chapter.

"You remember that is a terrible chapter, dear. It tells about how Jehu beheaded all seventy of Ahab's sons and laid their heads together in two heaps by the gate and then put the two and forty of Ahaziah's brethren and all the worshipers of Baal to the sword. It is a very dark Scripture, dear, and I asked her couldn't I close up the book again and try for another. But she said no. She said that was what the book opened to and that was what she wanted to hear. She said maybe it would get more cheerful later on.

"I must have read half an hour or so. I couldn't see her too good in the dark where she was sitting, but I could hear her rocking back and forth in her chair so I knew she wasn't asleep. After a while she said, 'Read me about Jesus, Brownie.' She said it in a kind of drowsy, restful way. It was the last words I ever heard her say, and at that time I was real glad to hear her say them. Second Kings never does get what you'd want to call very cheerful, dear, and I turned to the Gospels with great relief. I opened up to Saint Mark and started reading right from the beginning. I read how Jesus got baptized in Jordan's waters and was tempted of Satan and how he started gathering unto himself the disciples. Then all those miracles, dear. I read how he drove out the unclean spirits and cleansed the leper. How he cured the palsy and the withered hand. All the time I was reading I could hear the chair rocking so I knew she was awake. Anyway, she wasn't a person to let you go on if she wanted you to stop. So I went on and read her how the Savior taught us faith is like a grain of mustard seed which, when it is sown in the ground, is less than all the seeds. The Gadarene swine. The feeding of the multitude. I don't know how long I went on. When I get reading Scripture, I lose track of time. But finally I must have stopped to give my voice a rest. The chair had stopped rocking. She was sitting there with her head back. I thought she just had dozed off, dear."

The smell of Brownie's after-shave. The sky-colored glasses. The gun-barrel sheen of Herman Redpath's organ pipes, and Bebb sitting up straight and stiff in his chair with a plump hand on each knee and his face like something carved out of Ivory Soap. You try to represent the truth of a moment by drawing a line through such points as these. I was sitting next to Brownie on the sofa, and as he paused, I couldn't help remembering that fatal night on the sofa next to Tony: the springy, salt-stiff hair, the *I'm sorry, I'm sorry*. In some queer way, I thought, all moments are one moment. Outside where the sun was going down, there was the sound of tightly packed coins chinking in a sack.

Brownie said, "It was the wrists, dear. All that rocking back and forth—I suppose it acted like a pump. All over her dress, the rocker . . . There wasn't a thing in the world you could do. 'Read me about Jesus, Brownie.' Those were her last words, dear. What a blessing to know she slipped away with the music of Scripture in her ears."

Bebb got up from his chair. He said, "Thank you, Brownie. I'm much obliged."

He walked over to Herman Redpath's organ across the room from where Brownie and I were sitting. He had set his borrowed sombrero down on the bench when we'd come in, and he pushed it to one side to make room to sit down. When he sat down, the sombrero started to fall off the end of the bench, so he picked it up and set it on the back of his head. He pulled out several of the stops and pushed in several others. He settled his hands down on the keyboard and started by pressing out several vague, overstuffed chords.

Then he sang,

> *"Ten thousand times ten thousand,*
> *In sparkling raiment bright,*
> *The armies of the ransomed saints*
> *Throng up the steeps of light."*

There was something about his singing voice that always reminded me of the Gothic radios of my childhood—reedy, maybe one tube a little loose, the amber light of the dial.

He sang,

> *"'Tis finished, all is finished,*
> *Their fight with death and sin.*
> *Fling open wide the golden gates,*
> *And let the victors in."*

Sixteen

SOON AFTER we returned to Sutton, Bebb moved in with us, and Sharon said, "It's like there was a shipwreck and this house is the desert island where everybody gets washed up." We were in bed, and it was raining outside. There was a magazine near the window, and the damp breeze kept lifting the cover with a papery noise.

I said, "You can even hear the palm trees."

Something like two weeks had gone by since the night I found out about Sharon and Tony, and we had been sleeping together all those nights but we had not made love together. It was a long time for us not to have made love. It was not that the idea of sharing her with my impulsive nephew made her less desirable. If I had been thinking in those terms, that might even have made her more so in some dim and unsightly way. It was not that I was out to get even with her by withholding, such as it was, the solace of my flesh, or to get even with myself by refusing the solace of hers—Tony and Sharon continued to live together in that house so much as though nothing had ever happened between them that I began almost to believe that nothing had and that the guilt was therefore mine for having dreamed up the gaudy thing in the first place. I think we had not made love together because getting his horns is only the first stage a cuckold goes through on his way to becoming like the beasts of the field. The second stage is getting gelded. For two weeks making love with my wife had been an occasion to which I simply wasn't able in any sense to rise. In fact it wasn't till her remark about the desert island that the possibility even occurred to me. I suppose it called up all the old business about the girl you'd most like to be marooned with, the old *Esquire* cartoons. Add to that the wet wind rattling the magazine cover and the sound of the rain.

Sharon was lying on her side with her back to me speaking at least half to her pillow. She said, "The Dead End kids, I mean. They got washed up here because their mother kicked the bucket. Because Charlie's sinuses are all he can handle plus Mrs. Kling and her big boobs. And now Bip's gotten washed up. He's like Robinson Crusoe up there on the third floor with his suitcase hanging on the door and his portable TV. It's like he's just roughing it up there till some ship comes by and rescues him.

"The baby," she said. "He's the only one of them that's here on purpose. He got *born* here, for God's sake."

I was lying on my back with my hands folded on my chest. I felt just the way Lucille had looked in her box in Houston. I had an idea there was the same sort of thing wrong with my mouth.

I said, "How about you and me? Are we washed up too?"

I meant washed up marooned, that's all I meant, but it didn't come out that way. I knew it the moment I heard myself say it. Just *washed up* was the way it came out. It was too late to explain. I was like a man who happens to scratch his ear at an auction. God only knew what I might end up paying. I lay there knowing that within seconds I could be taken for everything I had.

Washed up. There wasn't a thing in the world I could do about it except just listen to the rain and wait to see how she'd answer, and then as I waited, and for reasons that will never be clear, there was that about me which after having been for two weeks as good as dead chose this moment to start coming slowly alive again, and there wasn't a thing in the world I could do about that either. Mr. Independence. I've heard that on the battlefield dead soldiers are found—and from the gallows men are cut down—in just such a state as I was in then as I waited in the dark beside Sharon, who lay on her side with her back to me and her knees drawn up. It was a kind of resurrection, I suppose. The crowing cock that puts the ghosts to flight.

"You and me, we live here," Sharon answered finally. "We weren't washed up. We're the native population." I don't know why she took so long to say it. Maybe it just seemed long. Anyway, knowing it or not knowing it, she gave me back my life again.

It might have been Ellie Pierce lying there beside me, I thought, Ellie with her yellow rose, her lovely Vassar French. Or it might have been Laura Fleischman, and for a moment in the lunacy of the dark and the rain I let it become Laura Fleischman, Laura Fleischman *en fleur*, gentle as falcon or hawk in the tower, that child lying there sleepy and shy with her knees drawn up. I remembered a dream I'd had about Laura Fleischman. It was deer season, and I was standing on a hillside. Laura Fleischman came running down the hillside disguised as a deer with antlers tied to her head. I thought what a crazy thing to do, and then I heard a gun go off. Laura Fleischman fell. Soon a real deer appeared, a big buck, majestic and proud. He slipped his antlers underneath her as delicately as though he was picking up a baby and carried her away down the hill on them.

But it was not Laura Fleischman lying there beside me. It was Sharon. Her hair smelled of sleep and home. She said, "We've come one hell of a long way from the Salamander Motel, that's for sure. My God, Antonio."

I remembered the Salamander Motel the way the Pilgrim Fathers remembered Plymouth Rock. At the Salamander Motel she had been Sharon Bebb of Armadillo, Florida, with illegal eyes and a somber mouth, and when I'd reached up and touched the towel she'd wrapped around her like a sari, it had fallen to the floor of the Salamander Motel not with a single movement but with two movements, like a leaf falling. And then like a king returning from long exile, I'd stooped to kiss the earth beneath my feet. "Thou shalt not commit adultery, dear," Brownie would have said, only it wouldn't have been adultery then. We were neither of us married in Armadillo, Florida.

The palm tree rattled on our island. Cartoon castaways—Sharon curled up there like a Playboy center-fold and me signaling for help with my flag in the air.

Sharon said, "How the hell much longer do you think Bip plans to camp out up there? And Tony and Chris, are they going to get married and move in with their wives, for Christ sake?"

I said, "Ah love, let us be true to one another." Always thc English teacher. I tightened the muscles in my calves as tight as they would go, and one of them began to cramp on me. I sat up halfway in the dark to work on it.

She said, "Do me a favor, will you? Rub my back. I must have slipped a disc at the swami's this afternoon."

I said, "For we are here as on a darkling plain. Swept by confused alarms of struggle and flight."

"The left shoulder," she said.

So I rolled over on my side and we came together like spoons in a silver drawer, and Sharon said, "Makes me feel all loose like a long-necked goose," which was what the Big Bopper had been singing when I first saw her coming down the steps of the Armadillo manse in her sailor pants. I put my hand on her left shoulder and worked around under it with my thumb. There was the sound of the rain at the window.

After a while she said. "It wasn't his fault, Antonio, and it wasn't exactly my fault either." The words came out slowly as though I was pushing them out with my thumb.

After a while more she said, "Bip says sometimes you've got to take crazy chances. I don't know what he means. Maybe he knows what he means.

"That Bip," she said.

I said, "Is it all over now?"

She said, "God I hope so, Antonio."

She said a few other things too, but I'd have had to be the pillow to hear them.

There were just two more words after that, one for the earth and one for the sky. They were too powerful to say in anything but sign language.

There were two adventures that night of which this was only the first. The second happened an hour or so later. Sharon was asleep, but I was still awake listening to the weather. The rain would almost stop and then it would start again—first a few random drops, heavy, like somebody throwing pebbles at the window, then the sudden rush and clatter of it on the roof. I didn't want the rain to stop. Every time it started up, it gave me back more than just the rain again.

Eventually I heard voices. I heard them first before I could tell whose voices they were or where they came from. It could have been one of the boys talking in his sleep or somebody outside in the wet. Like the rain, they started out slow and scattered, then got noisier. There were two voices, and they came from the hall. Through our closed door, I couldn't make out the words, but I thought I caught my own name. Antonio. One of the voices was Bebb's. I wouldn't have bothered to investigate except that I was afraid it might wake up the baby. I got out of bed without waking up Sharon and stepped into the hall. The light was on in Chris's room, and the door was ajar. I went in.

Chris never opened his window at night, and the room smelled of socks and breath and the medicated ointment he used on his pimples. His bedside lamp was on, and he was sitting straight up in bed. There were white patches of ointment on his face. He looked skinny and pale and scared.

In the center of the room with his back to me stood Bebb. It was the first time I had ever seen him dressed for bed. He had on a seersucker bathrobe with his bare legs sticking out and no slippers. He didn't seem to have anything on underneath the bathrobe. He spun around when he heard me come in behind him. He said, "Antonio, I'm afraid there's been a foolish misunderstanding."

"I was dead to the world," Chris said, "and then I woke up and he was here in my room. I didn't know what was coming off. I thought the house was on fire."

I said, "What's coming off, Bip? Is the house on fire?"

Bebb said, "Antonio, that's what I've been trying to tell him. There's nothing on fire. There's nothing coming off, and there's nothing to get fussed about." Bald, plump, barefoot, he looked like Friar Tuck in his seersucker bathrobe.

"What's a person supposed to think," Chris said, "getting woken up in the middle of the night that way? I was still half asleep. I thought the house was burning down."

Bebb said, "Chris, you're half asleep still. That's the whole trouble."

"So how come you woke him up, Bip?" I said. I closed the door behind me. "For the baby," I said.

Chris said, "You can't blame a person for thinking something must be wrong when he gets woken up in the middle of the night that way. I was dead to the world."

"Nobody's blaming anybody," Bebb said. "Antonio, I'm going to explain it all out to you just like I was explaining it to Chris here when you come in. Your trousers are unbuttoned."

I buttoned them.

There was a desk in the room, and Bebb half sat, half leaned, on it. There was a picture of Miriam on the desk. It was one of those posed photographs they used to take when a girl was coming out, and it didn't look much like her. She was wearing too much lipstick, and they had her looking down over one bare shoulder as though she'd dropped something. The background lighting was what they call in the trade dramatic. I thought that was probably why Chris liked it. The rain was coming down hard again.

Bebb said, "Listen to that rain come down." He tucked the flaps of his bathrobe between his fleshy, white calves. He said, "Boys, watch and pray that ye enter not into temptation, that's what the book says. Matthew twenty-six. I've always been a praying man. There's never been—Now I don't take credit for that," he admonished us, one finger raised. "It doesn't mean you're a better man on account of you pray more. Not necessarily. It may just mean you're a man that's tempted more. I pray nights mostly. I pray for the folks I know, specially the ones that's close to me, the ones I love. Selfish? Antonio, the way I look at it, it's like electricity. You've got a heavier-duty line strung out to the ones you love, that's all. The

Almighty can run more voltage through it than he can through the pitiful threads you got strung out to the rest of the world. To pray five hundred amps worth for the rest of the world—that takes a saint, boys. I'm no saint."

He said *I'm no saint* in a thoughtful way as if maybe things might have worked out differently. With luck.

Bebb said, "Tonight I was praying for the folks in this house. I knew the power was running strong. You can feel it when it's running strong. It gets hot inside. Like heartburn. I knew what the Lord was saying to me was Bebb, you get on up out of your bed and go pray for them in their rooms where they're laying fast asleep. He said to me Bebb, don't keep your candle under a bushel but carry it down there to the second floor where they are so it can give light unto all that are in the house. Sometimes even in hotels I've gotten up in the middle of the night and done it like that. It was taking a chance, opening the doors of strangers, but I done it anyway. Tonight it was Chris's door I opened. He woke up. Sometimes it's bound to happen that way. It's the chance you take."

Chris said, "I thought the house must be on fire." He was sitting up stiff in his bed with the white markings on his face.

I said, "It wasn't the house that was on fire."

Chris said, "I was dead to the world, and the next thing I knew, there I was with these cold hands on me."

Bebb said, "Cold hands, warm heart."

"You can't blame a person for being scared," Chris said.

Bebb said, "Chris, noboby's blaming anybody. That's the whole point of it."

"Why me?" Chris said. "Was I the only one you prayed for?"

Bebb said, "No, you weren't the only one. Sharon and Antonio here, I was in there first." His eyelid flickered. He said, "It's a fact when a man's asleep, there's nothing left in his face except the peace and goodness of him. Antonio, you were a real picture laying there dead to the world."

I have thought often since of Bebb's standing there in the dark of Chris's ointment-smelling room. His candle is out from under the bushel. It is burning. And I have thought too of his padding down the midnight corridors of drummers' hotels all the way from Memphis to Tallahassee taking his chances. If he was in Sharon's and my room that night too as he claimed, all I can say is neither of us saw him. But that doesn't have to mean he wasn't there. The way things were, it might be that we just didn't notice him.

Sharon was awake when I got back to bed. I said, "Bip woke Chris up praying for him, that's all. The laying on of hands."

What Sharon said was, "I wonder where to God he laid them."

Seventeen

WHEN BEBB announced around the first of June that he had decided to close down Open Heart for the summer and take Sharon and me on a trip to Europe with him, he presented me with a Bell and Howell super eight movie camera with a zoom lens and an optronic eye. He said, "Antonio, time like an ever-flowing stream bears all her sons away, but with a camera like this here, at least you can get a picture of it flowing." When I think of the events of that spring and summer, I think cinematically.

Even with as foolproof an instrument as my Bell and Howell, there are plenty of blunders an amateur can commit. He can overexpose or underexpose by failing to take into account not just the kind of light that's falling on his subject but the kind of light that's falling on him and his hopelessly literal optronic eye. He can get the distances wrong. He can pan too fast. He can forget to trip an important switch or neglect to turn a knob to where the two little black dots meet.

He can take movies of the wrong things, things that aren't moving or things that are moving too fast. A baby in its pen, for instance. He can use up his last twenty-five feet when all it's doing is lying there in the sun like an unbaked loaf and miss the moment of truth when it gets its foot in its mouth. Sometimes when interesting things are happening, he doesn't have his camera with him or gets too interested to remember to use it. Or he uses it and finds out later he forgot to put in the film.

Looking back over the movies I've taken in my life, I find that, as I might have suspected, the scenes I shot are usually not the really significant scenes. On Commencement Day, for instance, I didn't get Laura Fleischman walking across the gym stage with her diploma in her hand—she was wearing high heels and walked as though she was on a tightrope—but got instead fat Bill Urquhart with six inches of white cuff showing beneath each sleeve. The only time Laura Fleischman appears is in a crowd around a bowl of Kool Aid. She is shielding her eyes with a program. You can't even see her face.

I have found out something else which I suppose I might also have suspected but didn't. Although the scenes that I shoot aren't usually the significant ones, they tend to become the significant ones simply because I happened to shoot them. The same thing holds true of my memory. It's usually not the important things I remember best. The things I remember become important because I remembered them.

Take the day we found Mr. Golden in Bebb's barn, Sharon and I. A lot of the things he said have slipped my mind. What sticks is the barn itself. Open Heart. It was dim and shadowy with just a few bright patches where the sunlight hit. Like the Bell and

Howell optronic eye, what my memory retains best are those sunlit patches—Mr. Golden's porkpie hat, for one, the part of one wall that he'd painted red with vertical black lines running through it, the beat-up stepladder where Sharon had put down a spray of lilacs when we first came in. The lilacs stick especially, lying on that paint-spattered rung like wreckage at sea.

We'd driven over to pick up some lumber Bebb had said we could use. He was still living on our third floor with his portable TV and the suitcase hooked over the door, but he said the barn wasn't locked. We could just walk in and take what we wanted. There were some two-by-fours left over from the alterations he'd made, and I needed them for a tripod I wanted to put up for my monument which I'd decided to hang outdoors. Bebb had suggested it. He said, "Why make a thing like that and then leave it in a place can't anybody see it?" Like hiding your candle under a bushel, I suppose. So I dreamed up the idea of setting it up in the backyard where the weather could turn it gray gracefully. It seemed a better idea than painting it the way Billie Kling had suggested. The wind would blow it around and for all I knew birds might build their nests in it and children come and swing on it; but, as Bebb said, you've got to take some crazy chances.

We found Mr. Golden standing on a chair behind the pulpit. He had a can of paint in one hand and a brush in the other. He was in his shirtsleeves but otherwise dressed just as he had been the evening we'd met at the railroad station—the sneakers, the baggy pants, the porkpie hat. He was making a picture on the wall. There was a kindergarten look about it—the side view of a man sitting in a chair. The head was too big for the body, the hand hung straight down at the side with the fingers splayed out like an udder. There was another man sitting in a chair facing him. The man Mr. Golden was working on was yellow and the other man was white. They looked as though they had been sitting there facing each other since the beginning of time. There were other pictures on other parts of the wall.

Mr. Golden said, "Leo and me, we're like one of those old-time weather-forecasters with the little house. One man comes out with an umbrella when it's going to rain, and the other man comes out with a sunshade when it's going to be fine. I move in and Leo moves out. That's the way of it."

Sharon said, "Does he know you've moved in?"

Mr. Golden said, "He moved out, didn't he? He moved in with you folks, didn't he?" He stood on the chair smiling down at us with his lovely smile, encouraging us, now he'd shown us how to put two and two together. His face was furrowed and soft like a hand that's been in water for a long time. He said, "If there's anything half so much fun as being alive, I'd like to know what it is."

The barn was dark after the sunshine outside, and the overlapping petals of my memory's optronic eye slide back to let in as much light as possible, but it isn't enough. The reel I end up with doesn't do the scene justice. The walls were covered with Mr. Golden's pictures, but only a few of them show up clearly. The colors seem richer and deeper than they could have been in actuality—blues, greens, reds of stained-glass intensity. Stiff, flat figures are posed in all sorts of ways, but it is hard to make out who most of them are or what they're supposed to be doing. Mr. Golden himself is mostly his disembodied porkpie hat. He said, "I'm no Michelangelo but this isn't that whatchamacallit place either. Leo gave me leave to jazz the place up. He didn't care how I did it so long as I kept on doing it and stayed out of his hair. So this is how I did it. There must be twenty or thirty pictures no two alike, and I'm not done yet. What I put them up there to show is the story of Leo Bebb's life."

I don't think we would have known if he hadn't told us: the little flowers of Leo Bebb, in other words—the preaching to the birds, the stigmata, Brother Fire.

Sharon and I were shoulder to shoulder in the aisle between the two sections of folding chairs. Sharon had picked the lilacs by the porch steps and set them on the stepladder when we came in. Her right arm and my left arm, both bare, just barely touched—like a wedding—or the fuzz touched, or the thin sleeves of air that bare arms wear. She said, "My dad didn't mention about anybody staying here."

It was the first time I ever head her call him Dad. I suppose you didn't call anybody Bip who had his picture up on the wall of a church.

Mr. Golden said, "That one up there by the window is jailbirds, cons. Leo used to give it to them hot and heavy right through the bars." They looked less like birds than eggs the way Mr. Golden had rendered them—rows of shaved scalps like eggs in a box. Bebb leaned out over them big and white with

HARPER & ROW/Buechner 85-D

his wings spread. Mr. Golden said, "Sometimes after lights out he'd have the whole row belting out gospel hymns. It was enough to give you goose bumps."

Mr. Golden said, "In that one I'm still working on, it's Leo and me sitting in our little corner of perdition taking each other in the way we took each other in day in day out for five years. After that much time it's a rule of life you even start to look like each other. We used the same bucket for our needs. We worked side by side in the laundry. At night when we were asleep, his breathing and mine, it was like there was only one man breathing. Sometimes they even come in to check."

He said, "Pent up like that closer than marriage in a place the size of a box it gets to where after a while you don't have to *tell* the whole true story of your life to each other. You just catch each other's life from each other like a head cold. We used to play a game to make the time pass. It was a game of imagining. Leo would say something or I would. Let's say it was *raspberry* Leo said. Then we'd both start working on raspberries. We'd work on raspberries till it was like you could feel a raspberry in your mouth with the little red beads of it and the hole in the middle where the stem come out of. We'd work on raspberries till you could taste the true taste of a raspberry which is what a raspberry is, it is mostly a taste and shape in your mouth like summer and like all the raspberries you ever ate in your life. The first one of us that could say he'd dreamed up a raspberry lock, stock and barrel, the whole truth of a raspberry and nothing but the truth, he'd be the one was the winner of that round. You didn't even have to take it on trust he was telling the truth. You could tell from his face whether he was. Then maybe I'd say *sheets*. We didn't have sheets. We had sleazy gray blankets that looked like old newspapers that's been left out in the rain. They had about as much warmth to them as old newspapers. We'd commence working on the feel and smell and all of clean sheets. We'd get so we could hear the sound your toenails make when you slip down between a pair of clean sheets on a cool night. A brass band. A kiss. You name it, we imagined it. The game was to see which of us could get there first. It made the time pass."

A beam of sun turned the crown of Mr. Golden's porkpie hat gold, a golden crown. He said, "We'd try people sometime. People aren't for beginners. You got to work up to people. You can't just stop at their face either, though even the face isn't the easiest thing in the world to get—their *real* face the way it moves around in life, I mean, not just a snapshot of their face in some one particular look it has. You got to keep going till you can hear the sound a person's voice makes. You got to see how the clothes hang on him and the way he works his hands and feet. The way you know you've got him right is when you've got him so he starts in doing things in your imagination you didn't try on purpose to imagine him doing. Sometimes we'd spend hours on just one person. Once we tried our fathers. There's a picture for you. Two cons in the pitch dark spending half the night trying to dream up their old dead dads."

He said, "You don't have to believe this if you don't want to, but if you dream up a person all the way, sometimes it isn't just you yourself can see him.

That picture over there is the father of Leo Bebb the way I saw him though I never laid eyes on him in all my life."

Bebb's father was lying on his back with his arms crooked up into the air and a heavy head of hair spread out behind him. He looked like a fallen tree.

Nearby was what I took to be Bebb raising Brownie from the dead in Knoxville. Brownie's half-sitting figure was outlined in a rainbow of different colors. The outermost band of the rainbow was white, and Bebb was reaching out to touch it with his white hand.

Bebb was selling Bibles. He was driving a pickup truck with the Bibles piled up as high as the roof of the cab in back. The Bibles were red and looked like bricks. Each one had a small cross painted on it.

Bebb was standing under a palm tree with a swatch of blue sea behind him. There was a white balloon coming out of his mouth as though there should be some words written in it, but the balloon was empty.

Bebb was sitting on a bench beside somebody in black glasses with her hair sticking out like a sunburst. There was a baby lying across their laps. Lucille had the head and Bebb had the feet.

Bebb was shaking hands with a red Indian. The Indian had on a feathered headdress that hung down to his heels. The yellow paint of the top feather had dripped down into the blue paint of the one beneath it, and the feathers beneath those had been outlined but not yet colored in.

Above the door Bebb was flying. His arms stretched out straight from his shoulders. His toes pointed directly behind him. His face was round and white.

Mr. Golden said, "Thou knowest my downsitting and mine uprising. Thou art acquainted with all my ways. That's the story of that one."

I said, "Poor Lucille, she always said he was from outer space."

Sharon said, "She'd have gotten a bang out of that one."

"That one," Mr. Golden said, "is a whole lot of things in a nutshell."

Sharon said, "He looks like he's been shot out of a cannon."

I said, "He's got wings." They were small wings sprouting from the knobs of his shoulders and flattened out beneath the crossbeam. They looked inadequate to support his weight.

Mr. Golden had his hands in the pockets of his voluminous pants. He hitched them up, and there was the clinking of coins. It sounded as if he was carrying a small fortune in his pockets. He said, "If I take the wings of the morning and dwell in the uttermost parts of the sea, even there shall Thy hand lead me and Thy right hand shall hold me." With his oversized body and skinny neck, he looked like a turtle craning up out of his shell. He said, "If I ascend up into heaven, Thou art there. If I descend into hell, behold Thou art there."

I said, "Lucille had this crazy theory about elevators too."

Mr. Golden said, "It's a rule of life if a person comes to know as much about you as I come to know about Leo Bebb, sharing near to every living minute with him day in day out up to and including the imaginations of his heart, when you see him coming at you down the pike, you am-scray. It's a natural thing. All I'd have to say is Leo, fork out or it'll be all over town how you and me were roommates for five long years. Either you make it worth my while or I'll hang your downsittings and your uprisings out on the line for every Tom, Dick and Harry to gawk at. He ought to know I'd never say that. I've never said it. But that's what he's afraid of. These pictures, nobody'd know what they were all about unless somebody was to explain them out."

Sharon said, "Well, you can hardly blame him for being afraid the way you keep tailing him. How come you keep doing it anyway?"

Mr. Golden said, "Take a look at that one over there." Not flying or preaching or raising anybody from the dead, in the one that Mr. Golden pointed at with his delicate hand, Bebb was just standing still. His eyes were closed. He was holding his hands out with the palms turned up as though it was raining and he wanted to feel the rain in his hands. It was the only picture so far that approached being a likeness of Bebb, not just a white shape cut out with a cookie-cutter—the firm, tight H of his mouth on its hinges, the jut of his ear-lobes. But from the waist down he looked like nothing on earth. From the waist down he was a flaming meteor, a Ringling Brothers hoop of fire for lions and tigers to leap through, the concentric circles of an archery butt or wheels within wheels from outermost red through orange and saffron to yellow, to innermost white-hot bullseye. Underneath, his tidy black shoes stuck out like andirons.

Mr. Golden said, "They didn't lock him up for playing tiddley-winks, you know. They didn't lock me up for playing tiddely-winks either."

Up to this point I had thought of Mr. Golden as his face. I had thought of him as that keen, withered, oddly boyish face with that lovely, oddly girlish smile, and I had thought of the rest of him as a kind of cumbersome diversion or disguise. It struck me here that maybe it was his face that was the disguise.

He said, "Leo knows what I was locked up for same as I know what he was locked up for. For every picture I've made of him, he could make a picture of me. He knows my downsittings and my uprisings, and that's how come I'd tail him to Timbuktu if I had to. The way I see it, everybody needs to have a person knows the truth about him, the whole bare-ass truth and nothing but the truth. It's a fact of life."

"Why?" Sharon said.

Mr. Golden said, "Search me and know my heart, that's why. Try me and know my thoughts." On the wall behind him, Bebb was straddling his fire like a flying saucer upended. "See if there be any wicked way in me," Mr. Golden said, "and lead me in the way everlasting."

Sharon said, "You and Bip must have had a ball quoting Scripture to each other."

Mr. Golden said, "Of course this paint's all water-base. It'll wash off easy as pie if he wants to wash it off."

My idea that Mr. Golden was an angel died hard that morning in Bebb's barn. In a way I suppose you could say it never died entirely. Angels have been known to turn up in queerer places than jail, after all. Or he might have been a fallen angel. If Mr. Golden didn't look like an angel in any regulation sense, he didn't look much like anything else in any regulation sense either. I was never sure—and Sharon was no help—whether he was a very old man who looked remarkably young or a man about Bebb's age who looked remarkably old.

I didn't give up easily and to some degree have never given up the idea of Mr. Golden as the Hound of Heaven that poor Bip fled down the nights and down the days, down all the labyrinthine ways, and then some, that were rendered there on the walls of Open Heart: Bip as Happy Hooligan, Foxy Grandpa, Major Hoople, bluffing his way through frame after frame of that stained-glass comic strip which was his whatchamacallit, his life, and Mr. Golden as Mandrake the Magician or Mr. Coffee Nerves relentless in his pursuit, inexorable in his love. Bip on the wings of the morning like Buck Rogers, and Mr. Golden never far behind like Killer Kane in porkpie hat and sneakers.

The biggest single objection to my theory that Mr. Golden was really an angel is that he did go on and on so that morning, which raises the question whether anybody can be an angel who comes that close to boring you to death. He went on about jail. He reminisced to Sharon and me about the laundry where he and Bebb had worked shoulder to shoulder day in day out drying and folding gray coveralls, about the view of the ice-cream parlor they could get from the exercise yard and how they played their imagining game through every flavor they could think of before they were done—fudge ripple, and cherry vanilla, pistachio, banana, maple walnut. He dreamed up old friends they had had and old enemies until Sharon and I—sitting by then on either side of the aisle in the folding chairs—could almost see them as dreams of our own. Pete Piscatelli baptized by Bebb in the big tub where the blankets were mangled. Snapper MacFarland who got them all put on crackers and water by dousing himself with cleaning fluid and touching himself off with a Zippo lighter in the mop closet. Young Bobby Cort and Teaser Sprague who came to Bebb one day and asked him to marry them. "Did he do it?" Sharon asked, and Mr. Golden's answer was to point to a kind of triptych where the sun fell—black bars on a red ground with Bebb in the middle and at waist-level, on either side of him, what looked like Kewpie dolls with big blue eyes and round cheeks and out of Bebb's mouth a balloon that had written on it *Suffer little children and forbid them not*.

Mr. Golden sat down too finally, the Bell and Howell zoom lens retracting until he looked about the size of a Kewpie doll himself, everything around him dark except for the jeweled blur of Sharon's lilacs in the foreground. He talked about his bladder trouble. He told us he couldn't take aspirin because it made him bleed at the rectum. He said Bebb had told him he could stay on there at the house as long as he wanted that summer, but he knew Bebb was going to Europe and he didn't want to stay on past that.

Which brings up the second biggest objection to the angel theory. Does an angel have a rectum? Can an angel bleed?

Whatever the answer to that, Mr. Golden eventually helped us carry the two-by-fours out to the car where the sun must have been too much for the optronic eye because my last shot of him is badly overexposed. Except for the merest suggestion of his withered, boyish face and the pale sand-color of his billowing pants, you can hardly make Mr. Golden out in the storm of light that rages all around him.

When Bebb sent us back to his place to pick up the two-by-fours, he must have known we'd probably run into Mr. Golden. He must have known there was a good chance Mr. Golden would unburden himself to us. He must have suspected we'd find out that he, Bebb, had been pulling the wool over our eyes all those months by making us think he didn't know who Mr. Golden was any more than we did. Maybe he wanted us to find out. Maybe it was just one of the chances he took.

On the drive home we discussed whether or not we should let on to him what had happened. Sharon was for not telling a word. She said it would be like calling him a liar to his face. I said that by not telling him a word, it would be like showing him that we were liars ourselves. She said he could swallow that better than the other, and I ended up deciding she was probably right. So when we got home, we didn't say a thing. Bebb did.

Some kids had come over to see if I would tell them how they'd done in English before the grades were officially out. Bebb was sitting cross-legged on the front lawn in his shirtsleeves with six or eight of them grouped around him. Tony was there. Bebb was talking in an animated way. Everybody seemed to be listening intently. You could tell he was enjoying himself. When he saw Sharon and me coming up the driveway, he stopped abruptly and waved in our direction. While his listeners' heads were turned, he got up and disappeared around the back of the house. He was moving fast, tripped over the garden hose as he went.

We stopped to talk to the kids, Sharon and I. Laura Fleischman was among them, and I think it was the first time that she and Sharon ever met face to face. It was one of many moments I wish I'd had my Bell and Howell to record. The life and loves of Antonio Parr. I'm not sure they shook hands when I introduced them, but say they did. It was that moment when their hands touched that I would have zoomed in on—Laura Fleischman's hand, dancing-school damp, that I had touched for an instant once in her mother's straw bag at Grand Central. And Sharon's hand. For a moment it was more than just their two hands that came together. It was the Salamander Motel and *l'ombre des jeunes filles en fleur;* it was truth and fiction, earth and sky. What the hands of those two young women held together in one piece for about a foot and a half of Eastman Kodak Kodacolor was me. But I didn't have my camera with me, of course, and I didn't have the grades they wanted either.

I didn't see Bebb again till suppertime. When he didn't answer Sharon's yell, I went upstairs and found him in his stuffy third-floor room. He was sitting tipped back in a chair with his feet up on the window sill looking at a TV aerial across the street.

Without turning around, he said, "I suppose you ran into Golden this afternoon."

I told him we had.

He said, " 'I was hungry and you gave me food. I was a stranger and you welcomed me.' Antonio, that's what Jesus said. It's the commandment he laid upon us—to treat the stranger just like it was Jesus himself. Now this Golden, he's some kind of nut. He's been dogging me since I don't know when. God only knows what he wants. But he has nowhere to lay his head, Antonio. So I went and took him in like he was Jesus."

I said, "He seems to have a lot to get off his chest, Bip."

Bebb said, "Show me the man that doesn't. Show me the man doesn't have his whole life to get off his chest when you come right down to it."

I said, "Have you got everything you need up here?" It was a small, bare room. There were no curtains at the one window, and the shade looked like something that might have wrapped a mummy once. I thought of the picture of Bebb and Mr. Golden facing each other in their chairs in a room like this, Bebb's hand hanging at his side like an udder.

Bebb said, "You don't want to believe more than half what he says. He's a lonely man, and he's a wound-up man. He's wound-up something wicked." He clasped his hands behind his neck.

He said, "You take those young folks I was shooting the breeze with out there this afternoon before you come back. They're wound-up too. Those crazy drugs they use—they come right out and told me so theirselves. The desires of the flesh. Don't any of them appear to know that stuff's dynamite, Antonio. It's enough to blow their life straight to kingdom come if they aren't careful. They go around touching it off with each other like it was three-for-a-nickel Chinese crackers. Fed up with school. Fed up with the U.S.A. Fed up with God. They're the hope of this world, Antonio, and most of the time they don't know their tail from first base."

He let the front legs of his chair come down to the floor with a thump and swung around to face me. There was more of the old Bebb in him than I'd seen since Lucille's death. A fly lit on his bald head, and he didn't even notice it.

He said, "Antonio, when we get back from overseas sometime round about next—" He interrupted himself and pointed one finger at me as though I was a place on a map he was trying to find his way on. "I'm not kidding myself. It's like I said to John Turtle, Open Heart hasn't panned out like I hoped. It's the right angle, but it's the wrong place and the wrong people. Jesus has not graced that place with his presence up to now. Next fall when school starts, I'm going to start something bran' new. The new generation, Antonio. I'm going to bring the gospel of Jesus straight to the Pepsi generation, hit them right between the eyes with it. That movie house down to the shopping center, I'm going to find out can I rent it afternoons when there's no show on. All that youth and beauty, Antonio. All that pep and pizazz. Kids like Chris and Tony. I'm going to head them out for Beulah Land if it's the last thing I do. I'm going to round me up an organ and somebody knows how to play on it. Maybe they'll let me have

Herman Redpath's shipped on from the ranch. I'm going to serve up good things to eat and drink, heathy things. I'm going to have balloons and ice cream and dancing . . ."

He kept on going until finally Sharon came upstairs to say the hamburgers were cold as a clam-wagon, and then he went on a while longer to both of us.

While he talked I thought of Mr. Golden back at the barn painting up the story of Bebb's life. I thought of all those pictures he'd already painted up and of all the ones he'd have to keep on painting up as time went by. Like Flash Gordon or Captian Marvel, Bebb might go on for years. I tried to think of Mr. Golden the way Bebb said he thought of him—a lonely, wound-up Jesus with no place to lay his head, no place to hang his porkpie hat. And then, not for the first time either, Bebb seemed to read my mind. He spoke Mr. Golden's name.

"Clarence Golden," he said. "I might just put old Clarence Golden on the payroll to stay on and be my new Brownie. I'll need all the help I can get. He may not be Dwight L. Moody or Gypsy Smith, but he knows his Scripture, that's for sure. Leastwise he ought to know it," he said, his eyelid fluttering. "God knows there was a time he heard enough of it. Day in day out for five years give or take a little."

Eighteen

SHARON said, "Hey Antonio, guess what. I was changing him in his crib and he was laying there with his little pecker pointed up and when I leaned over to put the powder on, he let me have it right in the eye like a water pistol. Laugh—he almost knocked himself out. Don't tell me he doesn't have a lot of Bip in him. Sometimes I wonder if I was really adopted like Bip says. I mean I was adopted all right, but maybe Bip's the one got my mother in trouble. I wouldn't have put it past him. Anyway I hate like hell leaving the poor kid here with Billie Kling to look after him. Having her give you a bath would be like falling in the Electrolux."

I said it would only be for a few weeks and after all Chris would be around too. Mrs. Kling and Charlie had agreed to move in and look after things while we were away.

She said, "With that blockbuster for a mother and Chris for a father—it's going to head him straight for the shrink when he grows up. I think I'll stay home and let you two boys go off by yourselves."

She didn't, of course, but at the time I believe she

really thought she would. She'd given herself a shampoo and was on her knees in the backyard with her forehead on the grass and her hair spread out in front of her to dry.

She didn't give up the trip but she gave up Evelyn Wood and the swami and Anita those last few weeks before we left. She said she needed her time to bone up on where we were going, which was to be England mostly with a week in Paris at the end. Bebb said England was the place we ought to concentrate on because it was the country our country came from, and Sharon said she didn't know a damn thing about England. She said they didn't tell you a thing about England at Armadillo High because they hadn't heard about it yet. So I gave her books to read which she used her Evelyn Wood on, zigzagging her hand down page after page at a speed that made it possible to cover centuries in an evening. The history of England must have passed before her like those time-lapse movies of flowers blooming or caterpillars turning into butterflies—Hastings, Bosworth Field, Waterloo, VE Day, melting into one continuous free-for-all, kings and queens tottering by on the run like old newsreels. Elizabeth, grainy and out of focus, flickering by with her white horse and her red wig, to inspect the troops at Tilbury on the eve of the Armada. Charles the First stepping, light-struck, out of a second-story window at Whitehall and bouncing like a ball up the steps of the scaffold. Victoria giving birth the way a slot-machine gives Juicyfruit, her lumpish successors with their eyes too close together waving to the crowds out of limousines.

After a lot of reading Sharon said, "I don't know a hell of a lot more than I knew to start with. All I know's how much I don't know, and I knew that already."

Which raises the question what *did* Sharon know, if not about English history, then about herself, about me, about the whole comic strip of things that as far as I know may be running serially somewhere.

One day I showed her Lucille's *très riches heures.* I'd never so much as mentioned its existence to anybody before. Evelyn Wood herself couldn't have zigzagged her way through Lucille's handwriting, especially with those flowers scattered all through it, and Sharon read it over, word by word, sitting at the kitchen table with Bill in his playpen drowsing over his bottle and the rattle and whir of a lawnmower from across the street. When she finished, she went back and read out loud the part where Lucille had made lists of things: the things she had to hold on to, her good memories, her blessings.

Sharon said, "Poor Luce. I didn't know any of that. I knew there had to be things like that, but I didn't know what they were. I guess everybody's got things like that there isn't anybody else in the world knows them or wants to know them or who you even want to have know them. When Bip finds out about those pictures in the barn, he's going to have a shit hemorrhage."

Except for the time I was with her in the hospital just after Bill was born, it was the only time I had ever seen her cry. Just her eyes cried. The rest of her face went about business as usual, whatever that was, the shady business of Sharon's face. Her tears might as well have come from the outside of her, like rain, as from the inside of her. She didn't give them the time of day.

She said, "Sometimes when we make it together at night, I think about how it's like when you ride a surfboard. When the water's rough, it can be dangerous as hell if you don't know what you're doing and sometimes even if you do know what you're doing. You better damn well hold on tight if you know what's good for you."

She rolled Lucille's flowered stationery back up into a tube and looked at her bare foot through it. She said, "Sometimes I just shut my eyes and hang on to you in the dark like you're the surfboard."

She knew other things.

When Miriam and I were little, we had a game we often played. You needed two pieces of paper and two pencils to play it. Miriam would take one piece of paper and, closing her eyes, would make some kind of a scribble on it, some haphazard snarl of line or crisscross or whirlamajig. I would do the same on the other piece of paper, and then we would exchange them. The game was for each of us to turn the whirlamajig into a picture, to incorporate the scribble into a drawing that looked like something. It didn't matter what it ended up looking like. The trick was to make it end up like *something*.

Our getting married for instance—the sheer fluke of it. Me, Tono Parr (not Antonio in those days because Miriam said it made me sound too much like an organ grinder) taking the Silver Meteor down to Armadillo with a half-baked idea of writing an exposé of Bebb and his diploma mill. Me fresh from the ritual embraces and stately pecks of Ellie Pierce, from the endless box-step of our engagement. Me very Madison Avenue, very Central Park Zoo with all the lions and tigers and crimson-assed baboons safe behind bars. My twin sister in the shape of an A dying under the care of a cancer specialist who looked like Groucho Marx. My cat left to smolder in solitary at the vet's. My fifth of Dewar's in case the going got rough.

And Sharon. Sharon Bebb fresh from God knows what but fresh as the world's first morning in her white sailor pants and bare feet. Her sleep-smelling hair that divided over her ears, those Public Enemy eyes and shattering, hambone smile. Daisy May with all the local Li'l Abners laid end to end at her feet. Jai alai at West Palm. The beach at Fort Lauderdale. Rum and Coke. Sea and Ski. Elvis Presley with green fuzz down one cheek on Lucille's TV. The gift shop next to Holy Love where she worked part time selling shrunken heads, seashell-studded wastebaskets, coconut husks carved into cannibals. Brownie to teach her Scripture through a cloud of after-shave, Bip to take her on occasional trips on the Lord's business to Atlanta, Memphis, Charleston, once to New York, where she saw Marlon Brando getting into a cab. Without knowing it could we have passed each other on the street then?

Bebb, of course, was the one who introduced us. We dallied twice at the Salamander Motel and once in her bedroom in the Manse with Ringo Starr and Oral Roberts looking down from the wall. Later in a moonlight-colored dress she came toward me with her arm in a sling at Herman Redpath's barbecue, and Bebb said, "Behold new Jerusalem coming down out of heaven like a bride adorned for her husband," and for lack of anything better I asked her to marry me, and she did.

That was the whirlamajig. The trick was to turn it into a picture.

All this Sharon must have known better than I knew it. I was the one who located the Sutton house, landed the teaching job, took in my two nephews to live with us, but then all I did was let it lie there like a scrawl on the page. She was the one who tried to make it look like something.

She took up yoga, took up the guitar, took up speed-reading, to fill in some of the empty spaces, I suppose. She drew in a line between Chris and the baby, tried to strengthen the thin curlicue between her world and mine by coming to all those swimming meets and football games and track practices. At first anyway she fitted Tony into the picture by surrounding him with shapes that anyone could identify at a glance—her quick, semi-comic rages over his messy room, his poor grades, his late hours and early loves, followed by precarious reconciliations, interspersed with weepings together over grade B movies and the gags they played on each other, war-games, like the time he hung up the African violets in his jockstrap, the day she filled his Wildroot Cream Oil bottle with Elmer's glue. It wasn't the most artful picture in the world, but granted the scribble she had to work with, it could have been worse. It was a picture anyway, a picture you could live with, at least for a while.

She changed it later. She changed a line here, an empty space there, shaded in areas that had been blank before, darkening them, until the shape that came to enclose her and Tony was a shape that for a while I don't think either of them could identify. When she did identify it, saw the shape of what was probably to come as well as the shape of what had certainly come already, I think she incorporated it into a new and different picture mainly because a *ménage à trois* looked to her more like a living, breathing *ménage* than the earlier, vague tangle had.

Looking back, I give Sharon credit for knowing at some level of her being that in a marriage maybe any shape is better than no shape at all, and I suspect that her infidelity with Tony had a basically geometric impulse behind it, that there was more Euclid than Eros for her in the triangle she put together out of herself, my nephew and me.

What I had put together was also a triangle of sorts, my monument, my Thing, and following Bebb's suggestion and using his lumber, I set it up outdoors before we left for England. Tony helped me. We bolted the two-by-fours together into a kind of tripod and then lugged my masterpiece out of the shed to hang it up. It weighed a ton, and the day was so hot and humid we were dripping with sweat before we were through.

At one point in the process Tony tried to lift it not by the base but by the slender, slatted crosspiece that the wooden tongues curved down through. That crosspiece snapped in his hands and one of the tongues snapped with it.

I said, "Watch it, Tarzan, that's my life you've got hold of," and before I knew it, he was saying again,

"God I'm sorry, Tono. I'm sorry," with his face glistening. For the second time, like the night I asked Sharon if she thought we were washed up, I found that I had precipitated by accident a conversation that otherwise I wouldn't have touched with a ten-foot pole.

I said, "Forget it. It's nothing that can't be fixed," and he said, "I don't know what's wrong with me. Everything I touch seems to turn to shit."

I said, "The trouble is you don't know your own strength."

He said, "The trouble is I'm a natural-born yuk."

He said, "You put it together just the way you want it, and then I come along and fuck it up."

I said, "You haven't fucked it up."

There is a piece on the sinking of the *Titanic* that I sometimes used to read my English classes when I ran out of things to talk to them about. It ended with a description of the iceberg itself the way the survivors saw it from their lifeboats. "Tinted with sunrise" is a phrase I remember—the great pyramid of ice as it floated there, glittering and majestic, on the heaving blue breast of the sea. Some such words as that. And there we stood, my namesake and I, looking at my monument swaying idly from its chain with the raw pine turned almost gold in the sunshine and all those knobs and dowels and disks passing each other by as it slowly rotated. It seemed to be involved in some obscure and fearsome action. You hardly noticed the broken part.

"There is no excellent beauty that hath not some strangeness in the proportion," I said. "Maybe you've even improved it."

Tony was watching the thing with the same inward-looking frown that I've seen him run the last lap of a mile with—half St. John of the Cross contemplating the Trinity, half a man when the dentist hits a nerve. He said, "You and Sharon won't have to keep on going away places. I'll be graduating next year. You won't have me in your hair forever."

I said, "The only reason we're going away is Bip asked us."

"Why do you think Bip asked you?" Tony said.

I said, "Why do you think Bip does anything?"

Tony said, "Does Sharon know I told you?"

I nodded.

"Ever since then it's like it never happened. That's almost the worst part," he said. "I go my way and she goes her way and it's like nothing ever happened."

I said, "Maybe nothing did."

"It did," he said.

He said, "If something like that's not important, nothing's important. People oughtn't to be able to just walk away from a thing like that."

I said, "If you'd just walked away, you wouldn't be talking about it now. You don't have to talk about it."

"That night I told you," he said, "you should have thrown me out."

"Would that have helped?" I said.

"I don't know," he said.

My monument had all but come to a standstill, and I reached out with my foot and gave it enough of a shove to set it in motion again, gave us something to look at besides just each other.

Tony said, "Either we ought to be in love with each other or we ought to steer clear of each other, but she's just the same to me as she always was and I'm just the same to her. We came the closest to each other people can come. There isn't any closer than that. It ought to make a difference afterwards. If it doesn't make a difference afterwards, you're not even people, you're animals."

I wanted to tell him that everything you do makes a difference afterwards including even the things you just dream about doing. I wanted to tell him that life keeps piling up till you can no more walk away from it than you can walk away from your own shadow just as at that moment Bebb's life was piling up on the walls of Open Heart. I wanted to say something useful and wise to the roly-poly child my sister Miriam had left me. He stood there with the muscles in his jaw working as he stared ahead at my monument majestic in the spring sun, and I wanted to tell him something that might save him years of confusion if not his soul, but all that came out was, "In one way it doesn't matter half as much as you think. In another way it matters a hell of a lot more."

He said, "I'd do anything in the world if I could make it like it never happened. Honest to God I would, Tono."

"You don't have to do that," I said. "That's for me to do. I'll do it for you."

"But it did happen," he said. "Nobody can change what's already happened. You said so yourself."

I said, "I can't change it for you, but maybe I can change it for me. In time I think I can make it for myself as if it never happened. At least I can make other things happen around it so it won't louse things up. It might even help somehow."

"What do you call that?" he said. Looking at me through Miriam's dark eyes, he stood there stock-still like somebody trying hard not to rock a lifeboat.

"Call it anything you want," I said. "Call it a going-away present."

With a shake of his head, he tossed his hair back. "How about Sharon?" he said.

Hearing him say her name put the whole thing suddenly to the test, seeing his lips shape her name in such a blurred and private way as if he and she were together in one boat and I was alone in another. For a second I wasn't sure I could put my money where my mouth was. *Husbands and wives, little children lost their lives,* the old song ran through my head, *it was sad when that great ship went down.* Then I found I could. Just could. "Sharon will be all right," I said. "You don't have to worry about Sharon."

I don't know what difference, if any, my words made for him, but at least they made a difference in his frown. He was still frowning, but he was frowning out at me now, not in at himself, and he started to say something when the kitchen door slammed and Bebb was there calling out from the back porch. Bebb said, "Antonio, take a squint at these passport photos. Yours makes you look like you haven't eaten a square since Noah."

"Brother, can you spare a dime?" I said.

Bebb had walked out to us by then, and he put one arm around my nephew's shoulder. He said, "Listen, boys, by the time we get back from overseas I won't be able to spare a nickel. I'll be broker than the Ten Commandments."

"That's what you call broke," Tony said.

Months later when I finally got around to editing and splicing together the movies I took of our trip with Bebb's Bell and Howell, this is the scene I would like to have started them out with. I would have superimposed the title on it—OUR TRIP ABROAD in block capitals and behind it a long shot of the three of us just as we were standing there in the backyard: Bebb with his arm around Tony, me with my passport picture in my hand, the dangling monument. More than when the whistle blasted and the *SS France* started to pull away from Pier 92, it was the moment when we actually set off for foreign shores.

Nineteen

BEBB fell in love on the boat. She was seventy-five years old, a widow, and her name was Gertrude Conover. She was vigorous and wiry with a habit of tilting her chin down toward one shoulder when she walked so that she always seemed to be moving sideways. She had blue hair, lots of money, and came from Princeton, New Jersey. She had a seat at our table, and the first day out she told Bebb that they had met before. "It was in Egypt," she said. Bebb said that he had never been to Egypt. "That is a matter of opinion," Gertrude Conover said.

Bebb in love. Bebb leaning over the rail of the observation deck mooning out at the receding wake. He said, "Antonio, think if a man was to fall overboard. A ship the size of this one, by the time it got itself swung around and headed back, a man would have drifted off so far it would be like looking for a needle in a haystack. Think how it would be bobbing around out there by yourself in all those acres of ocean with nothing to catch hold of. Think of all those fathoms underneath you full of creatures like the leviathan of Scripture who esteemeth iron like straw and maketh the sea to boil like a pot. The lonesomeness of it, Antonio. The awful lonesomeness of floating around out there all by yourself waiting for the end to come with not another living soul to give a hang whether you sink or swim any more than the ocean gives a hang."

The breeze bounced Gertrude Conover's blue hair softly up and down. She had a way of smiling at you as though what she was smiling at was not what you were saying but what you were going to say next. She said, "Whoever put the idea into your head the ocean doesn't care whether you sink or swim with all that salt in it to hold you up?"

Bebb said, "Salt or no salt, the ocean would just as leave drown you as wet your drawers. It's the nature of things like the ocean not to give a hang."

Gertrude Conover said, "Of course they give a hang. Sometimes people don't give a hang because that's the way people are, but everything else does."

Bebb said, "You're an optimist, Gertrude Conover."

Gertrude Conover said, "I'm a Theosophist."

One day at lunch there was the usual basket of *petits pains* on the table. After helping herself to one, Gertrude Conover took another, split it, buttered it, and placed it for Bebb on his butter plate. She did it in an absent-minded way, not even talking to him at the time, but you would have thought she'd given him the shirt off her back. He said, "I never set eyes on Gertrude Conover till the day we come aboard, but it's like I'd known her always. After she buttered the roll and set it on my plate, she looked at me and said, 'I don't know why I did that.' What would make her go and do a thing like that for somebody she doesn't hardly even know?"

"How about in Egypt?" Sharon said.

Bebb said, "Sharon, you know as well as I do this is the first time I ever set my foot outside the U.S.A."

He said, "She didn't go and make a big production out of it. She just went ahead and buttered it so easy and natural it was like I was her oldest friend."

I said, "Maybe she was just buttering it for herself."

Bebb said, "She'd already buttered one for herself. Besides, she put it on my plate. Then afterwards she said she didn't know why she'd done it."

"What's a Theosophist anyhow?" Sharon said. "She's the first one I ever ran into."

Bebb said, "I'll tell you one thing. If what she is is a Theosophist, the world could stand a pack more of them."

After dinner the four of us sometimes met in the lounge on the Pont Véranda to play bingo. Gertrude Conover drank *crème de menthe frappé* which turned her lips green. Bebb said he'd never seen a lady with green lips before. Gertrude Conover said, "My, wouldn't your parishioners be glad to hear that."

Bebb asked her once about the time she thought she'd met him in Egypt, and Gertrude Conover said it had happened ages ago. She said, "You were a priest of Ptah. Your name was Ptah-sitti. The Pharaoh used to take you on lion hunts with him because he thought you brought him good luck. You got to be one of his pets. You didn't even have to shave your eyebrows off like the other priests, and you had the run of the palace. Then you got into hot water."

They were reclining side by side in their deck chairs with cups of bouillon on their laps. A humid breeze was blowing. Bebb had on a sport shirt and the kind of sunglasses that look like mirrors from the outside.

He said, "What kind of trouble, Gertrude Conover?"

Gertrude Conover was leaning back in her chair with her eyes closed. She said, "The Pharaoh had a ward by the name of Uttu. He had killed her father in some free-for-all, and he took her in as part of his household. She wasn't pretty, but she was neat and clean considering the age she lived in, and she played the flute nicely. She and Ptah-sitti became intimate—they both liked good music and had many other tastes in common—and after a certain amount of time, she found out she was pregnant by him. My dear, when the Pharaoh got wind of it, it sent him straight up the wall. He threatened torture unless she told who her lover was, and though she might have let them torture her to save Ptah-sitti's skin, she was afraid for what it might do to their unborn child, so she gave the poor man away. He was condemned to be impaled. It was an open and shut case."

"That's some way to go," Bebb said.

Gertrude Conover still had her eyes closed. She said, "You were very gallant about it. You said it was little enough to pay for the pleasure of having known Uttu, but luckily you didn't have to pay after all. The

Pharaoh was afraid it might bring him bad luck on lion hunts to kill a priest of Ptah so he had the sentence reduced. He had one of your eyes put out instead, and called it even-Steven."

Bebb said, "He must have had a heart as big as all outdoors."

I was sitting on the other side of him trying to write a postcard to Chris and Tony, and he turned to me and shrugged. Then he said, "Gertrude Conover, look me in the eye and tell me you're not making this whole thing up."

She opened her eyes and looked at him, but she didn't tell him a word. If she hadn't said she was seventy-five, I would have guessed she wasn't much older than Bebb himself. She had a young mouth, relaxed at the corners. Her blue eyes were faded, but there was plenty of life in them as she lay there looking sideways at Bebb.

"Where were you while all this was going on?" Bebb said.

Gertrude Conover said, "I was Uttu. I died in a papyrus marsh giving birth to the priest's baby. The baby died too, poor little thing."

Bebb said, "I'm sorry."

Gertrude Conover said, "There's no use crying over spilt milk."

It would be nice to be able to report that the end of Bebb's and Gertrude Conover's shipboard romance was marriage—that after all the centuries that followed on the tragic liaison of Ptah-sitti and Uttu, they finally met aboard the *SS France* bound from New York to Southampton and made it legal. But their romance never had an end in either sense of the word. It had no end in the sense of fulfillment because they never got married. It also had no end in the sense of termination because they continued to keep in touch with each other from that time forward, and if Gertrude Conover's theosophy holds water, they may go right on keeping in touch with each other from one incarnation to the next indefinitely.

A book has an end in both senses. Page follows page, chapter follows chapter, and that is that. The end. And by the time you reach the last page, everything has ended up saying something too. The plot has been unrolled to its full length, the loose threads have been drawn together, and you close the book up with the feeling that the author has made the point which one way or another all authors always make, which is that for good or ill events have a shape. The characters have all *gotten* someplace. Maybe, as at the end of *King Lear*, where the good people and the bad people die, both, and just poor, hapless Edgar is left to stammer the final curtain down as best he can, the place the characters get is really no place and the shape is shapelessness; but that's as valid a way of making the point as any if you can stomach it. Even Lear's story ends, in other words, but Bebb's and Gertrude Conover's never did, and neither did Sharon's and mine, at least not in any sense you can put your finger on. All our lives that summer were less like a book that ends and more like a comic strip where episode follows episode without ever getting anyplace in particular. Or like a home movie where as soon as one reel is through, there is always another reel in the making, where one shot is apt to have as much or as little point as any other and that is probably all the point you're going to get.

When we got to London, we found a letter waiting for us from Brownie. It was full of news. Lily Trionka was pregnant again, and though Brownie was worried about her because it came so hard on the heels of her last miscarriage, he explained that she had given up ice cream and promised not to work out on the exercycle during her pregnancy, and those were good signs. Maudie Redpath had given her blackbird dance another try, and some said that this time the magic was so nearly successful that she was able to fly five or six feet off the ground from the barbecue pit to the swimming pool where she fell into the water and would have drowned if Harry Hocktaw hadn't fished her out apparently none the worse for wear. John Turtle had used some of his inheritance from Herman Redpath to start a Tom Thumb golf course and was making money hand over fist. Holy Love had put in air-conditioning.

In his last paragraph, Brownie wrote, "My prayers are with you folks over there on the other side. Here's hoping you have a well-earned vacation and find rest for your souls. Mrs. Bebb's untimely end came as a hard blow, but lo the rain is over and gone now and the voice of the turtle is heard again in the land. The Lord hath taken away much with His left hand, but with His right hand He restoreth much. Remember Job, dear, and if you get the opportunity, drop us a postcard. Your friend in Jesus, Laverne Brown."

Bebb said, "Sharon honey, remember me to pick up some souvenirs for folks back home like Brownie," and in the course of our travels—sometimes on our own, sometimes with Gertrude Conover in her rented Daimler—we picked up tons of them not even counting the movies I took. Here are a few of them. There could be almost any number more.

Westminster Abbey. Sharon said, "This place gives me the creeps." She was looking tan and hostile in a sleeveless pink dress with a band to hold her hair back. She said, "There was a used furniture place outside West Palm reminds me of it, full of beds and sofas that looked like people had died all over them and stuffed chairs with brown stains. Makes you want to get in here with some dynamite and clean the place up. You take your history, this place stinks of history."

I said, "That's Alfred Lord Tennyson you've got your feet on."

"I wouldn't care if it was William Shakespeare. Jesus," she said, "there's William Shakespeare."

I said, "He's buried somewhere else though."

She said, "He was smart."

The only one in the Poet's Corner who interested her was Thomas Parr. "He must have been kin," she said, and looked him up in the guide.

"He was known as Old Parr," she said, "and lived through the reigns of ten sovereigns, surviving to the age of 152. That even makes Maudie Redpath look kind of sick."

I was reading over her shoulder, and when she turned, our foreheads knocked.

I said, "The wife who outlived Henry the Eighth was a Parr too. It takes a lot to polish us off."

She said, "It better had." We had bought a bag of bullseyes at Boot's, and her breath smelled of peppermint. She said, "I don't want to be a widow. I don't want to end up dyeing my hair blue like Gertrude Conover and being too lonesome to ever stay home."

I said, "You're a long way from home right now."

She said, "You're my home."

Bebb signaled to us. He was standing with his back to one of the pillars in the nave. The bag of bullseyes bulged out of one of his jacket pockets. A pair of binoculars hung around his neck. He had his head tipped back and was pointing up toward the roof.

He had spotted a pigeon fathoms above us. It was perched in one of the arches of the triforium with its wings folded in tight to its sides, a gray bird hard to make out against the gray stone. It was poised up there like a swimmer poised on the edge of a flooded quarry.

There was a crackling in the air as a P.A. system was switched on and a canned British voice began to run through an announcement that once an hour visitors were requested to pause for a moment and join in the Lord's Prayer. The sound alerted the bird and it started a twitchy side-step back and forth on the high ledge. Then it belly-flopped into the brimming dusk and ferried out across the nave sinking slowly, a stone bird. Nobody was paying much attention to the Lord's Prayer or to the bird either.

As it neared the other side, it back-watered with a ruckus of wings and fought for altitude. Bebb had raised his binoculars. The pigeon batted against the clerestory windows a few times on the way up, then shot cockeyed into the topmost ribs of the vaulting. The P.A. system tapered off to a needle-sharp whine and switched out. The pigeon floated in quiet soft as rainwater a hundred feet above our heads.

Bebb lowered his binoculars. "Keep me as the apple of the eye," he said, "hide me under the shadow of thy wings."

Sharon had one bare arm resting on Bebb's shoulder. She said, "That pigeon's smart as William Shakespeare. He wants the hell out of here."

Simpson's-on-the-Strand. Gertrude Conover ordered London Broil. She said, "In Holland I order hollandaise. In France I order French toast."

She said, "Looking at you three just now, I couldn't help thinking to myself those people are complete strangers. For all I know you could be dope-pushers, poisoners, anything. Your appearance is especially unreassuring, Leo. That queer thing you keep doing with your eye."

Bebb said, "It's never been the same since Pharaoh had it tore out."

"I had forgotten about that," Gertrude Conover said.

Bebb said, "You know what I was thinking while you were thinking about that? I was thinking that for many years I was the number one person for two people. I was the number one person for my wife, and I was the number one person for my daughter. Now my wife's passed on, and my daughter's got herself a husband. That means I'm not anybody's number one person any more."

Salisbury. We motored there in Gertrude Conover's Daimler, and found a letter waiting at the hotel. It was to me from Laura Fleishman.

Dear Mr. Parr,

I am writing this on my 18th birthday. They say what you do on your birthday you keep doing all year round so I guess you're in for a lot of letters from me. [Here she had drawn a round, smiling face.] *I didn't get a chance to say goodbye to you at Commencement with all those millions of people around. I tried to, but you were always surrounded. I wanted to tell you I really enjoyed having you as my English Lit. teacher, and I think almost everybody in the class did. King Lear is the most wonderful book I ever read. My favorite line is "The worst returns to laughter," which I guess means it's always darkest just before the dawn. That brings me to the main thing I meant to tell you. Carl West and I have broken up. It was the worst moment of my life so far, but I can see now how it was bound to happen inevitably. He is a sweet boy in lots of ways, but he is very immature. He was never interested in discussing anything. For instance he couldn't stand King Lear. I don't think he even read most of it. It was a hard decision for both of us, but maybe it is all for the best. Do you remember the time I bumped into you at Grand Central Station? You probably thought I acted awfully childish and dumb, but I was never so surprised in my life to run into a person. You were so friendly and kind I hated it when the clock struck midnight and we had to catch the next pumpkin back to Sutton. I'll always remember our meeting on that occasion.*

Well, I guess that's all for now. I hope I haven't made too many mistakes, you being an English teacher. Have a grand time in Merry Old England and please give my best regards to your wife if she remembers who I am. Love, Laura.

Sharon said, "I remember who she is. You don't forget a face like that. There ought to be a law against a face like that. I'm getting damn old, Antonio."

Soon afterwards she said, "What happened in Grand Central Station?"

I said, "Would you believe we spent an hour together in a bar and I bought her a 7-Up?"

"Why shouldn't I believe it?" Sharon said.

I said, "Would you believe a long corridor with a door at the end of it and then more corridors beyond that and another door?"

As soon as Gertrude Conover had seen our room in Salisbury, she said it was haunted. There was a Jacobean four-poster, exposed black beams, and a washbasin with a mirror above it. Gertrude Conover said to keep an eye on that mirror if we were interested in knowing more about the room, and before we went to bed that night, Sharon plastered the mirror over with a wet handkerchief she had rinsed out. It was in the Jacobean four-poster that I read her the letter.

"Then more corridors and more doors," I said.

She was lying beside me with her hands folded under her cheek and her eyes closed. She said, "I wouldn't blame you if you shacked up with her in a hotel. You had one coming."

I said, "Would you believe a room looking out over the Park with the curtains blowing in and these two standing at the window watching it start to get dark outside? Would you believe them standing there wondering not what's going to happen next because in a way what's going to happen next has already happened but wondering what's going to happen next after that? She's left a straw pocketbook she borrowed from her mother on the bed, and she's got her hand at the nape of her neck holding her hair back. It's a queer, formal kind of moment."

Sharon said, "I could believe that."

I said, "I can almost believe it myself. If there really is a room like that someplace, I can believe it's haunted too. Only what's haunting it isn't something that happened there once. It's something that happened not to happen."

Sharon said, "Poor Bopper. That's one that could have been on the house."

The handkerchief dried and peeled off during the night, but when we woke up the next morning, the only thing it reflected was us.

At *Stonehenge* Bebb sat on one of the fallen lintel stones with a shilling guide spread out on his knee. It was approaching sunset, and the great trilithons looked black against the lemon sky. Not far away a family of three was sitting in the grass having their tea—a father, a mother, and their daughter. The daughter must have been twelve or thirteen in a sunsuit with bloomers that hung loose about her skinny thighs.

She was sitting awkwardly half on, half off, her mother's lap. The mother held the girl's cheeks between her thumb and forefinger and was squeezing them into a fishface to keep her mouth open. The sandaled feet and spidery arms wobbled as the mother spooned tea into her out of a plastic cup. From time to time she broke a small piece off a slice of bread and tamped it into the girl's mouth with her finger. Once in a while the girl got a chance to lean forward, and tea and bread would dribble down her chin. She made sounds then, and when she stopped, her mouth would continue to hold the shape of the sounds. The father sat with his back to them reading a newspaper.

Bebb said, "The girl's not right, anybody can see that. It's probably the only way they can get her to take nourishment. She's just skin and bones."

Sharon said, "There's got to be another way than that."

Gertrude Conover had bought a shooting-stick in London and was sitting on it. She said, "Once at Revonoc I had Thomas Mann and Albert Einstein both for dinner. Thomas Mann was visiting in Princeton at the time, and of course Dr. Einstein lived in that little house on Mercer Street for years. Neither of them drove, so when it came time to go, I drove them home myself. I remember thinking on the way that if I smashed into a telephone pole and we were all killed, I would become a footnote in history. Dr. Einstein and Thomas Mann were in the back seat talking German, and naturally there wasn't any accident. When I got back to Revonoc, I fixed a cup of Ovaltine and sat out on the terrace for a while to watch for shooting stars. I thought about all the biographies that would have had my name in them somewhere. I think that was the same year Hitler marched into Paris."

Sharon said, "That's real interesting, but what's it got to do with the price of eggs if you don't mind my asking?"

Gertrude Conover said, "Everything, that's all. Everything's got to do with everything else. Everything fits in somewhere, and there's no power in heaven or earth that can upset the balance."

Still in her mother's lap, the girl had bent double at the waist and was staring at the ground. The mother had put the unfinished bread and tea aside for the moment and was saying something to the father, who was trying to fold his paper lengthways.

Bebb said, "It says here on midsummer day the sun rises smack over that big block of stone and shoots a beam through the middle of the circle. Why it's been something like—" He paused to check his figures, tilting the pages to catch the dwindling light. "This place was near to two thousand years old when the little Lord Jesus was born."

A tourist bus was honking its horn, and beyond the trilithons I could see stragglers hurrying out of the postcard place.

Sharon said, "I wonder if they've got a can there. My back teeth are floating."

Bebb was looking off toward where the midsummer sun was supposed to rise. He said, "Those stones have been standing out here summer and winter for three going on four thousand years while mighty empires have come and gone like a dream when it is past. Napoleon Bonaparte, Nebuchadnezzar, Caesar, the whole pack of them. Makes a man feel about as important as spit."

Gertrude Conover said, "I am a rich old woman and, making allowances, I am a happy old woman. If I thought the way you do, I would still be rich, but I would no longer be happy."

Bebb said, "The first time I laid eyes on you, I could see right off you were happy. It makes me happy just you being at the same table."

Gertrude Conover said, "I am happy because I believe spit is important. I believe the universe is important. I believe you and I are important. Everything is important because everything is needed to maintain cosmic balance."

Bebb said, "Sometimes things get out of balance."

Gertrude Conover said, "No."

The mother had started to do the feeding again. She had the girl's head wedged back in the crook of her arm and was shoving something into her out of a jar. Her stuffed face was jacked open, and insect-like sounds were coming out of it. One sandal had fallen off. The sunsuit had gotten wrenched around so that it bit into her at odd places.

Bebb rose to his feet and walked toward her. When he got halfway, he stopped. It was as if he had taken Gertrude Conover's words about cosmic balance literally. Stonehenge was like an overloaded tray held on the palm of a waiter's hand. If Bebb had taken one step too many or one step too few, the tray would have started to go. The girl was pinned by her bruised mouth, and the mouth was the center from which her legs and arms rayed out like broken feelers. Bebb had gone about ten feet toward the center. If he had gone nine feet or eleven, it would have been disastrous. The looming stones, Gertrude Conover on her stooting-stick, Sharon with her back teeth floating, the tourist bus, all of it would have begun sliding. The tray would have gone down with a crash.

Bebb stood with his back to us. I could not see what he was doing, but I could see them seeing it, the father first and then the mother. The father slowly lowered his newspaper. The mother relaxed her hold. They looked up and saw Ptah-sitti standing there looking down at them. It would have been hard to say which had been standing there longer, he or Stonehenge. His pants had gotten stuck between his buttocks. What was left of the sun set a bright cap on his bald head.

The girl slid one hand along the grass toward something white. She took hold of it—a napkin, a piece of sandwich wrapper—and held it out in one hand as far as her arm would reach. Then she stretched her other hand out toward it so that she ended up holding it way off there in front of her in both her hands. Ptah-sitti stood his ground as squat and intractable as once in a wild animal preserve called Lion Country in Armadillo, Florida, I had seen him get out of his car and stand among lions.

One of the best movies I got, the last before we boarded the *Queen Elizabeth II* for home at Le Havre, was at the Eiffel Tower. First a shot of the whole great uncial taken from below, that soaring initial printed against a cloudless Parisian sky. Then a shot traveling up one of the legs in an elevator the size of a boxcar. Finally another shot not from the very top—you had to wait in another line for another elevator to get there—but from the platform halfway up where the restaurant is. Bebb and Sharon are standing against the railing. Bebb has moped around a good deal since we said goodbye to Gertrude Conover at Victoria Station. She said, "Don't be blue. We're all number one people. He has numbered even the hairs on our heads they are so dear," but it didn't seem to help much. Bebb said, "I don't have any hairs on my head, Gertrude Conover." But in Paris he got another letter from Brownie, which brought him to life again. Brownie wrote that the Federal Trade Commission had proposed new guidelines for private vocational and correspondence schools, and a Texas legislator had announced that nothing stood in the way now of ridding the Lone Star state of every fly-by-night diploma factory within its borders. A man had already been around to Holy Love to check on enrollment and tuition figures, Brownie wrote, but in Bebb's absence he had refused to give them out. This is what Bebb is talking about as I zoom in on him there at the rail somewhere between earth and sky.

He is saying, "That was a piss-poor move to make. Brownie ought to showed them every last figure he had. There's not a thing we do isn't open and above board just like it's always been. We don't have a particle to hide, and that pitiful Brownie knows it same as I know it myself—maybe," he says, breaking in on himself, "maybe he knows it, or maybe he's been up to some tricks since I took off overseas."

For emphasis he wags the ice-cream cone that he bought down below. He says, "Holy Love is in trouble, but we're not going to get into a sweat about it. Holy Love's been in trouble from the word go. But we got the First Amendment to the Constitution on our side. And we got Herman Redpath's great fortune too."

He looks straight into the optronic eye, and his mouth snaps shut on its hinges. Then it opens for the last time, and he says to Herman Redpath or whoever else, if anybody, happens to be listening. "Forget not the congregation of the poor forever, for the dark places of the earth are full of the habitations of cruelty," as the purr of my Bell and Howell breaks into the steady clicking that indicates the fifty feet have run out.